The Amateur Science of Love

a novel

CRAIG SHERBORNE

TEXT PUBLISHING MELBOURNE AUSTRALIA

textpublishing.com.au

The Text Publishing Company
Swann House
22 William Street
Melbourne Victoria 3000
Australia

First published in 2011 by The Text Publishing Company
This edition published 2014

Cover design by WH Chong
Text design by Susan Miller
Typeset in Garamond Premier Pro by J & M Typesetting

Printed and bound in Australia by Griffin Press, an accredited ISO/NZS 1401:2004 Environmental Management System printer

National Library of Australia Cataloguing-in-Publication entry:
Author: Sherborne, Craig, 1962-, author.
Title: The amateur science of love / by Craig Sherborne.
Edition: 2nd edition.
ISBN: 9781922147776 (paperback)
ISBN: 9781921834264 (ebook)
Subjects: Love stories.
Dewey Number: A823.3

This book is printed on paper certified against the Forest Stewardship Council® Standards. Griffin Press holds FSC chain-of-custody certification SGS-COC-005088. FSC promotes environmentally responsible, socially beneficial and economically viable management of the world's forests.

THE AMATEUR SCIENCE OF LOVE

They say men marry their mothers. Me, I fell in love with Tilda Robson.

Same eyes, I admit, but that's about it: twin blues below tawny moustache-brows.

My Tilda had a masters; my mother had TV guides.

She was an artist; my mother a drunken farm wife.

I was born in New Zealand at twenty-one years old: up till then my life had just been practice. I was supposed to be a farmer, but I never had the heart. I had airs of being famous, of being an actor.

'Pipedreams,' my father said. 'How could a solid man throw such a dreamer!'

I did so-so at school then dropped out of uni, which my father held against me but soon came round: I was home and he had hopes that home meant home forever. What a team we'd make—I was his only child—more blood brothers than mere son and father. 'All this will be yours one day,' he'd say, and fling his arm towards the jade-green vastness. The *our* jade-green, *our* thousand Waikato acres, *our* mountains where cloud-surf breaks on the peak and tears open with good steady rains.

He didn't realise that pipedreams themselves are green; they have mountains of their own where you see forever. He'd never keep me there at the bottom of the world, anonymous for all my future. Only if God himself said the sacrifice would be worth it, and promised to put me in the Bible, the ultimate famous.

My first pipedream was officer in the navy, a commander of men in epaulettes and whites. A warrior hero like the ancients. When the literature arrived I put a line through the notion: it was 1984 and only peacetime. I'd float my years away in the middle of nowhere. No one would ever notice I'd been alive.

The acting pipedream came from staring in the mirror. I was good-looking enough, if not face-perfect. I had my mother's ears, even though her ears were better. Mine stuck out too much, like capital Cs, the width of thumb and hooked forefinger.

I had my father's nose, but his was straighter, shorter, thinner. Mine, I was sure of it, was worsening above the nostrils: the bulb there fattened each time I checked it in the mirror. And I checked it in the mirror on the hour.

They, my parents, Norm and Marg, were their true likeness in photos, still handsome in their bickering fifties. I was puffier in pictures. Side-on I had a flabby double-up of jaw skin. The old girl envied that as baby fat, said she would swap it any day for her wrinkles. But I never saw much justice in the compliment. What were photographs to her with the old boy her main audience? Or to him with his public of cows, sheep and horses?

I taped the Cs flat, scrunched up rugby-like at night so sleep would make the ugly things go smaller. As for the bulb, I tried to clothes-peg it narrower. I learned to nod off through the watery pain. I wore a headband chin to crown as if I had toothache, but there was no sign the chin was going to lift. The clothes peg sprung free whenever I turned over. I had to sleep on my back, which made me snore my throat raw.

I had a real name I didn't exactly spit to say, but I was no Colin any more than *common*. As for Butcher—it made me sound like sausages. I renamed myself after many tries—first Kirk Mane (too pretentious), Bradley Aurora (the same), Stephen Spire (too effeminate), Carl Tremain (not bad, not great). Then it came to me like a two-word poem: John Adore. John suggesting masculine. The Adore for what I wished for.

I didn't know for sure if I had any talent. In school plays I always got applause—I could hold a tune, yell loud and get angry. One problem was I'd shake from being so nervous, as if the stage lights were shorting up through my shoes. That's what I blamed—I blamed stage lights, I blamed incompetent electricians.

My father blamed school for putting ideas in my head. It put ideas in when it should have put in a few clues. For just as he invests in 300 acres, buys out neighbours to build a bigger pie, so a school builds a boy into a viable prospect: puts maths into him so one day he's good with money. Science so he knows how his house and sheds keep standing. Good English so he won't miss the fine print in a contract. What else is a private school for!

He blamed my mother for being Mrs Melodrama. Too much 'If I had my life over again I would have aimed at better than a farmer husband.' Too much buying me floral shirts and saying, 'Oh, let him grow his hair.' Too much swanning about pickled like those TV Americans, saying, 'You be Snapper, honey. I'll be Paige' as if she's in those idiot soap operas.

When the literature arrived to audition at RADA, my dad blamed her for being too encouraging. Too much rolling her gin-drowsy eyes and Rs: 'The R-R-Royal Academy of Dr-r-ramatic Art.' The Peter O'Tooles and Roger Moores in the booklet made her swoon. Alumni, I called them. She called them a bit of all right. 'My son is following in such distinguished footsteps. Next stop, Hollywood.'

She called my father 'dense' and 'spoilsport' when he told her to stop going off with the fairies. They were her usual trump words to best his 'fairies'. He trumped back with his usual work speech: how he can take a broken water pump and make that work. He can run 600 dairy cows, 1.4 of them to the acre, and make *that* work. He's bred twenty racehorses for a total of twenty-five wins from 150 starts. *They* know about work. But his own son? He can't make him work. He thumped his fist into his hand on *work*.

I studied the slap-jab of that action and mimicked it in my mind. Same for the slit of his accusing mouth—his lips bitten together between words: 'I can take a broken water pump (bite) and make that work (bite and thump).' I memorised how frustration jammed his breathing. He took a deep breath through his nose, held it in, then sighed it loose. His eyes became a pucker of lid skin, the dark bullseye of his pupils set deeper in his head than normal.

Sometimes my mimicking slipped out onto my face and I puckered and bit and breath-jammed back at him. He'd make fists of both hands and warn me not to mock him or so help me. I wasn't mocking him, just storing for acting what a face does when a man's in fury.

I tried to tell him as much but he'd stomp off for a few strides. I took a stride after him, storing every tic and motion with my camera-mind. His left fingers hooked on his belt. His right hand lifting off his brown pork-pie, too old and finger-smeared now for

4

race meetings, but still good enough to enclose his paddock-blown hair.

I took three hours to hose the dairy shed when it should have taken one. I didn't muck out stables, I shirked in them. The definition of shirker, that was me, he bit and breathed. 'What do you do in those stables all morning?'

Practise, I told him. Practise. How to bow to an audience (to the soaking muck sack). I practised *bravos* to the stable broom. I kissed my fingertips to the spotlight sun, thanking the experienced god who worked it and shone dust motes on me like confetti. I up-ended the yard rake for my microphone. 'Thank you. Thank you,' I bowed and begged. 'Please, please, no more applause.' My voice was getting toffier with each morning's horse-box session as I ticked the days off towards London.

So that's what I do, I said. Practise. I had perfected a pitchfork as a soldier's spear (I stood to attention, an invisible pitchfork to my shoulder to demonstrate). I'd have to start out in small roles and develop things from there. The better parts will come one day, the ultimates, the Hamlets.

'Wouldn't you like a famous son?' I winked.

He said he wouldn't know his Hamlets from his arsehole.

But he stopped asking 'You a queer?' after the Caroline business.

Three wild knuckle-knocks on the door and there stood vengeance, a fist-clenching ape-man, our cleaner's husband. 'If that boy ever comes near my missus again, then I, Stan Muller, will cut his nuts out like a pig's.'

He lifted his shirt to show his hunting knife holstered. His black-haired gut hung down like a carried animal.

For the first time my father said *fuck* in front of my mother. 'Our Caroline?' he rasped. The old boy's eyes had filled with water. His puckered lids were red from it. 'She's almost twice your age. She's got grown-up children.' He added *fucks* and *Christs* to the sentence and doubled over as if I'd hit him. He'd raised a home-wrecker for a son, he groaned. Had I no decency in me, no shame? He told me to get out of his sight. It made him sick to utter my name. I'd never amount to anything, it was plain to him as day.

I tried the line that I was practising cads for acting. That just made him chase me to knock some sense into my skull. It was the kind of sense he called 'some medicine'.

My mother turfed my bed sheets in the rubbish, though I confessed that we never did it there. *It* was four times in the garage; three in the garden shed; twice on the cellar stairs. She had the carpet dry-cleaned and vowed never again to ride in the Statesman. 'How can we ever show our face in town again!' She poured Beefeater after Beefeater, and fell asleep in front of *Coronation Street*.

If I was practising with Caroline, I was practising for Tilda.

They say we're ninety per cent water. But that's only our bodies. It's the other ten per cent that causes bother. If we could x-ray inside there we might see a person's thinking, spy out the bits of feeling in them that apply to us.

If I learned anything from Caroline it was the basics of taking x-rays.

I learned a blouse is not just a piece of clothing, it is a signal of information. If it Vs open to halfway then it's for my sake. Between hoovering and brushing the loo she reapplied makeup: my sake. Her rump of jeans was filled tight but not too fatly. When she kicked off her shoes she had glisten-gold toenails. Her skin was many colours, from mottled pink on her ankles to oak-leaf brown on her arms. I didn't desire girls the same age as me. They wanted to get pregnant and call me husband. Caroline had done all that. She wanted lust with me, not a family. I learned I had a thing for older women. Pleasure with no responsibility.

When she got sweaty from scrubbing she stripped to a bra-less frilly top—my sake. She cooled off at the clothesline hanging washing. Always my clothes first—was she giving them extra handling? Her nipples showed out like two permissions. At least, they read that way to me.

I recited my audition for RADA for her—all that clever-sounding schoolboy Shakespeare: the *put money in thy purse* speech; the *why should a rat have life?* She called them heavy and a little over her head. 'You must be so smart to remember such old words.' Smart. When had I ever been called smart! It's like being looked up to, and having the right to look down your nose.

Whatever stewy part of our ten per cent works out the rights and wrongs of our actions it didn't qualm us from starting kissing. She had the use of me, and left her wedding ring on, and twenty-one's too young to have morals.

I had never felt so...so...sophisticated. Movies, TV and books and I were now related. The sins in their stories had become my own. 'As long as my kids don't find out.' That was Caroline's only worry. That's the rule, that's the small-town code.

That's how I got there, in short: London, 1985. In short, and yet it's perfect—my life shrunk down to this written form. Here I am in my home on Main Street in Scintilla, Australia. It is 1993. I am sitting at my little wood desk, upstairs in a nook beside the bathroom. I may be in Scintilla but right this minute I am in London in my mind. I am about to fall in love all over again in sentences. Fall in love, fall in pity, fall in anger, hate, fear, pain. I bet Shakespeare that's all writing is: you live life out a second time, make sense of it to clear your conscience, square your soul.

To start with, the thrilling part, the love part. I swoon just thinking about it.

London was a bitter place in October 1985. I don't just mean the cold. Unemployment queues, a miners' strike—there was no Empire any longer if you took notice of the news. Me, *I* had a job. I had initiative. I had thirty pounds a week, with a room and food included. If the English didn't want to work I would do it. I would clean a youth hostel, and that is exactly what I did. I wasn't so proud I couldn't sweep corridors. Cow and horse stink prepared me well for toilets.

I was promoted to cutting the lunch ham. You had to hold it very softly to the mechanical slicer. If you squeezed it would slime away, you could lose a finger in the blade.

I had no idea Tilda existed. She was in New York, going to galleries like churches. She had pipedreams of her own, of being a

Pollock or Rothko. The other matter, RADA—even now I squirm to think of it. I jump on one leg and hit 'Get out!' to my temples to be rid of those four letters trapped like swim-water in my head.

At the time I convinced myself my failure was a blessing. It was bitter fate doing me a favour: I should be happy it happened, the shorting-foot-nerve problem. Such a violent attack I almost fainted. It rattled my leg bones and sent my nerves into such a spasm all my words got tangled: I recited, 'Put rats in thy purse.' It was humiliating.

Even if I had been accepted I would have turned them down. Or so I said at the time to my vanity. What kind of building was called Royal Academy and yet was shabby as an old town hall, flaked plaster and peeling paint? Where was the spruced, grand glamour?

And as for the two who sat and judged my shake-tangle show. I had dressed in good shoes and white shirt. I wore a duffle coat for the outside chill, but only for the outside. I carried it serviette-style like a gentleman when in. *They* wore jeans rubbed out at the knees. Jumpers moth-holed and letting through elbows.

I had combed my hair down, parted it at the side for a dash of drawing room elegance. They had matted mops, and beards with patches of baldness showing, the way beards are when you're young. They must have been under thirty and yet were magistrates of me. And no proper speaking either. They had cockney vowels. I was expecting Sir-someones with impeccable language. I was taller than they were but they looked down at me and smirked. I was thankful that at least they didn't laugh in my face.

I could not get out of the place quick enough. My legs were

awobble with nerve-water but I swayed down the hall and barged through the front doors onto the street before my legs gave way and I slipped on fish batter and rain spit.

It occurred to me to do myself in. Just a thought-sip of suicide, nothing more.

My room was tiny; I nicknamed it The Box. Four strides by three with a camp bed in the corner. I had to sleep with one shoulder hanging over to fit the rest of me. The hostel clientele were Italians, Germans, Australians. A hundred of them a night stacked in rickety bunks. Girls in the north wing; boys the south. My shift began at 6.30 each morning, serving breakfast with Polish Lily and Dirk from Rotterdam. At 10 we did the cleaning. The main rule was, if we slept with guests they still had to pay the bunk fee.

I hadn't slept with more than my passport under my pillow, but that was about to change: Tilda was coming. She was bringing my future with her. It had hatched in her hair, was growing down her limbs and about to make contact with me. She had arrived at Heathrow. Her purple haversack was hitting the carousel, *Tilda Robson* printed across it in gold texta. Flat 4, 14 Lyndon Street, St Kilda, Melbourne, Australia.

I was washing cups and saucers, scraping plates free of butter foils and marmalade plops. Cracking coins into the dining room till. What was love doing picking out me? I who smoked fifteen cigarettes a day now to burn away failure, to put up a screen to the outside world. I who pretended to swagger when I walked, for false confidence. A little skip in each stride as if swinging a dandy-man's cane. I who combined this with keeping my fringe over my eyes, a face curtain for aloofness.

Tilda was only ten minutes away. A train had set her down at Blackfriars Station for the uphill trek to the hostel. The sky was dripping greyly as always. It was Sunday. You could hear St Paul's bells practising their scales. She was mounting the laneway steps, the hostel sign in view. I should have kept my face curtain down for both our sakes.

But it was too late. There she was. Here she is once again in my mind, such a tall woman, her black boots adding at least an inch of heel. She is yellow—her clothes, I mean. Blink-bright yellow. A blouse of flower patterns—sunflowers and green and red tropical petals. Who wears a blouse those colours in London, city of drab? Tilda did. She was short-sleeved despite the goose-flesh rain.

The yellow continued up past her shoulders and became hair. Paler yellow than her clothing and pulled into a three-strand plait. An orange band bound the stump of it. Her ears stuck out more obviously from the tightness of the plaiting, like two little cupped hands. It was on purpose. A way of stylishly spoiling the beautiful rest of her.

Others stared, not just me. She was used to such staring. She pouted like a sour kiss to the air around her, rejecting the attention. Her lips were red by nature, not by lipstick.

She was in the age gap of my ultimate preference—ten or so years my elder. I was not intending love. I was *playing*. I was thinking how a woman like her would, for me, be aiming higher than usual. If I even got a kiss from her it would be an achievement. I enjoyed the idea, then let it fade. I went back to drying dishes.

Tilda finished admission. She dwelt on the spot a second, read the directions to her bunk room on the brochure you got with your locker key. Off she went. For all I knew that was the end of it. My rightful place was dishes. My face curtain returned to its down position.

My father would think I had my tail between my legs—that's why I hadn't rung him. It was time I did, though I knew what he'd do. He'd say, 'You've had your little adventure, son. Be responsible, come to your senses. Fly home and settle down to a good productive life.' There had been talk the Mullers planned to leave town to save their marriage. Perhaps they'd already done it, clearing the way for my return.

My conversation with the old boy was a masterpiece of lying. 'Norm,' I said. It sounded more confident than *Dad*. 'Norm, I did it. I was accepted into RADA. That's right, accepted. I was quite impressive. My practising paid off.'

He yelled out for my mother, 'Marg. Marg. He was accepted. I'll be blowed.'

She made a tearful speech about being vindicated before I had the chance to calm her down.

'But I am not going to accept their acceptance,' I told her. 'I know, I know, but you have to understand something. It disappointed me, Marg, the place itself, the people. I have other opportunities I want to take up and explore.' I didn't say what other opportunities. I let the conversation fizzle. Norm offered to wire me money to top up my funds. I politely resisted before relenting.

I was using the hostel payphone by the stairs. Exactly timed on my relenting, Tilda appeared. Down the stairs she came, skipping off the last step. She spun left, heading for the common room. Her yellow blouse had been replaced by a long green shirt with fruit drawings on it. Green apples, coppery peaches and red plums. She paid me no attention, just swept on by. My mother had to ask, 'Are you still there, Colin?'

The next stage came ten minutes later and involved cigarettes. A cigarette implies risk and cheapness in a person; it says they are bold and vulnerable in one. Tilda was smoking. It seemed at odds with the look of her. You wouldn't think she'd want a smokescreen across her attractiveness.

She was seated on a common room armchair, leg over leg, talking in smoke clouds to a man with thick, hairy forearms. Spanish, going by his seedy sound. He flung his arms about and was old—at least forty. Tilda's grey breath licked up from her top lip to her nostrils. She raised her chin as if to drain each smoke puff like a drink. It gave the impression of keeping the world out and also inviting it in.

Since the RADA fiasco I had been sexless in myself, too dead in spirit to feel desire for anyone. I could not imagine anyone feeling desire for me. But a month had passed. I could feel my blood reheating. Blood or hormones or whatever they are. They squirted once again in the sudden way they do, down my back, prickling in my groin and anus. Queasiness bubbled in my stomach as if semen was produced there high up in the intestines, poisoning me sweetly with its gases, forcing its way down the penis in the hope of being expelled. Tilda with her smoking, her one leg spread in a triangle over her knee, brought the queasiness on more strongly. When she reached forward to flick ash from her cigarette her biceps were woman-thin but strung with lean muscle. A vein ran down each arm like an off-centre spine. She was a woman, yes, but with a bit of male in those arms mixed in. The monotone of her Australian speaking had a scratchy grain, the kind of voice that's called husky.

She was telling the Spaniard she had 'done' New York. From her baggy thigh pockets she presented two black books and opened them on a coffee table. I swaggered closer, changing a dirty ashtray for a clean one in order to peek. I wiped stickiness from the table.

'That's Brooklyn Bridge,' she informed the Spaniard, thumbing pages of ink drawings. 'This is in Central Park. These are some wonderful brownstones.' Her pen had photographed them with spidery blots and watery smears.

'They're very good,' I blurted. 'Very good.' And they were. It wasn't just the queasiness talking.

Tilda jerked her head up to take the compliment from me. Her plait bucked across her stuck-out ears. Her smile caused a pretty crease at each side of her mouth, and above her eyebrows too, like an extra brow of skin. At that instant I was sure there must be a smell called Welcome: for all the nicotine about her, a cinnamon hello lifted to me from her hair.

But there!—a wedding ring. A skinny band of shineless silver. Easy to miss among the state of her fingers, ink-stained as if her habit was blue cigarettes. Was she travelling with someone, or was the ring just for show? I admit there was an extra squirt of excitement through me in memory of the sophisticated sin with Caroline.

If we put on a swagger we can appear smarter than we are. We can turn a good phrase if we're swaggering. I swaggered and said,

'I don't know what I like but I know that's art.' Tilda laughed and I sensed it was a good time to walk off, part of the x-ray basics I learned from Caroline. If we turn our backs we can read what someone thinks of us. It may sound unlikely but it's the truth. If we glimpse over our shoulder and catch them looking and they avert their eyes—that's an x-ray taken. They have an attraction to us.

I did it to Tilda and she averted on cue, I was certain of it. She resumed flipping through her personal New York, noisy flips of ink-stiff pages; she smiled in that closed mouth way we do when we've been caught out. She shut her book and stood, put her chair in like a good girl and was marching off in the direction of the female wing. Her plait kept time, ear to ear, with her striding.

I did the sensible thing and checked her admission card. She was travelling alone. Duration of visit, three nights. I set myself up in the common room with coffee, near the door where I could see all comings and goings. When Tilda passed by I would take another x-ray and if successful move to the next stage where I swaggered more and perhaps tried some Shakespeare.

Two hours I lingered, reading newspapers with one eye. No sunflowers or plums appeared. Only a scraggy not-Tilda, a girl-woman with short hair and scabbed pimples. She waved her hands and babbled French—*Je m'appelle Yvonne* and *s'il vous plaît*—and tried to take my hands in hers. Her touch was cold and greasy. I pulled my hands away but she persisted with her *s'il vous plaits.*

'What's the problem?' I said. There was obviously a problem. 'Speak English. You speak English?'

She said she spoke a little English and started off with her name, Yvonne. 'I need money, sir. My money stole.' She made a pick-pocketing motion with her fingers and sniffled snot back up into her nose. 'Please help. I need home. Boat. France.' Her hands sailed a hilly ocean. A thick coughing crackled inside her. 'My brother, he sick. I need go home.'

She doubled up at my feet and I patted her shoulder and said it was dreadful her situation but she should call the police.

'No,' she grunted. 'Money. Please.' Her hair smelled of not being washed of its oils. There was dandruff in the skin of its parting. Her maroon jacket had absorbed a layer of damp grime.

It was this moment, of all the two hours, that Tilda strolled by to order coffee at the common room counter. My first impulse was to fend Yvonne away—I didn't want Tilda seeing me associating with beggars. I stood and stepped free of the girl. But she followed me, shuffling along on her knees. I took a handful of change from my pocket and presented it. I said, 'There you go' loud enough to make a public display of my charity.

Yvonne poked the coins. Her nails were eaten down and dirty in the quick. 'Twenty fucken P,' she complained. 'Twenty P.' Her English wasn't French-English now, it was Liverpool or Manchester. She got to her feet and called me a tight-arse bastard because twenty P is like handing out nothing. She was so loud Tilda and others in the room stood still to watch us.

To save face—a childish thing to do over twenty P—I demanded she give the money back. I took her hand to tip the coins into my palm. She made a fist and screamed thief and rape and help. I let go and appealed to the room for witnesses that I was the victim here, not this fake French urchin.

Yvonne switched her attention immediately to Tilda at the coffee counter. Or rather the wallet in Tilda's hand. *S'il vous plaît*, she begged, fingers steepled together, using the same routine she'd tried on me. She could not take her eyes off Tilda's wallet and even reached out to touch it as if it were hers to claim. Tilda protested but Yvonne kept coming, ranting that the wallet was hers and that Tilda was a thief and must be arrested. She then made the mistake of trying to snatch the wallet. Tilda was not going to let it go, she had a two-hand grip on the thing. Yvonne persisted, but she did not have man-arms. Tilda's veins were popping out along her biceps and she sent Yvonne to the floor with an elbow jolt.

Yvonne screamed and swore she was being assaulted but Tilda kept wrestling her on the ground and retrieved her wallet with a yank and grunt. Yvonne was furious and tried to get back into character to continue her accusations but by now I had gone over to ask if Tilda was hurt. She had opened the wallet, removed her Australian driver's licence and said, 'There, you lying bitch. There's my ID. How dare you!'

I stood between them both, my arms out like a referee who favoured Tilda and was acting as her shield.

Yvonne hit out at my arm. ''E tried to touch me,' she said in her silly accent. ''E, how you say, try to rape me?'

'That's absurd,' I said. My leg nerve began electrocuting me.

Tilda was suddenly at my side. She placed her fingertips on my forearm. My bare forearm. Her bare fingertips. Our first skin-to-skin connection. She steered me, such a light touch, back, back, please, taking charge. 'He no more raped you than you own this wallet. I am his witness. So you go and call the police, because I'll be delighted to fill them in on your *s'il vous plait* rubbish.'

She turned to me. 'Will you be my witness? She's a con artist.'

'Of course I'll be your witness.'

'We can sit down and write out statements.'

Yvonne started shuffling in a circle, clockwise, a dozen granny-steps then back the other way. She knocked on her head like a door and shouted at the floor for us and everyone else in the world to go away. She granny-stepped out of the room, up the exit stairs and was gone.

Yvonne, you don't know what part you played in me and Tilda. You were our accidental matchmaker.

'It's an affront,' Tilda said, karate chopping the common room table. 'Your possessions are your possessions. It's like an invasion of me.' She shivered *invasion* like a sudden chill. Her eyes squinted against tears coming. She poked her plait to re-tuck burst hair as if tears were controlled in the knotting. She said she was determined to return to her afternoon plan. She would finish writing her statement, no matter how pointless—surely it was the last we would see of Yvonne—then she was off to any gallery that was open. The National. The Tate—all those Turners. 'He was abstract before abstract was invented. Have you seen them?'

'No, not yet.'

'You don't like him?'

I had never heard of Turner. But I remember Mr Lipshut at school used to say, 'With art, boys, there is no such thing as *like*. No value judgments or rash generalisations.' I said as much to Tilda.

'That's true. Very good,' she nodded, and with this came the offering of her hand for a formal introduction. She had a man's grip in keeping with those arms.

We signed each other's statements. 'It's been quite cathartic actually, writing this,' she said, taking a deep breath of musty hostel air as if it were a forest fresh with blossom. 'Just like art. You get something off your chest. You make something clear.'

I smiled, though I didn't know what cathartic was. It sounded like arthritic.

'I'll tell you what is not cathartic: crying.' She had managed to squint back her tears. 'When I came on this trip I promised myself two things. Number one: no crying. Do nothing to bring it on. This is a holiday.'

She buttoned her statement into her pants leg. Her right index finger began tracing out her talk in some table salt-spill, like a doodle. 'Let me get this out in the open. So there's no misunderstanding. Because, I sense you are, you know, trying it on. Which flatters me, but my number two for this trip is: no men. No flings. This is an art trip. No men. My marriage has recently ended and I'm enjoying being man-free.'

Blood blushed and burned in my cheeks from the embarrassment. I let my head hang lower behind my face curtain. 'You've got the wrong end of the stick,' I said. 'I wasn't trying it on.'

'You weren't?'

'No. You've made a mistake.'

'Really?'

'It was the last thing on my mind.'

It was her turn for burning cheeks. She tapped a full stop to her doodling. 'I just presumed. I'm sorry. I just thought you were trying it on.'

It was me doodling now. I felt mild nausea below my solar plexus, as if I had eaten bad food. A sinking from the heart like a glob of blood gone down the wrong way. I did not know that love enters us like this. It must have slipped through my skin while we were talking. My dry mouth was a symptom. My pulse quicker and irregular in my neck veins.

I don't think Tilda had any symptoms. She took my wrong-end-of-the-stick comment as a snub, or so I x-rayed, though I was not confident my x-rays were accurate after all. I could not tell if my being younger appealed to her or not. I suspected not. I suspected she considered me a safe male for uninvolved company and little more. I was invited to be her gallery partner when my shift finished.

My portrait of Tilda viewing pictures at the National Gallery, Trafalgar Square:

She preferred no talk during the process. She stood well back from a painting. Then five paces closer to it. Then sideways two paces, then back to her original position. She glowered at chit-chattering school children—would they please not block her line of sight!

She glowered the same at elderly people craning so close to a Picasso they almost nosed it. They passed judgment that 'the paintwork looks kind of rough to me. I like big signatures on a painting. Where are the Monets, Bert? Can you spot any? Myself, I prefer Constables.'

Tilda held her hand at arm's length to block out any realism— a shed or peasant, a donkey and cart. She wanted colours to sing for her and they can't sing around carts. 'See how that turquoise sings?' she said. Her lips were puckered in concentration. Her tongue poked through as if she were suckling.

'Yes, I see.' I copied her, my arm out the same way.

'Rembrandt's black is not really black. It's so dense it's blue and green and silver all in one.'

I chimed in with a Mr Lipshut quote. 'Colour is the suffering of light.'

'I like that. It's quite erudite.'

Erudite? I would have to look that up with cathartic.

From birth we hear so many famous names: Shakespeare, Jesus, Rembrandt, The Beatles, Mozart. Compared with the others Rembrandt was only pictures. He was not even music. He said nothing wise—he was just decoration on a wall, and disappointed me, though I didn't say so to Tilda. I watched her close an eye and aim down the rifle of her arm at colours.

She said they inspired her, pictures. She wanted to draw something right this second, that was how strongly she reacted to pictures. 'I want us to go out and sit at the feet of those stone lions of Trafalgar and I'm going to draw you,' she said.

'Me?'

'You.'

I liked that, the notion of being a model for art. Recorded in Tilda's black books where she sketched landmarks. So we sat on a lion ledge in the evening's street-lamp light and she captured the ghostly haze of my breath-chill forming a halo about me. She took a plastic bag from her shoulder bag and unwrapped from it a mini quiver of pens, a bottle of ink, a vial of water, a small tin. She tipped the blue ink and water together into the tin and smeared and scratched an image of my face onto paper. A splash for my hair, blotty with shadow. My big Cs and double-chin jaw. Making these features deliberately worse with distortion.

'I think we should stop this now,' I complained, straining my voice through a smile. 'I'm getting uglier by the minute.'

'Nonsense,' said Tilda. 'That's the way of art. It is not good enough simply to reproduce what's real. We bend and twist, bring out the essence of our subject. It's all about interpretation.'

Going by those smears and blots she interpreted me as ugly.

'I don't think you're ugly.' She touched her forefinger to the tip of my nose, delivering a cold dab of ink. I wiped it, my eyes crossed until it was gone. 'You're vainer than women,' she laughed. 'My ears are big as plates, and so are yours.'

She measured her left ear with the same hooked-fingers technique I used, and placed the hook to my ear like a shell. 'I would say we are just about equal.' She turned side on and asked me to describe her profile.

'Erudite,' I said.

'Oh, thank you. That's an artist's way of saying it. *Erudite* rather than good or nice.'

She patted another thank-you on my knee.

And so it was starting. We were starting. Tilda was relaxing her number two. She sketched another page of me and let me pry with a question about her married life.

'Off the scene' is how she described her husband. She had left him for what she called a very good reason. A 'let's not talk about it' reason. No lawyers were involved. No children to complicate matters. Sounded all very sophisticated. She was nine years, six months older than I was and she had *lived*.

I felt unlived. I fixed that by raising my own 'let's not talk about it' matters. 'I was accepted into RADA, but it wasn't my thing. Let's not talk about,' I said. 'There was a woman called Caroline in my life. It ended badly. Let's not talk about it.'

Tilda took the lead. She slipped a chilled hand into the crook of my arm and we walked London's higgledy cobbles in a hip-to-hip embrace. We leant into each other as if it were the cobbles' fault. The sweet poison was in me, working its way down my innards. 'Let's go to the Samuel Pepys Tavern,' I suggested. I had been there a few times but this time would be different: I would be drinking under the influence of the sweet poison.

The walls were amber-coloured at Pepys. The dim lights turned us that colour as well, sitting there side by side in a private corner. 'Pepys,' Tilda said, putting her thinking fingers to her lips. 'Mmm. That's a mustard-coloured name.'

'Names don't have colours.'

'They can in an artist's brain.' She said Tilda was red for fire and passion and ambition. I asked what my colour was. She decided on blue for me—'Blue boy', like the painting. I was still 'boy' to her then.

We drank whisky. Whisky is the hottest drink. It spreads the sweet poison through people quickest, whether a man or woman. Soon enough it helped us kiss. It opened our mouths and we connected with a click of teeth and gave over to the meaty swapping of our tongues.

That night we pulled my narrow mattress to the floor. There was room then for her to spread those veiny arms as she sat astride me. She did not want me inside her. She did not want to lie on her back, her feet stirruped the normal way as if giving birth. She wanted to be astride the scoop and pommel of my groin with no entering allowed. 'Keep outside,' she insisted.

'Why?'

'We don't have condoms.'

'You're not on the pill?'

'I stopped it.'

'I'll pull out.'

'No.'

'I promise.'

'Too much risk. I might be ovulating.'

'Just for a second.'

'The AIDS thing too.'

'I don't have that shit.'

'Keep outside.' Her blue fingers fiddled the ends of her plait as if her hair too could be aroused. 'No,' she bossed me when I wanted to change positions. I followed her directions, excited by her ordering and my failure to bob and budge between her legs. She folded her arm under her breasts. Just one arm, her left, and sat up straight upon me.

There is nothing that can be done about a first expelling. Tricks never worked for me to stop it happening too fast. It is not like clenching your bladder against urine. They say use mathematics, complex algebra puzzles, but puzzles were never a distraction in my case. I was no good at maths, it only ever delayed me one or two heartbeats. There is nothing to do but let the first one go, a process lasting sixty wonderful paralysing pulses. Simply give over to the mosquito-bite sensation it gives, the icy itch in an unscratchable place inside the testes.

In five minutes I was ready for more. With Caroline I once had four in fifty minutes. By three there was no need for trying mathematics. With Tilda that night I didn't go further than two because of the effort to stay outside. Tilda didn't have for herself the female equivalent. Didn't get close by my reckoning. She let me out from under her and lay there with that one arm still crossed over her front like some quirk or protective barrier of displeasure.

I kissed her nipples and asked, 'What's wrong?'

'Nothing's wrong.'

'Do you do that crossing-arm routine with everyone?'

'Now I'm really self-conscious.'

'About what?'

She sucked in a breath and let it out, saying, 'Well, you...you are...younger than what I'm used to.'

'So?'

'Parts of me look older than I'd like.'

Her breasts, she meant. She hated her breasts. Ten years ago they bulged in all the right places, but now they dripped off to the side whenever she lay on her back. She used her arm to try and hoist them higher. She had no children to blame for their state. 'It's just from being thirty-one now, not nineteen anymore.'

I assured her they were beautiful breasts. I nuzzled my way past her arms, said her nipples were a lovely peach colour and kissed them. Peach with pretty crinkled freckles. I kept kissing them and eventually her arm retreated to her side. We were two people having pleasure for the night, I said. Let's not have breasts distract us.

But one night became two. We did not want to end on just one, not without fully consummating our friendship.

So, the next night we did consummate it. It was good but a notch or two less than great. I had never used a condom before, but Tilda insisted and bought the pack herself to make the point that having sex with her was on her terms. Condoms let the warmth from inside Tilda in but kept any true feeling out. It did not feel like we had joined our skins.

As well, Tilda's arm went back up to its barrier position. One night together had not troubled her so much where breasts were concerned—she did not expect ever to see me again. Two nights were different. Two nights meant she wanted to look her best for those moments when we talked barely above a whisper, our faces so close we were breath to breath. She perched statuesquely across my lap, sucked her stomach in and held the pose while I teetered between mathematics and letting go. I could tell she was performing pleasure rather than truly feeling it. She could not fully give herself over. Not bodily anyway. Not yet. In talk she could, but not the rest of her.

In talk she gave over more freely than I liked. 'I felt I was sacrificing my life,' she said, propping herself on her elbow. 'Was I supposed to sacrifice my life?'

It was not a real question, it was a plea for me to understand her plight: to be married as she had been at only twenty; to be a gorgeous twenty and courted by a man who himself was little more than a teenager; to say *let's spend our life together* when it's just puppy love—it's expecting too much. Didn't I reckon so?

'Yes,' I said without even thinking. I was warm in the huddle of our breathing.

She wanted me to know that her husband, Lionel, was a kind and decent fellow. An architect. He came from the same mould as her St Mark's Church parents. But what is art to Melbourne suburbia? It is for hobbies in the holidays. It is for old ladies' lounge rooms, pleasant watercolours at Rotary fetes. 'Put your talent into your garden beds and cooking, dear. Get a lovely home in Camberwell and please spare us the whingeing about wanting more.' She put a finger, pistol-like, to her forehead, pulled the trigger and slumped down. 'I must seem really stupid to you. At twenty-one that was my life, and here you are at that age and you're picking and choosing about RADA. I was supposed to make my husband a father. But you, you're out in the world. You're living. Well, I took the pill no matter what my husband said.'

She stretched and smiled that life had become a banquet: to be lying on a London floor naked with a young man, how delicious. She propped back onto her elbow. 'I want you to know one thing, though: I'm not a slut or anything.'

'I didn't think you were.'

'I mean, I was a virgin when I married. Don't think I never had innocence is all I'm saying. In the whole time Lionel and I were together, a decade together, we would have had sex not more than twenty, thirty times. Seriously, maybe forty, that's all. And I can't recall ever coming. No orgasm with him in all those years.'

I was about to ask if she'd got close to it with me but decided she would have said if she had. I worried I was just another Lionel. Or was I to take the lead more? Get her going with my tongue perhaps, like an experienced animal-man?

She put her head on my chest. 'Anyway,' she said. 'That's my excuse for the wilder stuff I've done.'

'What wilder stuff is that?'

'Experimenting. With men.'

She made it sound scientific, as if test tubes and white coats were involved. She had slept with an electrician who fixed the lights in her kitchen; and an art lecturer who reckoned sex with him would 'radicalise her to extrapolations of linear impulse'. Whatever that meant.

'Enough,' I said. I put my hand gently over her mouth. I didn't want to hear about her wilder stuff, her fleeting lovers. It brought on more nausea.

They say we fall in love. But really we fall in sickness. I lost appetite for food when I was with Tilda. We spent a third night together and my stomach was sunken in its wishbone cavity. Me, I was never sick, but I was sick now, the strangest sickness that made my eyes gleam green with excellent health. They had shiny white edges. My cheeks were glossed in a fresh oil of pink. My brow skin was cleansed suddenly of its pimple dots and squeezings like a miraculous washing from within.

The thought of other men with her angered me. They had no right to have touched her, their butting cocks and loose belly hairs sticking to her. I could have murdered them in my imagination. If they no longer existed on this earth then Tilda's past would die with them. So goes the sickness.

I thought a cure might be found in countering her past by laying out mine. Not just details about Caroline, but the local farm girls—'*they* let me go inside them and I would time pulling out to perfection.'

Tilda moaned. 'Don't tell me all that.' She covered one ear with her palm and blocked the other by leaning harder into my armpit. It was happening to her too, the sickness.

She turned onto her back. She tapped my waist to urge me onto her, into her. 'Go inside, then,' she whispered.

'No condom?'

'I trust you.'

'Seriously?'

We consummated us. Properly. Flesh to flesh.

I did pull out, though for a paralysing instant the bliss was almost too much fever to resist.

Tilda got paralysis too: she lost control of her Ss in the reverie. She whispered, 'Tho good.'

'What?'

'I juth had one.'

'Had what?'

'Came.'

'You did?'

'Yeth. A quiet one.'

Dawn next morning she was packing when I woke, buttoning her orchard shirt so hurriedly she missed holes. 'I have to go,' she said. 'Sorry, but it's best.' She flicked her messy hair through her fists—in, over, in, over, plaiting, two elastic bands in her teeth.

I stomped away blankets. The off-smell of our sleeping bodies hung in the stuffy air. 'Why do you have to go?'

'I have to go, and that's that.'

She broke a band in her haste and mumbled a series of contradictions: no, there was nothing wrong. Yes, of course there was something wrong. These have been the most superb few days for her. They have also been disastrous. 'This is an art trip. Art is not *this*.'

My wishbone sent a burp into my mouth. I wanted to sweeten my breath with toothpaste before holding her and kissing her to please stay, but there wasn't time. 'Let me bring you breakfast. Let's have breakfast here in bed,' I said.

She stroked my chin with the inside of her fingertips, then the knuckle side. I kissed her fingers, their faint ink odour. Forever ink is her scent to me, the personal perfume of her skin. She said, 'You're a beautiful boy. But you are just a boy.'

'I'm twenty-one. I am not a boy.' I did not feel a boy. I did not feel a man. I was me. I did not feel any age.

Tilda stroked some more. I flinched from her touch. 'Three days ago I was free,' she said. 'I was free and open to life. Now I just want to stay in this room with you and make love and never see or speak to the outside world. I need to get out of here. Now. I have Venice and Florence waiting for me. I have Madrid and Amsterdam. Goodbye, my lovely, lovely boy.'

I shook my face curtain down. She unzipped her black books from her bag, opened one, the one smeared with pages of crinkly me. She tore out two pages for my keepsake. 'Please take them. Remember me with them.' She closed the book. 'The rest I will keep.'

She unzipped her yellow flower shirt, another keepsake. 'Try it on.' She attempted another stroke of my chin. I let her. She helped me dress in the shirt. It was too tight a fit, but that wasn't the point. It was *hers*. She took a step backwards to watch me button up.

I stepped forward. It was me who did the stroking then. She fended me off with a soft push. 'No,' she said, and swung her bag on. She kissed her fingers in my direction and without looking me in the eye she uttered goodbye and left at a walking sprint down the corridor.

My nausea was a different kind now. It came with cramps. Cramps as I put out the butter and croissants. I wanted to fold up in bed but there was my shift to do. Cramps as I brewed coffee in the vat. The smell of it was enough to make me retch. My innards needed food but I couldn't take food.

I folded the ink mes into my wallet. I vowed to rip them up for the garbage, deface them and thereby erase Tilda from my mind. But I put them in my wallet. I thought of wearing her yellow shirt as an apron, of doing the dishes in it until it was crusty from wiping my hands. Instead I washed the thing on gentle cycle. I ironed it for hanging on the hook on my door.

How long would they last, these cramps and retching? I had no previous experience to go on. Would a nasty bout give me immunity? Good riddance to her, I told myself. Who wants a woman with 'little experiments' in her history!

A week went by and still I had the sickness. I became desperate for an antidote. The obvious one was to go out on the town, go searching for a Tilda replacement. I felt more attractive than I ever had in my life. I had been physically transformed—a peculiar quirk of what ailed me. My face had lighter shading, like naturally occurring makeup. My skin was tight and polished-looking. My eye-whites gleamed regardless of poor sleeping. I was ill and super-well at the same time.

I believed I had developed a new power. I called it 'being in season', the livestock term for when an animal puts out mating odour. What else could explain the interest female patrons of the hostel showed in me? I had not drunk any special potion.

Melissa, for instance. Tilda's first replacement. I thought Americans would be beyond my reach: they were from the capital of the world; I was from the opposite. But I was in season. And what an antidote Melissa was. Americans are not a curious people. They do not waste breath on talk not centred on them. They have a speech ready for advertising their own existence. Melissa's began with how her long black hair was from her Shawnee heritage, and ended with how Marlboros kept her thin and the sugar in Coke kept her energetic. Her teeth were a picket fence of whiteness that New Zealanders only got with dentures.

Inga from Hamburg had man traits bigger than Tilda's: hands you get from manual labour, though Inga had never lifted more than law books. It must have been racial.

The next was from Wales (Moira or Myra—I have forgotten her name). I took each replacement to the National Gallery and held my hand at arm's length to block out realism. I found art cathartic, I said. I informed them that Turner was abstraction's pioneer. I took them to Samuel Pepys and explained how his name was mustard because it hinted at hotness. I kissed and fondled them in the amber privacy.

They let me go inside them and there was no pulling out. I promised I would but never bothered. I was impatient to get them out of my room when it was over. I wanted Tilda's nasally accent in my ear, not theirs. I wanted her sun-speckled shoulders and the speckled front between her collarbones.

This desk in my little nook is where I go to tell the truth. It's an honesty box, writing about yourself. I hold it to my ear and it rattles with apologies like these: Sorry, Melissa, wherever you are. You too, Inga and Moira or Myra. I treated you cheaply. Imagine if my sickness had been the AIDS kind and not love. I could have infected you with my expellings. At the very least I might have made you pregnant. Sometimes I fantasise there'll be a knock on the door and there you'll stand with a child in my image to claim me as its father, and want some money. You were just fleeting to me, nothing more. And with fleetings there is this sexual rule: complications from a one-night stand are *their* problem.

After a month I decided to leave the hostel, so any *their problems* couldn't find me. Fleetings are addictive but for all the solace they give they can soon bore you and sour you with emptiness. I didn't know that Tilda had the sickness for me. I had submitted my resignation and on the same day an envelope was poked under my door, her elegant longhand on the front. On the back, on the V-fold, was a drawing of my face.

Dear Colin,

'Darling Colin,' I really want to say. I certainly won't write 'Sweet boy.' I know how 'boy' riles you.

This is not a letter I expected to be writing. I hate writing. Painters should paint not write, especially when they are overwhelmed by something. If I continue the letter in drawings will the images make sense? I hope they express what I am feeling coherently.

I unfolded four pieces of paper. They had furry edges down one side from being torn from her black book.

Page one had a violent theme. Tilda was seated on a plane or ferry. Her fist was reaching in through her plait, into her brain. Inside her brain was a curled-up me. She was grabbing and pulling to remove me. The drawing was titled 'Sweet boy, but good riddance.'

Page two had me again. She'd got my nose-bulb down pat. My face curtain was fanned out like a powerful wingspan. I was flying up into her body between her legs. The title of this one was 'Eagleman. Apologies to Leda and the Swan.'

Page three had Tilda asleep. I was asleep too, but asleep inside her, where her heart and lungs would be. The title: 'Insomnia. 3 A.M. Colinized.'

Page four was 'After El Greco.' Tilda was naked and crucified, though with one arm across herself in that protective way of hers. The other arm was nailed the Jesus way, beneath a crown of thorns which was actually a crown of mes. My head, a dozen of them, twined around hers.

There was another page of her longhand with its lean tadpole Fs and refined seahorse Ss, as if the lines were living and shining:

Sweetheart—four weeks of not seeing you and yet it feels so natural to call you sweetheart. Please forgive me for racing off on you the way I did. I had to. I had to cool off. I don't know what more to say except I want to see you again.

I was going to fly home from Frankfurt, but maybe I could go through London instead. Can I stay with you? I will ring you in a few days. Will it be easy to have you come to the phone? If it's not I will leave a number and hope you feel like calling.

Do take care. Speak soon.

Love, Tilda XX

I wouldn't put it past the future to have ears. Massive ears so it can listen in on phone calls and assess if two people are matching up. The measurement for success I bet is giggly standardised language: plenty of *How have you been?* and *I wish you were here* and *I miss you*. If the future was listening to Tilda and me it would have thought we were coming along nicely. From the first phone call we used *sweetheart* instead of our names. There were numerous pauses for sighing. We hadn't even finished the call and we were looking ahead to another one the next day.

Tilda was in Amsterdam. I was in limbo. I said I was moving on to better employment. I didn't know what employment that might be but I glossed over this using an optimistic air, big-noting myself that I could do anything I put my mind to.

'If you can conquer RADA, you certainly can do anything,' said Tilda.

There should be a town called Comeuppance. There probably is, where others like me go. My Comeuppance town ended up being Scintilla. We'll get there soon, but first there's Amsterdam.

And before Amsterdam there were five more *sweetheart* and sighing phone calls. Whispery *darlings* were added, and kiss-sounds when we said goodbye. I'd run out of big-noting—I was too busy thinking about Tilda to scour London for a job more prestigious. Those phone calls with her were the central focus of my days.

'You need a break, darling. Why not come here and be with me,' she said. She had a pension room all to herself near the Van Gogh Museum. She had 'an appetite', which is love talk for mad lust. I had it too, so strong an urging it could only be permanent.

I can't sit calmly at my nook desk if I'm to commit Amsterdam to the page. I have to stand up and walk around between lines. There I am: I have just landed, am about to be queued and stamped through the airport doors.

My blood is sprinting in-out of my heart. I am a few seconds from seeing Tilda. Even now, these eight years later, after all that has come to pass, my blood sprints in anticipation. I push my chair out and bounce on my toes. I wave as if seeing her among the hugging and handshaken greetings of others. I pace the elation out, one circuit around my nook. But I do it softly or else the floorboards creak and Tilda calls out complaints from her studio. My floor is her ceiling. It disturbs her concentration, my creaking. To paint is to need silence to order your thoughts and summon inspiration. Could I please pay her the courtesy of silence, for she has lost so much time? There is so much time to make up.

Floorboards are my enemy. But not the rickety stairs. The old wood there is friends with me should Tilda suddenly appear. The slightest footstep and my friend sets off his creak-alarm, my warning to hide these pages immediately and quickly wind other paper into my typewriter.

My short-notice hiding place is under the desk's tablecloth. I keep a pile of books handy to stack on top. From there I transfer them, once Tilda is gone, to places in the walls around me. The architraves are loose and skew-whiff enough to tuck pages behind and tap the wood shut like a secret compartment. I don't trust Tilda not to go through my things. Hiding places have become essential.

So I walk softly. And although my heart may be sprinting I sit down and close my eyes. I puff my cheeks out to get my breath back. I light a cigarette and jerk the window open to blow the smoke out the slit.

Tilda had hired someone to take us to her pension by car. 'Look at that.' She pointed to the night's colours in canals, street lamps dancing pinkly in water. I couldn't have cared less about Amsterdam's canals. I wanted my hands all over her, starting just above the knee and working up, but she wriggled and pushed me off. 'The driver,' she smiled and frowned. She shrugged my lips from her neck skin. She glanced at the rear-vision mirror to shoo the driver's eyes from our play.

I slumped along the back seat in mock rejection. Pressed my knees against her thigh to cork it gently in punishment. I sprang up and kissed her ear deep into its wax bitters.

'Don't.' Her protesting was not about the driver anymore. She put her palm on my chest, held it there, a fence of fingers. 'I'm sorry if I'm standoffish, but I'm shy. It's natural. I haven't seen you in weeks, and I think: Is it going to be the same between us?'

'You're confusing me. Have you got cold feet?'

'No. No. Let's wait till we get to our room. There's something that might dampen your enthusiasm.' She moved the fence to my mouth. She re-pointed to the canal colours. 'Aren't they gorgeous?'

I replied yes, sarcastically. Yes, the moon is very...moony. Yes, the water is...watery.

After a squabble with the pension manager we climbed the steep spiral to number 12. He wanted my passport for safekeeping. His safekeeping, not mine. 'You young people don't pay and one morning—*phut*! You are gone.' I gave him my passport to speed up getting onto those stairs.

The room had a low double bed covered by a black eiderdown with windmill embroidery. Window glass was the headrest. Through the glass was a ledge with red and green flowers in a planter box.

'Look at that,' Tilda said, kneeling on the bed. 'Across the street. You wonder how the whole façade keeps standing.' She was referring to a row of bulging buildings, cracked from the ages and kept from toppling by telegraph poles propped against them.

'Yes, it's fascinating,' I said. I knelt beside her, positioning myself to catch her lips with my lips when she turned. Sweet poison dripped through me. She turned and, lip to lip, we spoke into each other's mouths.

'Wait,' she said.

'For what?' I fingered under her jumper, arms wedging open the wool. I fingered a layer of cotton singlet to ungoggle the bra wire from her breasts. She bit my bottom lip with her kiss. Her man arms were quivering. The taut skins of her ribs and drum belly were quivering. I was quivering too. She had hardly touched me with more than her mouth but that was enough to pluck my nervous system like a thumb.

The ungoggling went smoothly; so too unbuckling her belt— one of those seatbelt arrangements that snapped together instead of a spur and hole. But when I slid my flattened hand down her

48

fly-front she jackknifed away just as I reached the saliva parting. My wrist was locked between her legs—I had to shimmy after her as she jumped off the bed or risk a dislocation. She held my wrist in her hands as if I needed controlling. 'That's the thing I needed to tell you. My period has arrived. I hoped it might start tapering off by now. It's tomato soup down there.'

'So?'

'So it's a mess.'

'So?'

'So it's not attractive.'

'I'm used to blood.'

'Ay?'

'Calves and lambs. What farm boy ever baulked at blood?'

'In my experience this kind of blood puts men off.'

'I have no idea.'

'You haven't done it with blood?'

'No.'

'It doesn't bother you?'

Even if it had I was quivering so much I'd have gone ahead whether blood or acid.

'Sweet boy.' She cradled my face. 'The good thing is, I can't get potted with it.' She kissed me, a peck on the mouth. Another peck. Each kiss got longer until it was one long kiss that kept going while she slipped her tampon out and scrunched a pocket tissue around it for my non-viewing.

The plastic bag from the rubbish bin made an undersheet beneath Tilda. Period blood smells the same as any other kind: rust, soil and briny water.

49

Art smells like turpentine. Like garages and machinery sheds. It dries into pictures, but turpentine, that's what art is to me. Old baked-bean and tuna-fish cans filled with the stuff. It keeps the painter's brush clean and makes the paint go further.

The smell fumes up through the nook's floorboard cracks, burns my eyes, makes my nose run like winter. My pacing circuit may creak and disturb Tilda's concentration but my pages—my testimony, for want of a better word—get wrinkled in spots from my turpentine tears. Not real tears—I am the opposite of miserable. The testimony is liberating. There's a jaunt in me, a skip in my mental stride. The swagger I once had is getting another life. It's the perfect state to be in to write about our high spirits the next morning in Amsterdam.

Sex, a café breakfast, then more sex—that was the plan. 'Congressing' was what Tilda preferred to call it. Sex was too impersonal a word for our activities. Making love was too ordinary, a term everybody used. Whereas congressing made us sound like a two-person nation. A parliament of us, all to ourselves.

Our congressing left us with some cleaning to do. The plastic bag had ripped, Tilda's muddy red had streaked through. Expellings are not just something men have. Tilda began having what she called 'explosions'; sets of them ten seconds apart, not my ten minutes or half an hour. A clear fluid bubbled and frothed as if I had popped something inside her. It became runny and mixed with her bleeding.

We scrubbed the sheet with wet toilet paper but the mattress was left brown through the middle. There were other stains on it, older stains from other people, but ours was a size we thought too large to leave; we'd be forced to pay for new bedding. Half the morning we dowsed it with bleach bought from a supermarket around the corner. It paled the evidence but took all of Tilda's perfume to spray away the ammonia stink. I found a shower curtain at the same supermarket that would do for plastic for our next session. We left the window open a fraction to help drying and stepped out into the midday rain.

Tilda wanted to take me to church. The Rijksmuseum, that is. St Rembrandt. St Vermeer. She jigged along the footpath so excited to be my guide she knocked into people, or danced around them. Once in through the church doors she went into worship mode, closing her eyes sometimes, as if prayerful. 'This is *The Night Watch*,' she said. 'You bear witness to *The Night Watch*. You don't simply look at it.'

I swaggered that I admired Vermeer's *Milkmaid* for the cloudy perfection of the woman's skin. Rembrandt was still decoration to me, so I kept quiet on him. I walked ahead of Tilda, bored and mischievous. I ambled past pictures without taking any notice, or went up close to read the label with the painter's birth and death dates on it. Sometimes I read them out loud, which irritated her. She shushed me and told me to stand back and witness. Witness and behave like a good boy. I wouldn't call it a tiff exactly. She was embarrassed by me, yes, but I sensed she was amused by my hide. 'The paint is all cracked in these pictures,' I said to tease.

'Don't be gauche. The paint's cracked because it's old.'

Pictures just hang there. They do not change or move. Why would I watch them when she, Tilda Robson, was on display? I could put my hand down the back pockets of her jeans and feel the real thing. Art had nothing I could touch.

I am not a thief, I am not a vandal, I am not a murderer, though Tilda has at various times accused me of each. The thief-and-vandal part I will deal with first. These two were never really serious claims, but in the spirit of the honesty box I do have this admission: somewhere in this house there is thief-and-vandal evidence. I don't know where exactly—it has been ages since I cared. For all I know Tilda keeps it souvenired in her own private architrave, a treasured speck of art history.

I have no guilt whatsoever: the speck was obtained by accident. It happened while we were in the Van Gogh Museum the next day.

Ah, Van Gogh! Even I saw there was a clever mind behind the childishness of his stuff—the blunt black outlines that made the paint seem colouring-in; four flicks of black and there you had an amateur-looking crow; dabs of puckered yellow making a fat cliché sun. Each worth a fortune these days but back then, nothing. Just the visual rantings of a no-count man.

Tilda got goose bumps staring at them. I felt jealous, which was ridiculous: who can feel jealousy over something not living? Besides, they gave me goose bumps too. Here were the world's most famous sunflowers. Here were the wheat fields I had seen in books since a kid. They called me forward like the priest of all paintings to worship their surfaces. The paint was so thick in places I wondered how it held together and didn't fall off in chunks from gravity. Van Gogh had once stood before them as I was now doing, his hand reaching to the canvas churning paint into something buttery. I was like another him, my eyes beholding what he beheld; my own fingers just an arm span away from joining me to him through the time warp of paint.

And suddenly I was touching it. I shut my eyes and my hands roamed over the rough skin of a picture.

'Don't,' Tilda panicked. She pulled my shirttail but I wasn't listening. I was with Van Gogh. I *was* Van Gogh. 'Watch out. Watch out.'

A tubby bald man in a green official jacket ordered me not to touch. 'No touching. No touching. Get away.' He waved his arm stiffly against his side to signal me back to an appropriate distance. I did as he said, but somewhere in the time warp a piece of paint got caught in my finger webbing. Not a big piece. More a flake, a dot. I could feel it wedged there but the guard was lecturing me on the etiquette of not handling paintings and I couldn't try to stick it back with him watching. He emphasised the words 'forbidden to touch' with a heavy stomp of his shoe.

I felt the flake digging into my flesh but was too scared to offer it up with an apology. I just moved along to the next painting. I expected any second the guard, having seen the damage, would yell *halt!* Damage being too strong a word: if he squinted he might see a tiny bare patch. I moved along nodding and mumbling my admiration for the museum's collection.

Tilda had tucked her head down and with that metronome plait of hers going quick-time ducked and shouldered past other patrons to get clear of me. I could see her peeping from behind a hedge of tourists, her face straining against letting out laughter.

I puckered my mouth in a whistleless whistle and strolled in the direction of the gallery exit.

The best course of action, the right and proper thing to do, was to go to the front desk and say, 'I found this.' Then I could walk out free of blame. I'm sure the museum had scientists who dealt with paint flakes. If it wasn't for the guard I might have done that. But he kept watching me. I was afraid of being arrested. How long would I get in jail for art defacing? I'd be sued for millions of dollars—the family farm would have to be sold for lawyers. So I kept walking, my pucker directing the air from my silent whistle up over the ridge of my nose, onto my brow and hairline where fear-sweat was beading.

The guard followed me out of the exit and stood at attention to see me off down the street like so much riffraff. I didn't rush my departure in case I looked guilty. I gave a performance of casual strolling that must have been convincing despite my leg-nerve problem flaring up and giving me a drunkard's gait. I turned left at the corner and strolled out of the guard's sight.

Tilda caught up. She was doubled over in glee that I had the gall to do it—to touch a Van Gogh, actually touch it instead of minding my manners and respecting rules. 'It must be like touching history,' she said, grabbing my arm and squeezing it as if a Van Gogh volt might transfer through her.

I showed her the flake in my palm. 'It's like touching this,' I said. 'It *is* this.'

At first she didn't twig. 'What do you mean?' she asked. Her voice petered out. Her eyes went so wide her forehead concertinaed into her hair. She muttered *fuck*, and *fuck* again. That's when she made her vandal-and-thief accusation. 'It's destruction of a master-piece. You're a vandal. A vandal and a thief of a piece of history.' She spoke in a trance, her mouth agape in the shape of an O. She stared at the flake in horror and wonder and awe. She touched it lightly, like brittle treasure that might shatter to dust if she pressed too hard. 'We have to do something. We have to reattach it.'

I swore it wasn't deliberate vandalism but Tilda wasn't listening. 'We can mail it to them,' she said. 'We can send it anony-mously.' It came down to duty as far as she was concerned. It came down to doing the right thing by Van Gogh and not defiling the very art she honoured and adored. She held out her hand for me to deliver the flake into her keeping. I carefully swept it to her with my fingertip.

Once it was in her hold she clenched her fist loosely, like trap-ping a butterfly and feeling the flutter of vulnerable wings. She clasped the fist-cage against her throat. 'You're safe with me,' she whispered.

So much for mailing the thing back. She called it her Vincent flake. Far from dishing out more blame, she thanked me for doing it—my vandal crime of paint. She sat on our pension bed and there it was in her palm with all its time-warping magic. She put it in an envelope for hiding in her luggage, though she couldn't leave it there more than five minutes before needing to take it out and have another look. 'Hello, Vincent,' she would say.

Among her drawing paraphernalia was a pen whose gold nib she knew to be exactly one inch long. She measured Vincent as a third of that in length and width. 'Thank you,' she said, kissing and pushing me down onto the bed. She yanked my hair and bit my ear. 'Thank you, you vandal. My darling vandal boy.'

Her eyes were closed, her teeth were gritted ecstatically. I couldn't tell if it was me she congressed with or a vision of dead Van Gogh.

Being in love is a kind of being famous. Famous on a small scale to just one person. You are looked up to by them even if you're really just a child-man. Love is having power over someone. You are the president of them and you are also their servant, and the person you're in love with is president and servant back to you.

Nothing mattered outside that pension room the week we spent there. We opened the window for oxygen but sent the housemaid from the door when she knocked for cleaning. At night we crept down for food and cigarettes and whisky. As we descended the corkscrew stairs we imagined all Amsterdam was saying, 'Oh yes, there they are, the couple in room number 12. They've been at it for days. They'll waste away if they're not careful.'

When you are president and servant you only have one need: to spend every second with your opposite president; except the toilet, when you can at last let your bowels open, avoiding too much splatter and stench.

'I'm tempted to make a confession,' Tilda said quietly. She was pillowed on my chest, giving my solar plexus hair a pinch. 'I'm almost scared to say it but I'll say it anyway: this is like nothing I've felt for someone else before.'

'Why are you scared of saying that?'

She went silent, just her breeze-breath rippling my nipple hairs and tickling. I realised this silence was to give me time to match her confession with my own. To say, 'It's the same for me' and therefore demonstrate we had equal feelings for each other, no imbalance. I was about to say it, because it was true, but Tilda prompted me. 'And you?'

'Same for me,' I said.

'Truly?'

'It's not like anything before.'

'What have you got to compare it with?'

I had no love to compare it with.

'So this is your first time, in love?'

'Yes.' I did not want her to think I was inexperienced so I reminded her about Caroline, which wasn't love but was experience nonetheless.

'Shsh.' A soft rebuking. 'The point is—and this is miraculous to feel—it's not my first time, yet I feel like it *is* my first time. Like I am beginning with a clean slate.'

Love's favourite word is more. It always wants more *I love yous*. It wants you to say it over and over. 'Say it,' Tilda kissed of me. And I kissed the same of her. 'Say it again. Say it once more.'

Just as sex was too crude a word and congressing was better, even the act of congressing seemed inadequate to express how obsessed we were becoming, how exquisitely ill. We reminded ourselves it was barely a month since the start and yet here we were panting 'I love you' in time with each thrust and each expelling, 'I love you' in the aftermath, curled groin to buttock in a foetal lull position.

Soon that was not enough. 'I want to be with you forever' and 'Never leave me' needed to be added. Her saying it, and me saying it in return. 'If I can't be with you I couldn't live. I'd be better off dead.'

That was not enough either. 'Can I tell you something?' said Tilda. 'I am about to be very serious.'

'Say it.'

'First say you love me.'

I said it and she said it right back, with a tender tap on my chin.

'Okay. The thing I want to say is, I would even want to make a baby with you. I've never felt that, ever.'

I was really famous now. I had been selected from the world's millions of males to join my self to hers and create posterity through our genes. I was too flattered to reply.

'Have I said too much?'

'No.' I was the most important man in the world at that moment. I wanted to savour it.

'Please say something.'

'I would be honoured to do that with you. I would be honoured to be its father.'

Tilda said thank you. She put her chin on her cupped hands upon my shoulder. She said it was a beautiful sensation to congress with me and have my sperm inside her. It was like being joined even when we physically weren't. 'We should start thinking about how we're going to live.'

'What do you mean?'

'How we are going to make money.'

I big-noted we shouldn't worry about that. *I'm a clever fellow, am I not?*

We didn't need to panic, Tilda said. She had $40,000 due from her half of her marital assets. But where were we going to live? London was so very far from anywhere she was used to. She was used to sunshine and clean air. If she had a child she would want the baby to enjoy those benefits too, not be closed in by snow and darkness and fog. 'But I'll go wherever you are.'

'I'll go wherever you are.'

'Don't you have prospects in London?'

'Of course. But not if you won't be happy.'

That's how I got here—Scintilla.

Say Australia to me and I still can't tell you much. It has a ground beneath your feet like any other place. The sky has a fiercer, whiter sun. I wasn't here for those things. I was here for Tilda. She was Australia to me. We were citizens of us. I know it is not a healthy way to live, but it is how we ended up living. If I want nature there are Tilda's landscapes decorating the walls, stripes and splashes of what she calls Abstract Passionism. If I want something to read there are Tilda's medical records to remind me of life and death. If I want sport I can jog for an hour in the forest. I can play jump-the-snake in summer on the forest track.

Straight off the plane from Amsterdam—it was late January—we thought we might settle in Melbourne. It had old joined-up houses like dingy London streets, frilly iron-lace edges and brick of reddish brown. 'Good ole Melbourne,' Tilda called it, like a fond putdown. But she preferred the flat plains two hours' drive to the west. There, if you ignored the barbed-wire fences, it was like beholding fields of wild dusty desert and not just farms. She wanted to strike out in that direction. We'd sleep off the jetlag and then head westward into the summer heat.

We camped in her studio in Fitzroy, a suburb with the dingiest London look of all. Her rent was paid up till mid-February, so that gave us planning time.

By 'studio' I mean a partitioned floor shared by four artists above a lighting shop. The rules stated no lodging was allowed—the property was for art work only, not bedding down in. But there was too much smell from turps pots and soaking brushes to give away the funk of our congressing and sleeping. We bought a futon and had it folded up long before anybody arrived. One artist, called Sebastian, who had a waxed antennae moustache like Dali and wore a three-piece suit and white spats, was particular about the rules. He was painting a portrait of someone famous. He didn't want to bring someone famous into a doss house.

Our planning time only produced one idea: Tilda wanted to live as a modern Van Gogh somewhere on the dusty plains. A region called the Wimmera-Mallee had, she said, Van Gogh wheat fields. He would have drooled to see how vast they were, sun-bleached and blazing bronze. Her $40,000 would surely get us a house of fair proportions. She planned to paint, eventually have an agent in Melbourne and make money that way. 'The perfect life,' she said.

There is no such thing, of course.

What was *I* going to do? This was the question which marred our setting out for home-hunting. 'How will *you* make a living?' Tilda asked. I big-noted in my usual way—'I'll think of something'—and let the sentence trail off. But two events put me in my place.

The first was my birthday, February 10. I was twenty-two. It meant nothing to me; there was no big to-do; I felt no different. Even the mirror thought so. I had no extra year of face lines, no thinning hair, no belly bulge appearing. My eye-whites still woke up bright and clear despite the night before's two bottles of cheap cleanskin wine. No matter how much I drank I never got headaches.

Tilda was another story. Wine made her skull throb; she became argumentative with it. She moaned and coughed under the futon's blanket, wishing I wouldn't gloat about how I felt so fit and in my prime. It was like an accusation, she said, that she was getting over the hill. 'You may not mean it to be but that's how I read it. Could you stop parading, please?'

'I'm not parading. I feel no different from last year, or being sixteen, that's all.'

'You'll know what I mean one day.' She rubbed her bloodshot eyes and pushed her burst plait into a bit more order. She fingered around in her toilet bag and took out a mascara pencil, a pocket mirror. She turned her back to me but I could still see her face cameoed in the glass, her eyes rolled upward for dragging black pencil lines around her eyelids. 'Anyway,' she yawned. 'I have something you don't. I have plans. Some direction. A purpose.'

Being talked down to like that made me argumentative. 'Fuck purpose.'

'Hardly a mature attitude.' She pulled off the T-shirt she used for a nightie and began dressing, keeping her back to me for privacy. 'We've been together a few months now. We can't keep doing nothing but congressing all our lives. What will you do for a living?'

Was this the point where love's *more* ended? I had a flattening-out of feeling in me, an unspecified disappointment where blind excitement had been.

We began turning on each other in a scratchy, squabbling way. I sat on her studio table and lit a cigarette to show I was so fit and young I could enjoy a cigarette first thing in the morning. Tilda needed till noon to clear her lungs for it. She jigged her jeans on, sucked in a breath for the effort of the tight zipper. She waved that the smoke was making her feel sick. I blew louder and further into her breathing zone.

She suggested I consider her for a moment. She didn't mean the smoke; she meant the money issue, the issue she called 'the pragmatics'. When she introduced me to people they were going to ask, 'So tell me, Colin. What do you do?'

'What are you going to say?' she asked.

I shrugged. 'I don't know yet.'

'What am I going to say? "Oh, Colin just moons about being cuntstruck, and expects me to moon about being cockstruck."'

'What people?'

65

Tilda closed her eyes, exasperated. 'Listen. I love you. This has been such fun and so wild, you and me. I've loved it. But if we want a perfect life we have to start thinking sensibly.'

'When you say you've loved it, you mean it in the past tense? I've come all this way to Australia and you're regretting it?'

'No. That's not what I said.'

'You implied it, then.'

Her voice went up a key to a pleading tone. 'My parents, for instance. They will ask, "What do you do, Colin?" I wouldn't want you just shrugging.'

This led straight into the second event. Tilda had garaged her Escort van at her parents' while she was overseas. It was a dented, rattly thing, she said, but reliable enough to tackle the trip west. We'd sleep in the back—much cheaper than hotels, given it could take weeks to find a home.

She wanted to pick the van up that afternoon and thought it best if I didn't accompany her. We would hardly project an image of practicality at the present time, would we? They might think I was botting off her, and she'd saddled herself with a no-hoper. Which was so far from the truth, she knew, but it's all about image.

'I embarrass you?'

'I never said that. Come on, it won't do us any harm to have a breather from each other for a few hours.'

I thought I knew everything at twenty-two. Twenty-two is a know-all number of years. Back then it never caused me cringing but I am thirty now and can see the fallacy. There were things not normal about Tilda and me that were starting to show but I didn't pick them.

It is normal for two people to think no one has ever loved so powerfully as they have: theirs is a true and blessed union. All those *I love yous* have built up resistance to doubt. But love is not simply sensations of the skin. More is demanded of you than sensations. I must have expected food and drink would fall out of the sky without me working for them; thin air would create money.

As we drove west I sat in the passenger side and pondered plans. I feigned napping to come up with a plan to keep Tilda happy. I nagged myself to conjure an idea, but nothing came. Not a one. The van's radio commanded me to get down to Dimmeys for sensational bargains on towels and bedding, and I told it shut up and went back to the sleepy chore of plans.

I blamed Tilda for pressuring me. I didn't say a word but that's what I thought. Plans get blocked if there's someone pressuring you. I blamed the drugging motion of travel, the van's rotor-blade rockabye. I blamed the heat, the sun's oven-blast on full through the window, the miraging waters of the tarseal up ahead. Two days, three days, four. Six days and still idealess.

Tilda and I didn't speak about the matter. We didn't speak

much at all, which at first I took as normal: we'd got used to each other and so had less to say. But our conversations would have confused the future if it was listening: are those two a cosy couple or soured lovers about to end? Their conversation amounts to little more than aimless chit-chat.

Chit-chat about weather and cloud formations. 'There's a cloud exactly in a cello shape, Colin.' We still used *sweetheart* but reverted to using given names as well.

'Those trees are very black, Tilda.'

'Bushfires. Aren't these old towns quaint? Most were gold towns at one stage.'

'Really,' I yawned in open-eyed sleep as we drove past shanty, lean-to places with boarded-up shop windows and cottages wrinkled with peeling weatherboard. They had drought-dead lawns and black swans cut from car tyres for landscaping. Some had wild roses trained over the porch where men in grey singlets sat on sofas and smoked, and women with hair in scarves watched us drive past as if driving past was a strange occurrence.

Larger towns had real estate sections in the Elders Farm Supplies window. There were always plenty of shanties for sale, and most second-hand cars would be dearer than they were, but they weren't close to what Tilda had as ideal.

Talbot, Dunolly, Bealiba, Ouyen, Wycheproof, Sea Lake, Speed. To chant town names had a nursery-rhyme rhythm. Tiny three-house, one-pub Speed being my favourite, just for the irony.

Our congressing habits changed. Tilda suggested we shouldn't do it without condoms, just in case: let's face it, we were living in a van like the poor. It might be best to get settled before any baby.

'Fine by me,' I shrugged.

'If we want we can have a break from doing it at all,' she said.

I shrugged. 'Okay.'

She sucked her lips into a pout. I didn't know what the expression meant, whether she was relieved or disappointed. She'd felt unwell the last few days—a belly bug or bad Chinese. I expected the last thing she wanted was congressing stirring her up inside.

Then we found Scintilla.

Welcome, it said on the outskirts. Every town says that, but Scintilla was different. It had three signs:

Welcome, we are a Tidy Town.
Welcome, our pop: 2,200.
Welcome, our motto is Grow! Grow! Grow!

The third sign included a logo: a wool bale, a gold nugget and cow horns, all wreathed in wheat sheaves.

The main street was one minute long if you drove at 35ks. On each side there was fancy iron lacework on the bigger verandahs; rusty tin roofs on the smaller. The largest verandahs were attached to hotels, six hotels, each open for business though business was slow: I counted only ten cars the whole town long. 'It's Tuesday,' said Tilda. 'Ten's probably normal for 11.30 Tuesday morning.'

We bought a fish-and-chip lunch from the takeaway and asked the cook, 'Is this a nice town?' He had a foreign accent more like gargling than talking but we understood him to say, 'In life you make your own nice.'

We ate walking along the town park's crunchy figure-eight path. Tilda was so taken by the park she wanted to get out her ink and pens and capture it. 'Don't you love weeping willows?' she chewed. 'What lovely tall gums. This one's a lemon-scented. There's a plum tree. Jacarandas too. I love the way they've put lilies in the duck pond. It's a well-kempt town, I'll say that for it.'

Historic was how the road-guide literature described Scintilla. 'Settled in 1883 it has much to offer the curious visitor. It has its own little museum with a nineteenth-century parasol collection, primitive Aboriginal tools and native animal skulls.' We counted only three shops boarded up, which made it a boom town. It even had back streets for housing the down-at-heel, new cement-board homes behind a billboard reading *Government Welfare Project.*

A ridge of ironbarks and brown-blue bush ringed the town like a wild garden. Beyond it the wheat fields spread for miles without the slightest undulation. Tilda marvelled at the vista. 'In spring you can just imagine the whole world swaying with wheat to the sky's edge. And rapeseed too, with such bright yellow flowering.'

She extended her arm, the entire earth now her art gallery.

The Elders window had the usual shed-sized hovels for sale, and three-bedroom 'older-style' dumps needing guttering and a good going-over. But it had finer dwellings too. Places called 'renovated' and 'mock-Colonial' priced above the $50,000 range. That was proper money. This was indeed a prosperous township, just as the road guide said: 'The hub in a cartwheel of districts blessed with the rich black soil you need for grain growing.'

In the top-left corner of the window, faded from being stuck up so long, was a photo of a grand-looking two-storey building. The Old Australian Rural Bank, Main Street location, $42,500 or nearest offer.

'We've just walked past that place,' said Tilda, pointing back the way we'd come. 'It's very big. It's cheap for very big.'

It was grand, all right. Tilda called it decadent. Decayed was more accurate, with its wall plaster falling out, floorboards rotten in places—your foot went through if you trod heavily. The ceilings bulged down from windstorm sand in the roof space. Doors were broken off and dust fuzzed every surface like thriving bacteria.

Tilda loved it at first sight. Her heart was set on it. She took my hand and led me around, excitedly decreeing her studio would be in the front room where teller drawers still lined one wall. 'My own studio. My own, very own studio all to myself.'

'Not so loud,' I advised her. The estate agent was behind us up the hall. 'He'll think he's got two live ones here and be able to hold the line on price.'

She looked at me with one eye arched to mean *What do you know about buying property?*

I whispered, 'I have learned a thing or two from watching my father.'

That got rid of her arch. I could hear Norm's voice in my ear. I could see him give me a wink and a nod: 'You've got to screw 'em down, Colin. Smile but never give an inch.' I hooked my thumb in my belt in Norm's manner and winked at Tilda: 'Make out you're not interested.'

The agent stood in the door frame and bent over to hitch his cream walk-socks tighter under his knob-knees. 'So, what do you *do*?' he asked me. He had a plump grey moustache tarnished by nicotine. It curled into his mouth when he breathed.

'Do?' My hooked thumb and Norm manner must have fooled him that I was a man of means. 'I *plan*,' I said with an airy sweep of the hand.

'What, an engineer or something?'

I didn't answer. I turned to Tilda. 'This place needs work. Lots of work.'

The agent kept on with his questions. 'And the lady, does she do anything?'

'I'm an artist.'

There was a chesty guffaw from the man. The hairs in his mouth blew out and got sucked back in. 'Artist. Bullshit artist?' He reprimanded himself for laughing, waved his hand to make his laughing go away. 'I shouldn't make jokes like that, should I? Couldn't resist it. Artist. Bullshit artist. No, I shouldn't say that sort of thing. Love a joke, though, don't you? If you can't have a laugh, what's left in life?'

'Her name is Tilda Robson,' I said with a toff-vowelled flick of my fringe. 'She is an artist. *Not* a bullshit artist.'

'Shit, I mean, goodness, is she famous then, the lady? Are you a famous artist, lady?'

She was measuring out the room in her mind, dreaming about her studio. I answered for her, 'She is highly respected.'

The agent put his hands in his pockets. 'So, you interested in the place?'

'Like most things, Mr...I'm sorry, I've forgotten your name.'

'Clinch. Ken Clinch.'

'Like most things, it comes down to price. What's the best you

73

can do?'

A Norm favourite after that question was to shake his head even before the answer, and say, 'Actually, come to think of it, I might pass on this one today.'

I nodded to Tilda that I knew what I was doing. I did not look Clinch in the eye. All part of the next Norm stage: 'I tell you what. What's the asking price again?'

'Forty-two and a half.'

I gave a grunt and a headshake and launched in to the ambit-claim phase. 'Tell you what—thirty-two and a half. Tell your client take it or leave it.'

'I reckon they'll take it,' Clinch said, extending his hand to shake on the deal.

'They will?'

'Bloody oath.'

'Oh. It's...it's Tilda's money, so I better check with her.'

There was no need for checking. She was suppressing squeals and leaps. She was joyful and proud: her perfect life now had a home.

And she was proud of me. If I had to list my finest moments—
there have not been many—I would select that day, however sham
was my businessman's bluff. Clinch probably shouted the bar that
night: 'Thirty-two and a half. Vendor can't believe his fucking
luck.'

Tilda and I congressed for the first time in three days, parked
on a gravel stretch south of Scintilla cemetery. She dubbed me
Rockefeller: 'You've been hiding your light under a bushel.' I was
carried away enough to believe it and advise her that she could
make a decent dollar if she turned that old building into a viable
concern. What was the one thing the Wimmera-Mallee lacked, as
stated in the road guide? Good accommodation. There wasn't even
a bed-and-breakfast within an hour of Scintilla. 'You can do one
just for artists. Call it The Artists' Colony. Get the local council to
pitch in for renovations. Advertise in the city newspapers—*Paint
the wheat fields just like Van Gogh did.* Frame the Vincent flake, use
it as an attraction.'

'Would you help me with all this?'

'Of course.'

She said she was sorry for ever doubting me, for harping on
about me and no plans.

I was so deluded I wanted to phone Norm and boast that his
son was involved in an investment in Australia; he's a doer not a
pipedreamer. I slept deep and stirless that night despite the usual

disturbances: heat, stars and moonlight so bright they could be suns; moon moths butting my skin as if wanting to be let in. I might well have rung if not for what happened next morning.

Tilda woke belching bits of food brown. She caught them in her T-shirt and managed to lean free of the van before vomiting more. She knelt naked in silvery grass and retched herself empty. I attempted to drape a shirt on her in case traffic came past but she ordered me away. She walked on her knees a few stub-strides to block the sight of her puddle.

When the retching was gone she stood pale and sweaty and asked for water to rinse her sicky mouth. She hated when our water got warm and bitter from being kept in an orange-juice bottle, but this time she rinsed and drank it like nectar. It was 8am and already the sun was high, poaching the blue sky white, yet Tilda's sweat had turned icy on her. She shivered her way into the van, into our body-damp bed—two chequer sheets, two folded eiderdowns for a mattress. 'My period's late,' she shivered.

I may have furrowed my brow in reaction, but little more. I hadn't clicked to the significance. I was still full of myself over my big-business antics. I wanted to congress if possible, if Tilda was better now.

She crooked her arm over her eyes. No, she was not better. 'I'm two going on three weeks late.' She wiggled her fingers, counting on them. 'Two's not unusual for me, I've never been clockwork, especially if things are emotional.' She belched and coughed weakly. 'But I feel very strange today. Like nothing I've ever experienced. I feel inhabited. I feel pregnant.'

I sat on the van's passenger-side seat. Tilda adjusted her arm to observe me eye to eye. I acted a smile, more close-lipped grimace than anything happy. I blinked myself free of her gaze, bowed my head as if the piece of gum leaf blown in from the road and sticking to my shin was more urgent an issue to deal with.

'Probably just a false alarm,' she said.

I drove us to Scintilla. The chemist would be open by 9; they'd have a test we could buy, which, Tilda explained, might not be perfect but a pretty good sign. She rode reclined in the back until the puttering and lurching of travel got to her and she climbed into the front to get air. She let window wind beat on her fringe.

I asked, 'What are the odds?'

'We've been flying without a net. What do you think about it if I am?'

'What do I think? It's amazing.' But my true thinking was: It's terrifying; I am not ready to raise children; I am still raising myself.

'In what way amazing?'

'Amazing as in me having the power to do that.' This part was true to my thinking. What I didn't say was: I'll be trapped for the next however many years. Yes, I loved Tilda, as best as I knew to call a feeling love. What if love had several levels? What if our level was just lust-love, just temporary, not love fit for breeding, sitting at the kitchen table budgeting for school expenses, other childhood bills?

'All the drinking I've been doing, the smoking and shit food, any baby I had would be a mutant with two heads and six arms. I'd have a miscarriage, probably.'

'That's a terrible image.' I had a reprimanding tone but I was hoping she was right. Is a miscarriage dangerous? I knew it to be dangerous in horses. Cows just go on eating, lick the dead calf and leave it. 'Sensible people, I suppose, plan having babies well ahead,' I said.

'I thought we did plan.' Tilda's eyes contained a flash of fury. I couldn't see it—I was concentrating on driving—but the side of my face had a sense.

'We talked about it. In a carried-away sort of way.'

'I'll tell you what you're doing. You're changing your tune.'

I told her it was not a good time to argue with me behind the wheel. She repeated, 'Changing your tune,' and went quiet.

Scintilla had park toilets of such bluestone distinction they were included in the road guide: 'Former gaol cells, now public conveniences.' Tilda tested herself there. She told me to walk off while she did it. I can't remember how long I walked, an hour, two hours, fretting on fatherhood. I did laps of the main street. I was starting to make up some plans, though they were a dark variety. I hoped God, if there was one, had turned his face away.

I wanted more proof than just a toilet testing. I wanted doctors and written evidence. How could I even be sure I was the father? Who knew what Tilda had been up to behind my back?

Stop it, I said to myself. There have been no behind-my-back episodes—it was just the fretting talking. It was advising me to go home to New Zealand and leave Tilda to cope with pregnancy alone.

At the same time, I was dazzled by the notion there could be part of me in that woman. How grand to imagine the round form of her abdomen. To be a father, an elder at twenty-two, a protector of new human life. To be able to say 'This is my son' or 'This is my daughter.' No matter who you are, how poor or stupid or ugly, that is surely the ultimate status.

I ended up back at the old jailhouse in that latter mood. Tilda was waiting in elm shade, sitting chin on knee. She said, 'It says I am. You've potted me.' She looked at me, searching for leadership. Fear, hope, trust, pride—all these were contained in that look. But the main one was pride. She gleamed with it. My own breathing quickened with it; I swelled up at the shoulders. I had that *famous* feeling but it had multiplied: I would be famous not just to one person now but two in nine months' time.

There is no intimacy like it. Not ever have I felt that way again. No matter how deep a kiss or tender the congressing, the simple act of walking along hand in hand with Tilda that afternoon could never be matched for delirium. We paraded more than walked around Scintilla. When Ken Clinch swerved his jeep to the kerb to confirm our offer had been accepted—'Congratulations. Thirty-day settlement suit you?'—Tilda quipped, 'It's quite a day for news.' We let Clinch be confused by our in-joke chuckling.

We ate at the Scintilla Arms—T-bone steak to keep Tilda's blood full of iron. She drank lemon squash and warned me off smoking around her because smoke was not healthy to breathe in her condition. We discussed baby names. What a purifying activity, baby names! A boy could be Richard because Richard is dignified. A girl could be Alice or Elizabeth or Clare.

The bank's rooms would be cold in winter. The building had fireplaces—we would have to keep them alight to make the child toasty; have to de-mould the walls, patch plaster so the air wasn't dusty.

We didn't congress that night because, in the purity vein, it felt dirty to have me prodding and expelling with a Richard or Alice inside her.

Next day, Tilda signed the sale contract. 'Initial here. Sign here,' said Clinch, tapping his finger on the pages. Tilda's stomach, her flat, pregnant stomach, pressed against his office counter as she followed his instructions. I stepped away from the counter. I did not wish to be involved in the signing. I did not want to join in her excitement. I equated that signing as a signing-up of me. I tried clinging to the delirium but it was slipping from me. Purity had emptied from my heart. The dark planning was recurring, darker than earlier, much darker.

By law she had three days to change her mind, a cooling-off period in which she could render the contract non-binding. I set myself the task of unbinding it and thereby unbinding myself. I felt entirely justified. Yes, I loved Tilda but not in forever terms, the kitchen table kind of love I've mentioned. As she bent over that contract a beam of sun put a microscope to her face. It homed in through the open door, right in on her cheeks and magnified what normal light doesn't show—the creases and crumples that are only going to worsen. I didn't have markings like those.

In five years I would be twenty-seven and she thirty-seven. That was old, even sounded old to say—thirty-seven. When I was thirty-seven she would be old as aunties. When I was fifty...on and on it went. The microscope discovered three grey strands in her eyebrows that needed urgent plucking. There was dandelion fur along her jaw—it would only get longer and thicker as she aged ahead of me. If she were twenty-two then at least we'd be even.

I began the unbinding as Tilda drove us back to Melbourne. She was fussing, 'There is so much to do.' The logistics of packing; getting professional advice on floor repairs. I sat on the passenger side with my dark planning. For just as love has its *more* stage, getting out of love has the opposite: there is a ratcheting-down to do. There is dismantling to inflict, breaking of heart and faith. I was new to this as I had been to falling in love. But I was a natural. I must have been to summon the ruthlessness so well. There was no intricate strategy involved. I knew instinctively to start out meekly, even if I appeared pathetic. 'I feel a bit dizzy,' I lied, pressing my fingers into my eyes. I shook and feigned fainting.

We were about 60ks east of Scintilla. I gripped my chest as if blood had stopped working in it. I put on such a show of face-clenching pain Tilda reached over for the orange-acrid water and splashed it on me, made me gargle and spit like a sportsman recovering. She stroked my hair and called me darling. The *darling* caused me to complain that her stroking wasn't helping. I shrugged her hand from me with genuine irritation. When you are trying to be ruthless you don't want *darling* to soften the momentum.

'I am not ready to be a father,' I said. 'I am not ready for father-hood or being a family man or anything like that.' I said it not as gently as I'd hoped, but there, it was said. My legs were shaking from the electrocution nerve being activated. I needed to gallop my sentences out before they jumbled like a fit. 'For Christ's sake, I've got no money, no prospects. I'm only twenty-two and it's not time for me yet.'

I didn't see Tilda's reaction. I couldn't look at her; I wasn't that brave. Her voice went strained, almost shrill. 'What's happened? How can you be like this? You were happy about it. Why have you changed your mind? What have I done? Have I done something? Did something happen?'

'I'm sorry, but it's how I feel.'

'You should have thought about that before you stuck your dick in me.'

That shut me down for a few seconds, the viciousness of tone. Such a crude image—'stuck your dick in me'.

'Charming thing to say,' I said with a disapproving shake of my head. 'Whatever happened to *congressing*?'

'Please don't do this to me.' She hunched over the steering wheel.

'Concentrate on your driving.' I was fearful of the cars coming our way.

'I don't care.'

'Well, I do care.'

'If you are old enough to get me pregnant, you are old enough to do the right thing.'

'I *am* doing the right thing. I do not feel ready to be a father and therefore it is the right thing to tell you so.'

'I feel ready. It's the right time for me.'

'You've fucking well lured me into this, haven't you?'

She yanked on the wheel. The van swerved left sharply onto the road verge and slid to a stop. A horn mooed, a truck behind us blaring because Tilda hadn't indicated. She thumped her hand on the dashboard. 'Why are you doing this to me, Colin? I never lured you or trapped you. Don't do this to me, please. Don't take something beautiful like us having a baby and turn it on me.'

I shoved the passenger door open with my shoulder. It was sticking but I wanted the aggression of the barging action to scare her into silent submission. It didn't. She shimmied across the seat after me. 'I'll do anything,' she pleaded. 'I will get a job until it's born. What a time we'll have doing up the place. Okay, you're young, you're overwhelmed at the moment. But that's just temporary.'

Nature thought us a comedy. Parrots on the bleachers of dead branches, crows on the other tiers, all laughing with mechanical croaky jeering. I had bare feet and tilt-walked over painful stones towards some grassier cushioning. Tilda followed. I cursed 'piss off' to the jumping-bean flies on my face but the curse was really meant for her. I tiptoed between ants, stomped on the smaller ones and rucked dust at the bull ants which were more like infant fingers fidgeting around than insects.

'Do you want me to get rid of it? Is that what you're saying?'

I acted dim, as if not understanding the question.

'Do you want me to have an abortion?'

'I never said that.' Never said it, but was thinking it.

'You do, don't you?'

There was such a thinning of her lips and eyes it occurred to me she might hop in the van and drive off, leaving me there, stranded. I returned to the vehicle, just in case.

She said, 'Well, I'll tell you something. I'm going to live in Scintilla and have my Richard or Alice with me. And I'll say, "Your father? He was the man who wanted you dead before you were born. No better than a murderer, that's your father. We're better off without the bastard."'

This hit the mark, of course. I sat there on the heap of our bedding, shamed. No sun, no heat from the van's metal frame could sweat that out of me. The only thing which would work was my saying, 'Abort the baby? I'd never dream of it, sweetheart.' But I wasn't going to say that. As bad as shame feels I knew a secret word that was worse: inheritance. Into the honesty box it drops with a thud.

For all my pipedreaming I always knew it was there. A backstop if I failed—a thousand acres waiting for its heir, for Norm's wayward prodigal to return from overseas. But a divorced and ageing Australian artist? No farming father would want that for his son, would he? 'She's just using you, you fool,' I predicted him saying. 'If she has your child, boy, she has dibs on half the property.' Disputes of this nature are regular farm scandal.

So I said nothing to Tilda. I took the shame into me and sweated on it and said nothing. I let her slump and weep and weep.

Two hours later in Ballarat I was at the wheel when the tyre blew—Tilda was sleep-sobbing in the back. I pulled over quickly enough so the wheel rim wasn't damaged, but the problem was getting the spare from the roof. Tilda kept it there roped on the rack she used for transporting paintings. She didn't know knots—hers you had to pick at to untie rather than one tug and the rope slips free. I picked and poked but the tightness wasn't budging. It needed fingernails longer than mine and a screwdriver to get a good purchase.

'I'll do it,' Tilda said as I climbed down. She elbowed me to get out of her way, gave a jump to catch hold of the rack and scaled the van's side. The decent thing to say would have been, 'Be careful, watch yourself in your condition.' In me, however, some indecent door had opened and in had walked all the wrong crowd.

I watched her pick the knots and swear at the roof for being so scorching with sun. I watched her stand and heave the spare out of its ties. She knelt to roll it from the roof edge. It occurred to me that if she fell now it might bring on a miscarriage. Not a serious fall: I wouldn't want a serious fall that broke a limb or got anywhere close to maiming her. Just a fall where the bump and shock of it churned her insides. It would be better than an abortion, wouldn't it? A more natural process. It would spare her something more medical. The strain she was putting into taking the tyre's weight in one hand and dangling it for passing to me might be enough to do the deed. It was my job to reach up and take the tyre from her.

I should have. But I didn't.

Tilda grunted and wriggled further to the edge. The rack rail must have been jagging into her pelvis but she didn't make a moan. She held the hanging tyre as if a test of strength, eyes and mouth slitted from the hurt of what she was doing.

She unslit an eye and stared at me. I could see exactly what that eye said. It said: *Are you watching? Are you seeing that I am thinking the same as you?* She let the tyre drop and roll into the ditch.

Her eye did say it; I wasn't dreaming. She had the miscarriage idea too. She was willing it. How else can the rest of that day's trip be explained? We didn't share a word for 100ks. No hostilities either; not a tear or cross word. She drove without one reckless jerk of emotional steering. Her bottom lip was pushed up over her top in concentration.

There was one sentence, Tilda's, but with no obvious sub-meaning: 'Cigarette, please. Can you light it?' There was a 'ta' from her once I'd passed it to her mouth. I wasn't about to ask, 'What are you thinking?' It might have been viewed too warmly as trying to bridge the distance between us. I was getting away with breaking her heart too well to risk that.

Or so I thought.

On the futon above the Fitzroy lighting shop that night we congressed. No, we fucked. There was no tender playfulness to warrant *congressed*. We did not kiss as such, more a light grazing of two limp tongues. It was all body, as you'd have with fleetings. I would swear she was willing that baby dead, as if there was something wrong with it now, because there was something wrong with us: we drank two bottles of wine, Tilda going two glasses to my one. She chain-smoked a whole pack of Dunhills. You don't do that and want good health for your unborn. She said, 'I have such a desperate need to be entered, hard.' I did as she wanted. It took place in the dark—we had dark to look into instead of each other's faces. Not once but three times before finally we turned our backs to each other for sleep. Of all the perversities, I wouldn't have guessed the lash of wanting a miscarriage was an aphrodisiac. The lash kept us at it all week. But no miscarriage came.

On the seventh night Tilda went to bed with her clothes on, didn't even let out the belt to loosen her jeans. When my fingers tried to do it, she said, 'No more entering.'

'Why not?' I reached out to the belt again.

'Don't touch me.'

'Why not?'

'Let me lie still and not be touched. Don't touch.'

I sat up and kicked the blanket down to my knees. I was naked and expected that if I pushed and rubbed against her she would want touching. She put her elbow into my side to keep me off her.

'I want this out of me,' she said. 'This is not how a child should be born. We are not what it should have. I want it out of me.'

I pulled the blanket back up, as if that was more dignified given what she was saying. I kept silent in case my relief in what she was saying showed in my voice. *It's her decision*, I told myself. *That frees me from being responsible. Or shares it between us. If I am a murderer (and I know what pious folk say—there's a God of wrath and a day of judgment on the issue), then Tilda is co-murderer with me.*

She said, 'I'll make a doctor's appointment tomorrow. They'll be looking up me, so no more entering.' She spoke quietly, no tears. You'd have thought we would have one argument at least. One outburst of pleading—'Change your mind, Colin. Let's have this baby.' Even some 'stuck your dick in me' savagery. But there wasn't.

Not mentioning Richard or Alice was like living a convenient lie. But live that way we did. The abortion was arranged for the following Friday. I sat in a café across the road from where it happened, just around from her studio. The café's still there; the doctor's place isn't.

I kept smelling the sewer under my feet. For all the concrete and tarseal, my mind had wind of it. Richard and Alice would be flushed down there, I expected. I lifted my soles off the ground. As if that would disconnect me! After all, sewers run to the sea. The sea gets turned into oxygen. My lungs would end up breathing it in. There was no escaping.

Ever since, if I go to Melbourne I avoid Fitzroy. I loop right around it.

I have a theory: Tilda adored the idea of motherhood but was relieved we never went through with it. She'd had a lovely, if brief, experience of having life inside her without the reality to deal with. If the episode haunted her she had me, Colin, to blame. She had the upper hand on me. Morally, I mean. She was absolved.

Makes me feel better, this theory. Why else would I have invented it, sitting in that café? It helped rid the sewer smell. It was a comfort once the abortion was done and I drove Tilda to a motel in North Melbourne. She was silent and pale in the passenger seat, head back, eyes closed. Her hand over her stomach as if nurturing it.

The motel wasn't some cheap dive. It had air-conditioning and a king-sized bed and six pillows for Tilda to treat herself.

'Treat myself for what?' she said. 'You make it sound like I've achieved something.'

'Treat yourself in the convalescing sense. We can afford two nights. I'll wait on you.'

Doctor's orders banned her from exerting herself or having baths for three days—baths can bring on haemorrhaging. She had pads between her legs, which made walking uncomfortable. She reclined, legs apart with the blankets over her and looked at the television, more staring at it than watching. She didn't laugh when the canned laughter prompted us. Or look sad when movie music wanted it.

The only food she felt like was wonton soup. I found a take-away place and ferried in two lots a day. She craved the salty juice and hardly pecked at the wontons.

I asked, 'Is there nothing else I can bring you?'

She shook her head, said no. There was an irritable sound in the no. My theory put that down to punishment. The more I wanted to do some little thing for her, the more she was determined to deprive me of the pleasure.

It worked too. I had never felt so miserable. I hoped that by telling her this she would converse with me, be finished with punishing. 'I want you to know I feel terrible,' I said.

'How does that help me?'

'I don't know.'

On one visit to the toilet her bleeding became heavier.

I panicked. 'Is it normal? You want me to call someone?'

'No,' she said. Still an irritable no, but she repeated it quietly and then said, '*I'll* make a call. I want to call my lawyer.'

Was she intending to sue me? I didn't know what law I'd broken. 'Lawyer? About *this*? We can solve this. No need for lawyers.'

'About Scintilla. I want to speak to him about my place. I want to check something with him.'

'If you want to get out of the sale, I'm sure they can do that.'

'Who wants to get out of the sale?'

'After what's happened. We, well, we wouldn't be going ahead.'

'I am going ahead. I want to speed up the settlement date.'

'What, go ahead alone?'

'Not alone. You're going to lend a hand for a while. I've thought up a businesslike arrangement.'

I frowned and shrugged my confusion and sat on the end of the bed while Tilda puffed up pillows behind her shoulders.

She said, 'You help me move in. I'm moving in to my Van Gogh garret and you must help transport my things in the van. And once I've moved in, the next part of the business arrangement can begin.'

'Are you ordering me?'

'Let me finish. You can putty the walls, plug the holes in the floors. Replace where the tiles have fallen off in the bathroom. I want to be able to get straight to painting my paintings. You can tart up the place for me. Patch the ceilings where the plaster's come down. Rehang all the doors. You owe me that, Colin. You bloody well owe me that.'

'For how long?'

'A year.'

'A year? A year of that?'

'A year of work to clear your Richard or Alice debt. Consider us business partners. We'll be assigned domestic duties. I will cook. You can plant a vegetable garden for me. I will pay the bills and do my art. You will work on my place and pay off your debt that way. We will be like friends. We will sleep in separate beds, in separate rooms. You futoned on the floor in one room. Me in my bed in another. I'm going to buy myself a nice four-poster one.'

A year. It sounded a long time, though in my heart I was convinced I deserved it. A year, and at the end of it my absolution would be the reward.

A convenience of the arrangement was money. I wouldn't need any: Tilda was in charge of that. Buying the Van Gogh garret meant there was nearly $8000 left over from her $40,000. She would top that up by painting. In no time her new studio would be wet with canvas paddocks and sunsets. She'd sell pictures to loyal aunties and cousins. Charge them $1000, which I called robbery given they were relatives.

The arrangement included guidelines for socialising. If either of us met a Scintillan who attracted us for dating, that was perfectly reasonable, part of the arrangement. Reasonable too if we wanted to bring them home for congressing. Or so we said—it was never tested. Scintillans took some getting used to for Tilda. I was accustomed to country people—hairy-eared, bull-sized men who talk rainfall as if rain was life's measure. Tilda's type was more... well...a feckless me. Besides, she was back to the Tilda I'd first met in London: art not men in life, that was her decree.

If only we humans didn't have the sweet poison in us, wouldn't that be simpler and save us so much misery?

Six weeks after we moved in Tilda made a suggestion. She couched it as a slight amendment to our business agreement. Did so not with coldness or unfeeling calculation; there was fondness for me in her face. At least that was my surmising. Her cheeks were blushed ashine from the cask reds of the evening. But the blush was also a red shyness and boldness blend.

It was late autumn, which still means summer if you've stoked the fireplaces. Your skin slicks with sweat after showering. Hot temperatures, I'm sure of it, thin the poison and flood the body with it easier. 'You can come into my bed tonight if you want,' Tilda said, her top lip teasingly attached to the wineglass rim.

The poison slushed through me. My breathing wouldn't behave. 'Seriously?'

'Seriously.'

Week after week and only me had touched me.

Tilda put her hand on the kitchen table as if swearing on a Bible. She said, 'Let's not call it congressing. Let's call it servicing. You can service me and I will service you.'

I said, 'You make us sound like Herefords,' though it was not a criticism. I was so excited no amount of mathematics was going to prevent me from having to let the first expelling go.

We serviced each other, nightly, then I would go back to my room.

But the servicing got more serious. One night, I did not go back to my room. I fell asleep in Tilda's arms. Same the next night. Our servicing became more like congressing again. We pushed the business arrangement out a bit, to thirteen months. Then fourteen months, fifteen. Then sixteen.

Month sixteen: that's when I discovered the egg.

It was lodged deep in her right breast, stuck against the breast-bone. For all our congressing I had felt no hint of it before. I must have groped harder this time, her arms reaching over her head in pleasure, arching her frame out. An egg like eggs feel when they're hard-boiled and peeled and have rubber give in them. Though this egg wasn't smooth—it had rough portions on it. Three kisses down from the nipple it made the skin bulge.

I flicked my fingers away as you do if suddenly touching a spider. And like a spider the feeling of it remained, tingling. I wiped my fingers on the sheets but the revulsion was too strong. I spasmed with flicking. I shuddered and hid the reason for doing so by groaning as if in the throes of a fierce expelling. Stomach to stomach I lay in the fork of her, my left side lifted up a little so as not to have the egg pressing on me.

A lump like that is just popped muscle, I reasoned in myself. A lump like that just goes away, no need to think of it again. A lump like that is not a growth, as in disease, as in old women's talk—*growths*. If it was a growth, wouldn't it be painful? Look at Tilda smiling, eyes closed, content to go to sleep now. No look of pain in her face, which you'd have if you had a bad lump.

I slid into position beside her. 'Everything okay?'

'Yes,' she yawned. 'Why?'

'Nothing.'

'Night.'

'Night.'

She turned rump-to-groin to me, wriggled in closer, reached behind herself to take my wrist and cross my arm under her arm to have my palm cup her breast. But it was the spider-egg breast, so I couldn't cup it. I cupped her hip instead, which was not very comfortable but clear of the cold tingle and crawl. Clear of obligation to have a proper feel, a more medical probe. If I touched it again, if it was not a mind trick but real and pronounced, then I would have to say so. I would have to point and poke, guide Tilda's fingers, asking, 'Is that normal, that lump right there?' We were two people who needed our sleep rather than be up all night worrying about egg lumps.

It was bound to be nothing, I decided. I slipped into sleep. After all, tomorrow I had a job to go to. My sixth freelance job reporting for the *Scintilla Gazette Weekly*. A dozen culvert pipes had gone missing from the racecourse—concrete and brand new. Someone had used a winch to uncouple a drain and thieve them. The day after tomorrow Tilda was off to Melbourne. Principally to hawk paintings around galleries, but also to tie in a doctor's appointment for the usual swabs and top-to-toe. Preparations, Tilda called it. Preparations and maintenance for her future pregnancy hopes. No Richard or Alice fiasco this time, but a proper planned making of a loved child. I figured if the egg was still there the doctor could appraise it.

The loved child plan involved an ultimatum to me: if I, Colin, was not prepared to take the step to fatherhood; if I was still the Colin of sixteen months ago and not father material; if I did not feel it in my heart and head, if the urge had not come upon me,

97

then, decreed Tilda, we should say goodbye once and for all. She would find herself a man more committed. Her body would not be in working order forever. It would dry up like a dam eventually and be barren.

She did remind me how I had let her down. 'Richard or Alice—do you ever think on it? It would be seven months old now.' She knew it was futile to force me into fatherhood. 'I could try saying *You owe me*,' she said, 'but what good would that do? If you don't want a child, deep down in yourself, *You owe me* is pathetic.'

I was not the same Colin of sixteen months ago. If you could have x-rayed my thinking, if all the wires and locks could be picked away to expose the very spot you'd call true-me, there had been alterations. I was warmer on the pregnancy idea. I had an inkling that I'd found my niche in life in Scintilla. That's what a bit of steady work will do for you. Not that there was an immediate hurry for pregnancy, surely. I committed myself to the idea, but suggested Tilda keep using a diaphragm until *Gazette* work became more frequent and lucrative. 'Let's get things bedded down,' I said.

She relented, 'Okay. As long as it's not an excuse. *Bedding down* is not *never ever*.' She agreed the *Gazette* opportunity was an exciting development, one I should not be distracted from at this moment. It gave her a sense of pride to see me march out the door so purposefully of a morning, pad and pen in hand like real tools of trade. My plastering wall cracks gave her a house-proud pleasure, but 'Look at you!' she smiled as I put a tie on. 'Mr Professional. Quite the respectable fellow.'

The *Gazette* even let me use its vehicle for assignments—a latest model Commodore with a CB radio, like police have.

'Assignments,' Tilda quipped. 'Sounds very James Bond.' She hated ironing but wouldn't see me walk out crinkled: crisp and creaseless is how shirts must be when there's a job to do that you call 'responsible'.

The work came via a chance conversation of Tilda's. Because of her art degree she'd been asked to judge the primary school's prize for collage. At the fairy-bread supper after the award ceremony a mother, stuck for conversational subject matter, asked, 'And your man friend, Tilda, is he of a creative bent?'

'Oh yes,' she replied. 'Goodness yes. He was accepted into a very exclusive academy for drama in London. He became disillusioned, however. He's more a business brain, that's his bent. He has thrown himself into renovating the old building like you wouldn't believe. He's a roll up your sleeves and get on with it sort of guy.'

The mother, it turned out, was the daughter of Hector Vigourman, grazier, *Gazette* owner, former state member of parliament for the district, amateur actor and president of the Scintilla Footlights Community Theatre Company.

Two days later there he was, knocking on our back door, stout and dapper in fawn cashmere cardigan and proper leather shoes—not the elastic-sided boots and flannelette shirt of a normal Scintillan.

He had a proposition for me. Would I be willing, as a favour to the town's few but passionate amateur thespians, to cast my eye over their new production of *Arsenic and Old Lace?* If I would perhaps sit in on a rehearsal? If I could perhaps impart some advice—a few tips I had gleaned from my experiences in London? In fact, would I be willing to review the play for the *Gazette*? As its proprietor he would be honoured to print me.

He described the *Gazette* as a very modest enterprise, smiling a mix of apology and boasting, and given that his sister was the editor he could assure me prominent placement on, say, page three or five. He would be delighted if I included a paragraph or two about my RADA days. It was bound to pique the interest of locals.

'I don't think so. Those days are far behind me.' I was too busy with my renovating project, I said.

'Oh please,' he persisted.

'I wouldn't want to be seen as a Scintillan newcomer who is blowing his own trumpet.'

'Not at all.'

Tilda elbowed encouragement. 'It's not blowing your trumpet. It's community spirit.'

'Too true.' Vigourman nudged me. 'Go on.'

'Sweetheart, go on. Do it.'

'All right then,' I said. 'A review. A short one.'

'Excellent.' Vigourman clapped his hands together. 'A review that gives us a little pat on the back. After all, we are not RADA material.'

I drew the line on the subject of RADA. I said RADA was a very unhappy time for me. I hated talking about, let alone writing on, the topic.

'Of course, of course,' Vigourman said. 'We don't want to stir up unpleasant memories.' We shook hands like two notable men agreeing on terms. 'The troops will be so excited. They're getting on in years, you'll find, but they are always willing to listen and learn.'

Getting on in years—he wasn't kidding. I sat beside him at the rehearsal worried about them surviving the ordeal of speaking lines: two or three needed to sit between scenes and catch their breath. One fell asleep doing it. All the lines were fluffed—sometimes the stage went silent for twenty seconds while the cast waited for offstage prompts.

'What do you think?' Vigourman whispered. 'Be honest. I know we've got work to do.'

I did enjoy his deferring to my authority. 'Nervousness is the enemy of the actor, in my experience. They need to relax. You can't underestimate the nervousness factor.'

I took my chance on that note of wisdom to excuse myself and slip out.

Review, my arse. I wrote twenty paragraphs with 'delightful' in the piece four times, 'charming' three, 'interesting' and 'energetic' twice.

'Appropriately diplomatic,' Tilda called it.

'Cheesy lies, more likely,' I said. I was embarrassed it bore my name. But Vigourman was chuffed, and he had influence. I was suddenly in demand: could I write some 'reflections' on living in Scintilla? If I filled a page my fee would be $25.

I got busy reflecting. I chose the town's bluestone buildings to wax about. 'Vertical cobblestone streets', I dubbed them, prose I thought poetic as sentences go. I described the Scintillan sun as 'chandelier material'. I said the people of the town were as friendly and as straight-backed and square-jawed as any humans I had encountered in my travels. My one quibble was to do with 'bending the elbow', though I never meant it as hard-hitting. You wouldn't find a boozier, noisier Saturday night on planet Earth, I wrote. The town's main street has more midnight argy-bargy than a boxing ring. London is like a graveyard in comparison.

'Exposed at last!' wrote clergymen in a joint letter to the editor. 'Are hotels now our places of worship? Why have our youth lost their way?'

In response to which, successive editions published letters dismissing me as a 'blow-in' and a 'snob' because I had only lived here a handful of months; you need twenty years to know the place;

you need to be born here. The controversy sold 106 more copies of the paper than usual. That only ever happened when Scintilla played the Watercook Cannons at football.

My mini-fame, my notoriety, lifted me up in name and spirits. I don't care what they say about big fish in small ponds, to be lifted up in any-size place is a powerful physic. It puts a drop of self-importance in your system. I remembered the famous feeling of first being in love with Tilda and how her being pregnant with Richard or Alice multiplied it, if only for a few hours. If the two were combined—pregnancy and this new small-pond fame, what a state of grace to be in. That's what I mean by *alterations*.

I bought a cash-register-looking typewriter at the Salvos and practised—thwack, thwack, thump—like morse piano until my fingers could produce 600 words in one hour. I rang home to my parents and big-noted, with some truth in the big-noting this time, that I was involved in a promising venture in newspapers.

Norm mumbled, unconvinced: 'A writing job? Where's that going to get you?' I did lie that I was earning $300 a week, which he liked the sound of. My fee was now $30 an article but I could not resist the exaggeration. It drew a 'You're back on track, by the looks of things' from him, which I appreciated.

Tilda appeared younger to me now. That was another alteration. When out in the sun she tanned and glowed. The dandelions became almost invisible along her jaw. Country life was suiting her. It smoothed her skin out and put pretty freckles on her nose. I counted them, twenty tiny freckles, the morning after the egg discovery. She lay beside me, eyelids closed, eyeballs fidgeting beneath them half awake. She looked too healthy for that egg to be of any significance. I should just put it out of my thoughts. Which I did. I had the great drain robbery to go to. I had to shave, shower, help Tilda load the van with paintings without getting marks on my good clothes.

Her phone call came the day after next. 'I have a huge lump. A huge fucking lump.' She hiccupped with tears, her voice blocked with terror-phlegm. 'There's a smaller lump near it. And under my arms, where the glands are, more lumps.' She said her doctor's face was furrowed when he found them. She'd swear he looked concerned and tried conceal it with 'Don't worry' but Tilda wasn't blind, she was no fool, she could tell his thinking.

She was phoning from her parents'. She desperately needed to curl up in her childhood bed. She wanted her childness back because there is only *living* in childhood, there are no lumps or tears too terrible. There are no tests and specialists who will do a biopsy on her in three days' time. 'Three days. They think they need to hurry, don't they?'

'I don't know. I couldn't say.'

'They think it must be serious, too serious to wait, don't they? I can't wait three days. Why do I have to wait three days? Why can't they do it now?'

'I don't know.'

These were not real questions from Tilda, it was the terror talking, for which all answers are stunned *I don't knows*.

'Something bad is in my body. I can feel it.' She spat the words with such revulsion she might have been spitting at her body. 'How can I go three days with badness living in me?'

'I don't know.'

She could not stand to glimpse any part of herself. She vowed to keep her clothes on for three days and have no shower so she didn't see or touch her gone-bad body. Her body had turned on her, she wept. Her body was the enemy within.

She instructed me to pack her blue nightie, the one she had never used but saved as if for special sleeping. Bring white knickers too. If none were in the clean pile then buy some. I was to use my initiative and pack anything else I thought she might need. Manners were obsolete to her now. There was no point in please or thank you. They belonged to the past, a kinder place than this new hell of worry. She wanted me to catch the train to Melbourne immediately. She wanted me to hold her through the night. Hold her and be gentle. She wanted to hold me and be mad and have the right to be mad. I'd have to sleep in her parents' study on a foldout cot because they were old-fashioned and we were not a married couple. But they would have to turn a blind eye and allow me to sneak in to her at night.

Just as screens are drawn around a patient's bed, so too a screen is pulled around that time for me.

Inside the screen there are only Tilda and myself. She is waking after whatever they do in biopsies. Her lips are dry and pale. Her eyes are dragged left and right slowly by the drugs. I sit on the bed edge and hold her hand, such a cold hand, from the pretend death of anaesthetic. 'It's over,' I say, smiling. I force myself to kiss her forehead—I should at least kiss her forehead until the medical smells have gone from her mouth. We will be back in Scintilla in a few days, I tell her to cheer her. The results will be negative and we can get out of this sterilised ward and go home; me to write another *Gazette* masterpiece, her to her canvas equivalents.

Outside the screen is Tilda's family: a brother, two sisters, her mother, Raewyn, with pearls twisted anxiously through her knuckles below her throat line. Her father, Eric, jiggles change in his pocket and reassures Raewyn that Tilda has pluck and fortitude. They mutter their own *I don't knows* and *Don't worrys*. Where I am concerned they use talk that avoids talking: 'What footy team do you barrack for?'

There is suspicion if can't answer that question in Melbourne. If you can't say the Dons or Magpies or Demons it's as if you're a threat, an alien. I said the Dons just to keep everyone happy.

In reality they were inside Tilda's bed screen but I have decided to keep things to just her and me or else I will get shuffled back from the bed at this point, as I was that day. They stopped short of saying, 'Can you step outside please, mate?' but I sniffed the sentiment. She had been theirs all her life; I had been on the scene five minutes. I was an impostor. When she clutched my hand I could x-ray jealousy, especially in her parents. I'm not retaliating here but they are now my impostors. I decide who gains admission to this testimony. They were not Tilda's lover. Nobody but we two could understand the intimacy to come. I want to get it on the record, that intimacy, because it's a finest-hour entry in my otherwise lopsided list.

Mr outranks *Dr* in the medical world, an anti-title they give to their royalty. *Mr* gave Edwin Roff's words added authority; he was surgeon law. His hair was white as prophets', his cheeks gaunt from the great burden of informing patients of what pathologists saw in their petri dishes. In Tilda's case they saw a large malignant tumour, a most aggressive, dangerous form. They saw two secondaries from the same breast. The lymph nodes in her armpit had cancer in them as well.

Roff said he was going to speak quickly and directly to get it all said—the facts, the course of action. If I, Colin, would be alert in case Tilda could not take it all in. Becky too please, her sister, sitting the other side of her at Roff's wide dark-wood desk. There were two schools of thought on such diseases. His was the school that advocated radical action—removal of the full breast. The other school preferred removal of lumps only. 'I take the view,' he said quietly, 'that the radical option is better. Removal of the affected breast, the lymph nodes stripped away: an aggressive attack to match an aggressive cancer. We will follow that up with chemotherapy.'

It was a game of numbers, he explained. Of percentages, of odds. If Tilda's cancer returned within twelve months then the chances of survival...(he paused to select the right word) fell. If in twelve months it had not returned, well, then there was a fifty-fifty chance it might not return the following year. The odds extend more favourably as years go by.

He permitted his lips to bend into a professional smile of hope and goodwill. Tilda did not return the smile. Roff reached across his desk and spread his long pink fingers in front of us as if to display his wares—his expert tongs for the removal of deadliness. Tilda bowed her head. He patted her forearm and leant back into his black leather chair, his fingertips testing his bow tie's straightness.

Tilda lifted her head. 'What about a baby?'

Roff's smile bent into reverse, into a frown. He jerked forward to look in Tilda's file. 'You're not pregnant, are you?'

'No.'

His face unfrowned.

'But I'd like to be.'

He frowned again. 'There are two things I would say about that. Firstly, a pregnancy could very likely speed your cancer on. It would also make treatment more limited.'

'So you're saying I can't have children, ever?'

'I would advise against it, ever,' he said firmly, then tried to soften the blow. 'The other issue is the social implication. There are certain social issues, which I'm sure you can imagine.'

Ever was too much of a cobweb word for her to continue the conversation. She waved it from her face and convulsed into a hunchback of tears. Becky and I scrummed her shoulders and uttered useless comforting. 'It's all right. It's okay.' We kept it up for several minutes, language empty of truth or reason.

Becky began crying. I was not, which made me feel I was misbehaving. Crying is a measure of emotion, or else why do it? It was a measure of love for Tilda given her circumstances, but I could not cry. The miserable wonder of her suffering had me frozen, over-awed. To touch her sobbing shoulderblades was to touch death close-up. I knew cancer was not contagious but I wanted to take my hand from her body and stand alone, at a safe distance. Then maybe I would cry.

To compensate I became practical. Roff had caught my attention with a slow nod of his head. He said there were certain questions he would like to ask Tilda and obviously this wasn't the time. He folded a sheet of paper—a questionnaire—into an envelope for my safekeeping. The questionnaire covered many of his queries, he said. Queries relevant to research, of establishing 'links and causes' and 'correlating patient history'.

I was relieved to have a helpful role. He passed me pamphlets on preparing for a mastectomy; the side effects of the operation, physical and mental. Emotional side effects, the sense of woman-hood being challenged. If I could make sure Tilda read them he would appreciate it. 'Keep her spirits up,' he said. 'The next few weeks will test her spirits beyond the ordinary.'

'Social issues,' Tilda said with a contemptuous snort. 'What have social issues got to do with me?' This was back at her parents' place. They were out grocery shopping or getting their crying done in their car without upsetting Tilda.

But Tilda was not upset. She was whistling and laughing. She had turned the TV on and flicked channels for a distracting program. She was fine, she said. Fine. She just wished she knew what exactly was meant by *social issues*. She stared at me for answers. I tried some *I don't knows* to avoid the subject. She was no fool. She had worked out what Roff meant. She was looking for an argument, not answers.

'He means, if I die, I would leave a motherless child behind, doesn't he? He means I'm definitely going to die, doesn't he? He means there is no hope, doesn't he? My death would be like abandoning a baby. I would be guilty of abandonment. It is so fucking cruel, Colin. Why is this happening to me? I do not deserve this happening to me.'

She paced the lounge room, yelling and pointing at east, south, west, north. At all the women in the world in all directions. 'Why not *that* woman or *that* woman or *that* woman instead of me? Thousands of useless, ugly bitches breeding like farm pigs to ten different men. Why not them or women in prisons? Give them cancer. They deserve it. Give it to them and take it from me.'

She knelt in a corner of the couch. She wept herself silent. Then wept herself angrier: those vile, revolting tits of hers, they were to blame. She always hated them. Now one was being taken from her. 'Good fucking riddance to it,' she punched a couch cushion. 'Men are lucky. Men don't have tits.' She laughed that soon she would be part man. She laughed that she might as well start practising: could I get her a beer, please? Wine is much too feminine for men. She slapped her thigh as if making a manly decision, spoke with her voice forced down an octave: she was going to stop wearing makeup and not wear bangles or shave her legs.

'My hair will probably fall out from the drugs, won't it? I'll be very masculine, very bald.' She put her hands on her head like a finger cap to tuck her fringe away. 'What do you think? Will it suit me?'

She got off the couch and came up close to me, peered into my face, my eyes. She let her finger cap go. Her fringe sprang out and pounced at my cheek she was so close. 'Why don't you cry? Not so much as a single tear. Everyone else has, but not you. Not a drop.'

I thought it part of her funny male performance. 'Men don't cry,' I smiled.

It was no performance. Her nostrils flexed open and closed with snotty breathing. 'I know very well why you're not crying. You're not crying because you don't really love me.'

'Not true.' I leant sideways to escape her gaze. I may be six foot three but her questioning was intimidating. Plus, if someone has cancer they have privileges over you. You can't just tell them to settle down or shut up or be reasonable. They have a licence to glower and rage.

Tilda touched my cheekbones. I couldn't lean sideways any

further. 'Not a hint of wet,' she said quietly, with an offended gaping of her mouth. 'Not a single hint of wet.'

'There's been so much to take in. I've been holding back crying.'

'Cry now. Go on. Do it now.'

'I can't cry on demand.'

'All I am to you is servicing, aren't I?'

'No.'

'Not love, just servicing.'

'No.'

'Say you love me, then.'

'I love you.'

'I don't believe you.'

'I do.' It was true enough—remember my alterations. I repeated three *I love yous*. Tilda refused to hear them. She shook them from her ears.

'Do you want me dead?'

'Dead? Of course not.'

'Is that why you don't cry? You want me dead so you don't have to bother with this?'

'No.' The only words she would believe were her own. I could have pledged *no, no, no* a thousand times but as far as she was concerned I was a liar.

'I'm damaged goods now, aren't I? What man wants a one-titted woman?'

I touched her shoulder to rub it, pat it. She slid away from me.

I had the idea of putting water on my face. If my not crying was troubling Tilda then rubbing tap tears on might placate her. I said I needed to go to the toilet. She said, 'Do what the hell you like.'

She flicked TV channels again. A *Hogan's Heroes* rerun came on with a burst of canned laughter, which Tilda took personally. She switched the set off. 'Why are they so fucking happy?'

I closed the bathroom door and leant against it a few seconds, grateful for the peace. I dug water into my eye sockets, creating a damp, bloodshot appearance. Not so damp that water would stream falsely down, but damp enough to look like raw feeling. I tilted my head back to look as if I was trying to stop tears from welling. I stepped into the lounge.

Tilda was sitting cross-legged in front of the TV. She had turned it on again and was watching a newsbreak. She held her hand up. 'Shsh.' She pointed to the screen to a girl in jodhpurs mounting a pony. I sniffed and cleared my throat to keep my acting going but got the shush treatment. Three years ago the girl had been given two months to live, and look at her now—happy and healthy; her cancer, to the amazement of doctors, was gone.

'Gone,' cheered Tilda. 'Gone.' She leapt to her feet, skipped a few strides and flung her arms around my neck. She kissed me with such butting suddenness my top lip was squashed. She had never been so exhilarated in her life, she cheered. All this talk of Roff's, this cancer talk, his social-issues jabber, the gloom and fear and panic of it all, and there was a little girl who was expected to die and instead was riding her pony to Sydney for charity. 'Don't you think it's exciting?'

The water was drying tightly around my eyes. My performance was past its peak. Tilda skipped and laughed as if all her woes had vanished and her lumps had gone into remission by television. 'Don't you think it's wonderful? What's wrong with your eyes?'

'It's the emotion. It's all coming out.'

'Don't be like that. Don't spoil this moment. How can you be upset when there's such hope from that little girl? It's like her story is my story, or will be. You should be happy for me.'

'I am. I am.' I switched to smiling. Tilda held her arms out for me to lift her and dance a triumphant jig.

Dear honesty box,

With regards to the president-servant principle. From that night on its balance became different. The president side was tilted towards Tilda. I was more servant now—it was part of her privileges. No great discord was created by the tilting, not at first anyway. In fact, quite the opposite: I felt privileged myself. I felt important, called upon in someone's hour of desperation. To be used in the service of someone's very survival, to have purpose of that magnitude is to have life beyond our own needs: a greater, nurturing cause.

I patrolled her hospital bed once the operation was done. I ensured blankets were over her toes and not so heavily as to cut circulation. I ran ice around her lips to ease her thirst. I read her the newspaper, the arts section if there was one on the day, or else a few pages of the book she'd brought for comfort reading: *The Memoirs of Sherlock Holmes*. I brushed her hair so it haloed her on the pillow. When food was allowed I cut the crusts off her sandwiches.

I dared not touch the tube draining blood from her wound but I did make sure her smock covered it so she didn't take fright. When Roff paid a visit I was suitably servile. I stood up and almost bowed to his reverent presence. He had the habit of not looking directly at the face of the person he was speaking to. He peeked under Tilda's sheets to check his handiwork. I offered to step outside the screen as he inspected her but no, he said, he wanted me to stay: 'We'll have a little talk in a second.' This had a forbidding ring to me, as if he had grave news to impart.

It wasn't news—it was advice. He studied the tube and said, 'Good drainage,' and asked if I would take a seat on the end of Tilda's bed. The operation had been a success, he reported. The cancer was no longer there. He was confident he had got it all. Tilda whispered, 'Thank you. Thank you,' though the effort made her wound hurt.

'Now,' Roff said to me, as if I was his patient's translator. 'A few things. In a day or two someone will come, one of our lady helpers, and she will have a mirror. She and Tilda will look at the scar together. It's important this is done as soon as possible so Tilda gets used to the sight of it.'

He put his hands in his pockets and strolled towards me. 'And may I give you this advice...'

'Colin,' I prompted him.

'Oh yes, Colin. On the anecdotal evidence we have, it's important for Tilda to show you the scar before too much time goes by. Don't let it drift or it becomes dreaded and affects her wellbeing.'

'Understood.'

Tilda was muttering 'Thank you, thank you' sleepily. Roff nodded his pleasure at her gratitude. He reached down and stroked her hand, her right hand. He stared at the hand, at where a needle was taped to her vein connecting her to a baggy drip with a spirit-level bubble of clear liquid in it. He became agitated. He tugged his cuffs out from under his suit sleeves. 'Nurse,' he said with a raised voice. 'Nurse.' He flicked the bed screen apart. 'Nurse.'

He lowered his voice when the nurse arrived, spoke very quietly, but my cocked ear picked up the gist of his complaining. The needle should not be in Tilda's right hand, it should be in her left. Her right side was the 'removal zone' side. 'For heaven's sake, did you not check this? It's basic. Basic.'

He ordered the needle be changed this instant.

The nurse, chin tucked down, cowed by Roff's gentlemanly anger, hurried past me with a cool 'Excuse me' and did as he commanded.

I leant out of the screen. 'Is there a problem?' I asked Roff.

'Nothing. A minor matter.'

Fair enough, I thought. It seemed logical to me that the more status someone had the more minor matters would annoy them. I said as much to the nurse out of sympathy for her.

She had rust-red hair, a thick stack of curls. This ward, 7D West, was not a red hair ward, or a brown hair ward or black. All the patients were blonde. All had breast cancer, all were thin. Not sick-thin but fit-thin, as if they ran miles and ate properly. The blondeness was of the same yellow shading as Tilda's. In eight beds, eight women, none related but so similar. I almost said something to the nurse, a slip of the tongue about coincidence—'Is there a breast cancer look?' But I could tell she was too stern a breed for appreciating whimsy.

It is an honour to be taken into someone's wounds. Their real wounds, not their emotional gripes. Wounds that cut the body until it is less whole, less human and no amount of healing can make it complete again. To be taken into someone's wounds is to be trusted to recognise that only their flesh has been ruined. It may be revolting to behold, this wound, but it has not wrecked the rest of them.

I was about to be taken into Tilda's wound. I was about to witness the ultimate nakedness. I waited outside our bathroom door until I was called. We'd been back in Scintilla four days. It was time to get my first viewing over with. She told me to wait until she showered and gathered her courage. She warned me that her right side was like a breast without a nipple at the moment. This was because swelling remained on her. The idea of that swelling pleased her. Wouldn't it be wonderful if the swelling never went? A nippleless swelling is better than flatness and poky ribs showing.

I tapped on the frosted glass door. 'Your audience awaits.' I could see Tilda's shadow moving about in there, shuffling this way and that. I supposed she was deciding where best to stand.

'Okay,' she called. 'I'm ready. Careful what you say, won't you?' A nervous giggle parenthesised the request. She whistled a few tuneless bars. I could have been inspecting a new outfit she'd bought. I finger-brushed my fringe out of the way like I was going on a date. The death-awe returned to me. Death was about to show me its true face, the face of the god of disfigurement. I was determined to look it in the eye and not blink or turn my head or gasp. I may not be a crier when it's required of me, but, honesty box, this was my finest hour of intimacy.

I turned the knob and eased the door open, making the steam mist swirl out. Tilda had wrapped a towel around herself like a long bra. Her wet hair was furled in a bob and she had brushed blueness onto her eyelids. She smiled with a mouth of purple lipstick, though I could tell it was more scared grimace than smiling. She stood up straight and adjusted her bony shoulders back and forth, unsure of their correct setting for this occasion. Forward made her bust too concave, she said; the other way made it stick out too falsely. 'Here goes, then.' She closed her eyes, held her breath and let the towel drop.

It was just as she had described: a breast without a nipple. And yet not exactly a breast. More a bulge of pale pink skin with a thin scar running horizontally through it. Darker pink where the scar stopped in the middle of her chest. Whiter pink where it trailed into her underarm. The effect of the scar and the bulge together was like a pair of large lips pursed and permanently sealed from ever parting. I said as much to Tilda and she looked down and felt across herself. 'Lips?'

'Lips.'

'Yes. I can feel lips all right.' She remarked how the pain was so slight, the skin so smooth and so firm and so silky. 'Lips. Come and kiss them. Come and kiss them.'

I thought she was testing me, wanting me to prove I was still attracted to her. Yet there was no mistaking the other meaning in her voice, the groan which was caught in her throat and making her gulp. It was one of her usual pre-congressing mannerisms.

I did not hesitate. I placed my hands on her hips, bent down and kissed. I started at the centre of the scar, kissed along to the right of it, then back along to the left. I kissed into her armpit's bristle. The taste there was soap and cotton. The scar's taste was faintly metallic, the kind that blood leaves when a fresh scab is healing.

She turned around to have me kiss while she watched in the mirror. Was she checking if I was doing it under sufferance? I was not doing it under sufferance. There was ecstasy in this wound-kissing. It was the *more* factor making a comeback.

In the city you are anonymous. You can walk down the street and no one says hello. Country life is a different proposition. You can't turn a corner and not be recognised, greeted, watched. Which is fine if you want to live in public. But what if you want to avoid people's eyes?

Tilda wanted to avoid them after the cakes and casseroles began arriving. There they were at the back door with well-wishing messages:

Our thoughts are with you, Tilda. From the Croft family
(your neighbours over the rear fence). Hope you have a
speedy return to good health.

Thinking of you at this time—Pamela from the bakery.
P.S. These Neenish tarts were made with my hand. They
are not bought ones.

Hector and Filipa Vigourman left a tin-foil parcel of quiche. *We have both had family members touched by your illness. We know what you are going through. The Lord only gives burdens to those who can bear them.*

How did anyone know? 'Have they been spying?' Tilda railed. 'Has this town had its eyes pushed to our keyholes?' How could she walk down the street now? They'll be looking at her for defects. She always liked getting looks from men. She guaranteed being titless would disqualify her from being perved at.

I confessed it was me who let the word out. On the day I rushed to Melbourne to be with her I couldn't disappear without telling the *Gazette*; it would make me look unreliable. I took Gail at the office into my confidence. I asked her to pass on my apologies to Hector Vigourman: I couldn't write more articles for a while. I did mention cancer as the reason but I didn't say *Tilda* and I didn't say *breast*. I said *biopsy* and *woman's problems* and I suppose Gail guessed the rest. *In confidence* must mean *spread the word* in Scintilla.

Tilda called me stupid and naïve. 'You really are just a boy, aren't you? You had no right to say a thing.'

I apologised with over a dozen *sorrys*, but *sorrys* become like tears and smiling: you just do them to have the argument over with.

I did have an inspiration, though. What's the best way to deal with a rumour? Put out a counter-rumour. Get tongues wagging in the way *you* want, I said. Don't shut the door on the town, don't hide yourself away—it only feeds gossip. Step out, be bold and stroll down the street like you're Princess Di, chest out, not hunched up, big grin on your face. Tuck a soft sock or one of my old singlets down your blouse for a substitute mound; it should do until your scar is ready to have a proper prosthetic rub against it.

'Yes', Tilda said. 'A counter-rumour. What a brilliant idea!' But forget socks and singlets. She's a good carver, not just a drawer and painter of things. If she had some rubber sponge it would be an ideal material—the thick green sponge they use for fragile packing.

I fetched a dozen bricks of the stuff from Hobbs' Timber, Tacks and Twine, and Tilda sat down to carve with a Stanley knife and scissors. Three breast moulds as trials until she got the dimensions accurate. The finished article matched up perfectly in the mirror, tucked in her bra. 'Can you tell the difference?'

'No. It's like you have two normal breasts.'

'Promise?'

'Promise.'

'Both exactly matching?'

'Yes.'

And so we stepped out together, promenading like we hadn't a care in the world. Tilda had tanned herself with a makeup mixture to cover her pallor—her own invention of facial powder and ochres from her studio palette. Turps, ochre, cinnamon, face powder and tea. She looked Indian if you didn't get close up to spot the fakeness. Her teeth flashed Indian white as we saluted *good mornings* to cars and pedestrians, shopkeepers through their windows. I wouldn't have blamed people if they thought us strange; I expect we overdid acting happy. We stopped people we'd never even met and remarked how the sun had a fair kick in it today but we certainly could do with rain.

The false bonhomie turned real in us. We arrived home laughing and hugging. All problems should be solved like this—a dab of colour on your skin, a few *good mornings* down the street. It doesn't last but it's a holiday for the heart. Tilda admired her carving so much she left her bra on as an experiment and wondered, 'Can a woman be alluring if she never takes off her bra? What do you think? Am I alluring enough?'

'You are.'

'Truly?'

'Of course.'
'Prove it.'
We congressed.

I have become more protective of this document. Eventually I had to run out of architrave and that's what has happened—there is not a skerrick of space left. I've tried speeding up getting this thing written, secretly adding to it at work, pretending I'm typing up good rural copy. I smuggle the pages home and past Tilda by stuffing them down the back of my trousers. But I can't fit any more sheets behind the dry wood areas. There are damp wood areas on one wall where my nook abuts the bathroom but that would turn the paper to mushy mould. I am too far gone now to bother with fixing leaky pipes and sealing bad plaster.

Fortunately our hot-water system is permanently on the blink. It is a gravity-fed arrangement in the roof cavity, so ancient a system its tank is rusted and the ballcock lever doesn't shut off properly. Water drips through the ceiling and lands *plop* on the lino in front of the toilet. Up I go every third day, squeezing through the manhole to bend the ballcock arm down so it trips the water level to stop filling. I empty the tank's tray of smelly slime by bailing it into a bucket and climb back down, dangling my toe until it reaches the ladder. Normally I would get the plumber in but I have thought up a use for my ballcock routine. Tilda thinks I'm too stingy to pay tradesmen. I am actually hiding pages.

It is not too dark up there when daylight pours in. The roof holes are like stars, creating an outer-space effect. I can see every cranny. I can lean across beams and misty cobwebs and architrave my testament safely. Tin foil and Gladwrap should keep out the rodents. At the Salvos I found a metal briefcase and slung it through the manhole when Tilda was at the dentist. It should provide extra preservation.

But preservation for what? For whom? I own nothing of any worth. I have only this story. And in thinking that very sentence I have my answer! This story is my most valuable possession. Nothing is more valuable than squaring your soul.

I bet my soul was responsible for my touching habit. That and Tilda's proper prosthetic arriving two months after the mastectomy. I wish I could say, 'Colin, set aside a few minutes in the day when you don't have the urge to do your touchings.' But it's impossible. I cannot escape their tyranny.

I only touch wood and I touch it in threes. Three touches of wood with the flats of my hands. I rest for a second, do another three touchings. Rest. Another three. Pause. Sometimes the urge to keep going, keep touching, is so strong that many sets of threes are performed in sequence. The worst I've done is 600.

If I'm in someone's company I sit near wood. A table leg is my favourite position. I can touch wood while in conversation, keeping my hands down out of sight to touch and talk at the same time and not lose the rhythm of the counting. I don't think I've been noticed. If so, no one has said. My explanation would just be Swahili to them.

At first I enjoyed the ritual, like my own version of a religious tic—crossing yourself and the like. It soon developed into the curse of my waking hours. Even now as I type away I must pause to do my touchings. It takes so much longer to get things done. The legs of my desks at work and at home are smudged from the touchings, and showing wear.

The new breast came by post. A plain brown box with a body part in it. That's how real the thing looked, a credit to the designers. It was coloured beige to blend discreetly inside any shade of clothing. It had the weight of the real thing. It felt breasty in the hand. It was silicone but had a muscle-like firmness. Its skin wrinkled like skin does when pinched or handled.

'I'm perfectly balanced upstairs now,' Tilda said, jogging around the house. 'I feel more whole.'

What a relief to see her bouncing and in good cheer. She had been anything but cheerful since our bonhomie occasion. She had been bitter. It was the fear doing it. Fear that she would not be alive very long. The constant, exhausting fear of dying. Fear of living too, because each day there was the fear of dying. There were no pills for that. There were pills to help you sleep and get a break from the fearing. There were pills to pep you up a notch, but nothing to reverse life back to the way it was. And the trouble with sleep was the fear was waiting when you woke. Hating the fear was no good; Tilda tried it many times a day. 'Fuck life. Fuck life. I hate life. You know what life wants from me? It wants to torture me. It is a sadist, life. It is a fucking sadistic arsehole.'

Surgery just kids you along. It makes you elated because something is being done on your behalf, action is being taken. The relief it provides is short-lived, however. Tilda discovered there is a never-ending aftermath to it. There is *waiting* to do. Waiting for the tumours to grow back. Not the same ones, but their spider-egg brothers and sisters filling invisible spaces inside her. To delay that process more action was needed. There was chemotherapy to inject in her arm.

Mr Roff arranged for vials to be sent to Dr Philpott, Scintilla's GP. He lived a few streets away, had clinical rooms in the front half of his house. Roff thought it might reduce Tilda's treatment trauma if she just wandered up the road instead of travelling to Melbourne. If she felt sick after the injections she could lie in her own snug bed. Not that she should feel sick—she was on small doses. She might lose a little hair but not much, not baldness. It was rare to lose all your hair with the milder mix of drugs he was giving her.

Philpott's place was a walk of two minutes if you crossed over the rail line beside Hastings Road and cut through the Methodist Hall carpark. Tilda preferred to make the journey alone. She enjoyed the idea of being brave, of not needing me to hold her hand. She insisted I go to work and not fuss.

Her jeans, which a few months ago grabbed her thighs, were now a size too loose. Fear is the most radical of diets: Tilda said it made food taste like sawdust.

Walking home she wore a swab on the back of her left hand where the chemicals had been trickled into her. She kept that hand hidden in her jeans pocket. Her hair plait was untied for the purpose of blowing across her face to conceal her wincing queasiness. The drugs put an aluminium tang in her mouth. She licked at her lips from the unpleasantness.

By the time she reached our back door she was in two minds.

One, to go to bed like a cotton bath to lie in. She would pop her head around the nook door to see if I was home. If I was she would say, 'How's your day? I'm going to take a nap now.'

Two was a very different popping of the head. It was a hanging of the head, a banging of it against my door while she cried. 'My body has tried to kill me. It is going to keep on trying to

131

'kill me, isn't it?'

'I don't know.'

'It's not going to stop because of chemicals and surgeons. I don't want any more treatment.'

She held up her fist like a defensive boxing position and let out a burst of howling, a cursing howl at the world, head thrown back, the M of her throat visible. A sound so lonely it belonged to animals and darkness. It always made me jump up from my chair to shush her with hugs and patting. I learned to do it warily, approach her slowly as if we'd only just met, not been two years together. There was danger in it, that sound. If I laid hands on Tilda too suddenly she felt trapped, not hugged. She would howl more and I'd have to back off and wait and have another try. Once the shushing was accepted and hugging allowed we would rock side to side, embracing. I could feel her heart thudding through our clothes.

The first time we rocked I cried. Cried for real. Cried for Tilda, out of care for her, and love and sadness. It welled up and spluttered from me. Then she began to expect it every time we rocked. I still cried for real sometimes but it became more a crying for myself, especially when Tilda took her howling one step further. A step where she sobbed and said if I truly loved her I would help bring about her death. She saw no enjoyment in going on with life, so why not embrace death instead of fighting it? Why not buy a rifle or the strongest weedkiller and help her? I shushed *no, no, no* because I thought saying that displayed more true love than rifles ever could. I suspected she was testing me with the rifle and weed-killer carry-on, checking that I wanted her to live by having me shushing her and telling her I loved her. Yet how was I to read the next step?

'You would want to come with me, wouldn't you?'

'How do you mean?'

'If you bought a rifle or weedkiller and helped me go, you'd do the same to you, wouldn't you? You'd turn the rifle on yourself so you could follow me straightaway?'

'Sweetheart, please, that's crazy stuff.'

'You wouldn't?'

'Wouldn't what?'

'Want to follow me? Be with me always?'

'Of course I would.'

'Truly?'

'Of course.' I found this the best strategy. I'd say 'of course' with a kiss on her forehead. Matter closed, until next time.

The sign for mind number one, for popping her head around my door then going to bed, was hesitation. She would pause on the landing outside our bedroom door. She flicked her sneakers off and made the eleven-step journey up the hall towards me.

The sign for number two started out almost the same—there were flicked shoes and the eleven steps. The difference was she flicked the shoes *as* she walked the eleven steps. She flung them at the walls. By the time she got to my nook she was running, not walking. In between hearing her mount the stairs and reach the landing I would think: Touch wood she hesitates. She hasn't started running yet, touch wood. This must be a number-one day.

Even when it was a number-two day I touched wood in the hope she would not talk rifles and weedkiller. I shushed and rocked her in such a way that my fingers could reach the door frame behind her. It was painted cream but chipped in places, which gave me access to exposed wood. 'She hasn't mentioned rifles and weed-killer so far—touch wood.'

I started the sets-of-three ritual when only one touch didn't work. There's no logic in it, I know. Still, that's the way the touch-ings grip you: three touches of wood may have three times the power. When three didn't work I went to six sets of three, then nine sets, ten, twelve...

I got it into my head they would ward off troubles: Tilda would get well in body and soul; I would never get diseased; Hector

Vigourman would keep hiring me. If I stopped the touchings I was convinced the repercussions would be dire. Unspeakable horrors—a car accident, our house burning down—would befall us. If I failed to do the touchings then wood itself would get even with me for my neglect of it.

I should have sought help, an anti-touchings group or a prescription for medicine. Truth was, I never saw pills put Tilda in a state of peace, so why would they me? I know she took them as scripted at first. I used to count them out on her palm—uppers, downers, ones to make her sleep. I never twigged she'd started hiding them under her tongue. I wasn't the pill police. I didn't say 'open wide' and go peering. I took it for granted she wanted relief from fear. Turned out she fretted that pills were unwholesome. She needed healthy food to clean her out from the chemo—celery, carrots, oatmeal, fruit—not pills from American laboratories.

Roff assigned her a psychologist from the start but Tilda lied, lied, lied. She boasted to me how she spun them a stoic line: 'I'm coping very well, thank you. I'm faced with a huge challenge but am in a positive frame of mind. I don't think I need another appointment, thank you.'

Tilda was worried for her art: psychology and pills might steal it away from her, dull her talent as their side effect. They might alter her personality, turn her into someone bland and passionless. She would rather go crazy like Van Gogh than suffer such a fate. What's the point of living if your very nature is compromised? 'Don't let them ever do that to me, will you, Colin?'

I was probably competing with her. I'm not certain of it, but was it coincidence that my touchings tripled in frequency when

Tilda took to counting her hair?

She was convinced she was balding from the treatment. Forget Roff claiming it was highly unlikely. His chemical concoction may have been mild but she was one of those few who would go bald from it, of that she was adamant.

'Look here!' she would call me out of my nook. 'Look, look, look!'

There she'd be kneeling naked in our bathtub shower, dragging a dripping fingerful of hairs from the plughole. 'Two, three, eight, nine,' she counted, parting them with tweezers.

I told her it was not a large collection of hairs. 'You probably always lost that amount. You just didn't notice it and now you do.'

'Bullshit. You think I don't know my own hair? I would have thought by now you would know my hair.'

I said I didn't notice any difference in the thickness of her hair.

She took that as insulting, as me being too bound up in work to give a damn about her. No sooner had she said it than she apologised and conceded I was probably right. 'I'm just panicking about losing my looks. You have a breast taken off, you can cover it up. But baldness.' She smiled about how her lovely yellow hair had always turned heads, including mine. Losing it would be the cruellest humiliation. 'Just to make me happy, would you count them for me? Please, baby. Double-check my counting.' She handed me the dripping hair and tweezers.

Every second day—the times she washed her hair—she knelt and counted and jotted the figure on a page torn from her sketchbook. There were seldom more than forty hairs. I told her forty hairs is the normal number shed in showering. I told her I'd read it in newspapers, which was a lie but a good one—it satisfied her.

When her hair count came in at thirty or thirty-seven she would beam all day and I could head off to work confident that when I got home there'd be no histrionics. Work was still freelance but was getting interesting in its small-town way. I had freedom out on the road, the *Gazette* car radio blaring Cold Chisel and the Rolling Stones. I had interviews to go to: Old Meryl Furner and her cactus collection; for two decades she'd won best in wax plants at the Royal Melbourne Show. Mrs Doris Mitchell of Borebore Road turning one hundred and being awarded life membership of the Presbyterian Association of Crop Farmers' Wives. I was even called upon now and then to sell classified ads door-to-door to farmers. I wrote my own copy: *Lucerne round bales x20, good qual. $ neg.*

And there were puma sightings. Every month you'd get them—pumas running wild in Scintilla forest. Millionaires up north had bred them for pets then let them go. Always some farmer claimed he'd had sheep eaten.

If Tilda's count was over forty, reporting on flies climbing up a wall was preferable to staying at home with her. She would ask me to do a scalp check. It is not possible to add up every hair on someone's head. Tilda pleaded for me to do it, and I agreed after reaching a compromise that I would only count the crown. The act itself, picking and poking my fingers about, seemed to pacify her. I always lost count and made up numbers. The very fact that there were hairs to count and no bald patches gave her heart. When she asked, 'Does it feel thin?' and I answered, 'No. Feels like your usual mane,' she breathed easy and let me stop. I touched wood, grateful there'd been no rifle and weedkiller talk. To put time in on her scalp was worth the effort.

The trick was to be involved in the task without betraying a sense of duty, without sighing and appearing bored or put upon. If Tilda sensed dutifulness she would ask me to leave the bathroom immediately. She didn't really want me to leave. What she wanted was her desirability demonstrated. Asking me to leave the bathroom was supposed to prompt me into demonstrating her desirability. She wanted congressing, proper congressing in the way we hadn't done much of since the wound-kissing occasion. I felt like saying, 'This counting-hair nonsense hardly makes you attractive. I feel like an ape checking for lice.' I would never have heard the end of that. So I learned to count her hair and not make a complaining sound. I learned to escape congressing.

I got into the habit of running, long-distance running, around the hair-counting period. I laced on my Dunlops and jogged the forest paths. Not for fitness, not for self-preservation. I ran to be alone. You could say I ran from Tilda.

Two hours, seven days a week, from 5 to 7pm, regardless of weather, I ran. I carried a torch for when the winter moon wasn't working. For the record, I never saw a puma: they are the myth of simple men. But I did learn to tell dead sticks from live snakes. I learned that kangaroos don't come when you call them, even if you hold out grass or sugar cubes.

When running, I was temporarily free of Tilda, and the touchings and the hair-counting. I was sometimes tempted to reach out and touch tree bark as I scooted by but it wasn't until I got onto my home street that I stopped and touched telegraph poles—'Touch wood the drug of running never fails to get me high.' I worried that it would cease one day: the chemical that running released in me would dry up its supply. This chemical had been my main entertainment in Scintilla. I had others, but the chemical was precious.

Earthquakes were an entertainment. They still are. Minor earthquakes caused by cattle trucks rattling and rumbling down the main street at night. In the very dead of night when I can't sleep those earthquakes entertain me. I ask the dark, 'How strong can quakes be before the bricks-and-mortar world of buildings tumbles?' There is no figure, going by my count. 'How many quakes can there be in one minute before Tilda wakes to reach her arm around me for reassurance that they're only cattle trucks?' Six so far in these past eight years. Most of the time Tilda stirs but doesn't panic.

I listen for quakes arriving as far off as I can. It distracts me from the click in Tilda's sleepy breathing, the annoying mechanics of her throat. When love has worked its way up through all the *mores* and reversed back down towards zero, a click in the throat becomes a revolting feature.

Galahs were an entertainment. Flocks of them, pink-feathered on phone wires. I hold their flight dear to me. The speed they go turns them silver as they swerve. They fly like one aeroplane made of a hundred little planes. In a blink they explode, regroup, change shape from a plane into an arrowhead. I don't care if they do eat the farmers' seed, you have to envy a creature born not to think, just thrive. No ambition, no dos and don'ts. No knowledge except appetite.

Because, from that hair-counting period forward, ambition led me on. Freelance *Gazette* work was all very well, but a year of it and I had the pull of wanting something better. A city newspaper was the logical step but I needed more experience to go from Scintilla to there. I set myself a schedule to freelance at the *Gazette* another six months and then send off applications to Sydney and Melbourne. I didn't expect to sail in on my first try but I did expect a little interest, a phone call saying *we'll keep you in mind* or friendly letter of that nature. I sent my best *Gazette* pieces to prove my worth:

Meryl Furner isn't considered a prickly person, unless you criticise her cacti...

All I got were reject notes: two paragraphs that amounted to *sorry, not hiring. Your resumé is paltry. Sincere regrets.* Six months later I tried again. The same thing happened. Throughout the next year, rejection, rejection. I rang four editors but didn't get past their secretaries.

Who can blame them—cactus stories! Only hicks from the back of nowhere call that news.

My ambition didn't go away; it slowly fizzled into failure. I never let the failure show. I used my running chemical to dull it. It was my cure for everything. It kept me going for another three years, like a blank man.

Then the great mouse plague blessed me.

If I had to choose the best two weeks of my life I could not do better than the Scintilla mouse plague.

It was the mild autumn that did it. The right amount of sunshine, the humid drizzly rain. They bred in the stubble of the previous year's harvest and feasted on leftover grain. Billions of them, fat as small rats. Like an Old Testament curse they flowed over the ground, grey as living water. They ate green stalks, root and all, and left the soil like colander holes for miles.

My brief from the *Gazette* was 'the human angle. How does it feel to have your paddocks overrun, your home invaded by vermin?'

Holly, the paper's cadet, the only in-house reporter, was assigned the economic impact: the estimated loss in dollar terms; the tonnes of plant matter eaten; the cost of ploughing up the damage and sowing life back into the land.

We worked well together, Holly and I. I drove while she scouted for photo opportunities. I interviewed housewives about the mouse-flood that scuttled through their kitchens, swept through their bedrooms, crawled over babies in cots. Holly took totals from their husbands about destruction per hectare. She jotted quotes about their budgets being buggered and how the government better get off its arse with financial assistance.

She was twenty-one but looked fifteen, with her boy-short hair, military trousers cut off at the shins, Doc Martens boots and saggy socks she kept bending down to hitch higher. A crush on someone is merely a nice way of saying lust. Lust implies you intend acting on your feelings. I was professional with Holly. There were moments when I was close to sending explicit signals but I didn't have a hint she had similar ideas. There could have been ideas but I played it safe. The point is, I was being unfaithful. Not in body terms: in mind. Holly was the first time I developed those symptoms. I wanted the mouse plague to last until my crush ran out of fantasies.

'You're a really hard worker,' Holly said.

I wasn't working hard. I was pretending to need more inter-views with people. That way I could have Holly in the car with me longer, her bare calves and cleavage. A real cleavage that split into two proper breasts for a few inches down her shirt.

Another reason I wanted the plague to keep going was the gift it gave me of a disaster: I was a proper reporter now. Helicopters flew in bringing dolled-up TV journos but *I* was the one who could boast of being a local. This was *my* plague. I had been here with my notebook from scratch. I hate a mouse plague as much as the next person, I told them. But when they're in such vast numbers they're not mice anymore. When you stand in the current of them they're a force of nature. I was only big-noting myself but a tall shiny woman from Channel Nine liked my 'force of nature' imagery. Her brown fringe was frizzed so high, like a hedgerow of hair, she made me seem one foot shorter. She scrambled onto the roof of the *Gazette* car batting mice with her microphone and shoe heels. She wiggled her flick-knife fingernails in revulsion and said, 'Could you wade in amongst them all, Con?'

'Colin.'

'Colin.'

'In amongst them?'

In amongst them did not appeal to me but I was not going to lose face or pass up being on the tellie. I waded. With my teeth gritted I waded while they trained the cameras on me. I became 'Mice Man' on all the stations. I stood, hands on hips, and let the plague wash around my ankles. 'Not enough traps in the world to trap these,' I quipped. 'Not enough Ratsak to kill this many.'

That fortnight I was on air four times, using 'It is a devastating tragedy for the area' as my closing comment. I practised saying it with different emphasis on different syllables each time.

At first Tilda was encouraging. She had me wear a shirt with stripes going longways: long downward stripes make a person look leaner, apparently. The camera puts pounds on you otherwise.

Then she changed her attitude as the plague persisted. She fished a lot, in the mental sense of fishing. 'So, what's it like being around those glamour-pusses?'

She fished for what Holly and I talked about together. 'You spend so much time driving with her—you must have *some* conversation.'

'We're far too busy for conversation.'

'I expect she's too young for intelligent conversation. How old is she, twenty-one? She looks like jail bait.'

'I hardly pay her any attention.'

'Don't go getting tickets on yourself, will you? I mean, I think you're lovely to look at. But the camera hates your jowls. You're not the natural photogenic type. I'm just trying to help you, darling.'

Tilda's cleverest fishing was using role reversal. I first noticed it during the plague and it rattled me because of the guilt it gave. She said, 'If you were an amputee my head would be turned by other men, I expect.'

'That's a strange thing to say.'

'Tell me, do you ever look at a normal woman and think: That's a *whole* woman?'

'No.'

'You don't find yourself ogling them?'

'No, of course not.' I put a little scoff-laugh in the answer.

She asked, 'Tell me about your day,' and I would impart anecdotes about trainloads of charity hay arriving to feed starving sheep. Mice were migrating into the town proper: they had eaten farms bare and were on the scavenge. I made sure I mentioned Holly in these stories, but judgmentally, for Tilda's sake: 'She's good at shorthand but has hopeless people skills.' I complained she was a lazy kid and her big boots smelled of feet sweat. Lies Tilda never picked as lying. Or if she did she preferred believing them over not trusting me.

She had not been focussing on her artwork. Her hair-counting routine had produced a sculpture of sorts—samples from the plughole stuck onto drawing paper. She considered including them in a future painting, but not much painting was getting done. Her sickness had made her art sick as well. She had no patience anymore for pretty trivia like pictures. Van Gogh never had cancer, he was just mad and poor, she said. He was lucky. Mad and poor is not as disastrous as cancer. She'd take mad and poor any day over having death-fear relentlessly in her.

On the last day of the official plaguing—the Department of Agriculture had declared it come and gone—I remarked to Holly, 'I'm going to miss this, you know.' I would miss her too, of course—that was implicit in the comment, though I wasn't about to state it outright. I was doing some fishing of my own. I was hoping she'd say she'd miss the plague too. I could then follow up with a clever line. Exactly what that line would be I wasn't sure—I was too out of practice to swagger smooth lechery. I was grateful when she didn't speak: I hadn't embarrassed myself by making a pass; hadn't given town gossipers the chance of a field day.

Mid-afternoon the CB radio crackled and gasped. It was Vigourman, with a favour to ask. There was a gentleman at the *Gazette* office, a Mr Cameron Wilkins. Had I heard of him?

No.

Vigourman certainly had. Cameron Wilkins was a writer with a national reputation, he said. A poet and playwright originally from Sydney, now a resident of Watercook. The clean country air assisted in his health problems. Two years earlier he'd been felled by a nasty bone cancer. It had gone to his brain but drugs and radiation had zapped it. He was thirty-three years old and married, his wife pregnant with their first child. 'You never give up hope, that's the lesson of Cameron Wilkins' life. I don't need to tell you it's inspirational, Colin. Inspirational.'

The favour was this: could Holly and I give Mr Wilkins some

assistance? Could he be directed to the best spots in which to view the plague's devastation? The *Bulletin* magazine had commissioned a piece of literature from him—two pages of rhyming verse immortalising the resilience of the man on the land.

No problem, I said. Have him meet us in half an hour at the Barleyhusk Road weigh station.

Holly giggled, 'There's poetry in mouse plagues?'

'Pardon?' I said, though I heard perfectly well. I wanted her to lean closer and repeat herself. I wanted the tickle of her chewing-gum Ps popping breath on my ear.

Wilkins was hardly the most robust of men. He covered it up with a dense beard for a face wig, a dun cowboy hat for rugged panache. His shirt was a bushman's kind—flannelette with red-and-black chequer patterns.

It had buttoned pockets over his chest where pens bulged like helpful padding. When I shook his hand it was like grasping boy bones. I relaxed my grip early in case I sprained him. He smiled whitely enough, which made me think: Teeth. They're the last thing to go.

The main feature about Cameron Wilkins was not him but his wife. She stayed at their car after nodding hello, raised her face to get a blast of sun on it. She leant against the bonnet, hand across the belly dome in her T-shirt. It was like he was from hospital and she was from Spain—such a wickery mess of black hair, more wild shawl than human material. The U of her chin had a dimple at the bottom. Her face was wide and healthy-creamy. I thought: What does she see in him? I know what he sees in her. What does he have that, say, I wouldn't?

I looked at her, then at Wilkins, then back at her. She was twenty-eight, twenty-nine, not much older than me. For all his thirty-three he was cancer-old. 'Brains,' I said to myself. 'He must have brains and that compensates for a body gone bad. And he's going to be a father—he's still in working order down there. I bet he knows I'm thinking all this and feels cocksure proud.'

I had dumped Holly by now. I was too distracted by Mrs Wilkins. Mrs Donna Wilkins. She was a more respectable subject for ogling, being pregnant and therefore out of reach. I wasn't about to lean close for her breath poppings.

I led Cameron through swirling chaff between the weigh station silos. I said, 'Chaff. That's all the bastards left, chaff. They gorged on silo grain—don't ask me how they got in through the concrete but they did and they gorged. Ate themselves to death.' I took a standing position that kept Donna in my view, the sun behind me and in Cameron's eyes. Her face was still upturned, as if she was showering in dry sunlight. A spinning top of dust blew around her. She shielded her eyes and turned her back against painful grit in the wind.

I came to my head-shaking senses. 'What are you doing? Stop it,' I muttered, closing my eyes.

'Are you all right?' asked Cameron.

'Yes. Yes. Just dust.' I blinked and picked at pretend eye trouble and silently berated myself: you've got a sick woman at home— you should be thinking about her. You've got enough on your plate with hair-counting and rifles and weedkiller without being face to face with a decent fellow and feeling sweet poison in you for his wife.

'Listen, Cameron,' I said. 'I have to go. I'd like to show you around more but I have commitments.' I advised him to drive north-west to the most plague-ravaged places. Call in at the Mallock Mallock general store. The owners, Claude and Verity, would tell of how they slept in the bath because mouse feet couldn't climb the slippery sides. I promised to ring him if I thought of any quirky details he might find useful for his piece. I jotted down his number, shook his thin hand. I made a point of not even waving to *her* at the car.

When I got home I embraced Tilda. I told her I would cook dinner this evening, which was unusual—I can't boil eggs. It was all part of an apology she didn't know I was giving. I felt purged by it, if only until bed. We congressed. Or rather, we serviced. It was servicing to me. I imagined Holly beneath me, not Tilda. Then I imagined Donna, how gentle one would have to be to accommodate her tender belly. Holly, Donna, I alternated between the two. I had to concentrate not to let slip a moan of their names.

It's customary in Australia to abbreviate a person's name and add an affectionate O or Y, a gesture between people symbolising friendship: Vigourman to Vigo, that sort of thing.

No one abbreviated Tilda and me in Scintilla. We had the usual *good morning* and *gidday* and other pleasantries but we didn't socialise much, didn't seek out friendship. Nor did friendship exactly rush to invite us in. We wore a covering, I suppose. The prickly shell of loners. More Tilda than me, because of her worry about gawking. She kept sensing gawkers in the street. Not in cold weather so much, with her bulky oilskin jacket on. More the heat, when tops come off and we go around in loose singlets. She didn't mind her arms exposed—those veiny vines were her trophies—but for the rest of her it was always a shirt and denim overalls, baggy-fronted like camouflage. Even then she suspected a gawker could peek in at the edges.

On the subject of peeking, she wondered what my eyes did when in public. I glimpsed her watching me on occasions if I was talking to women of a certain age—anywhere between fourteen and sixty. She had tape-measure eyes able to calculate my line of vision. Any hint the line was intersecting with a bosom would get her fuming. 'Don't deny you were perving,' she accused. 'How fucking dare you perv. And in my presence.'

I swore to God I wasn't perving. And it was often true. I crossed my heart and hoped to die and said, 'This is Scintilla, for Christ's sake. Name one beauty who'd turn my head. Just one.'

Tilda couldn't, which left her satisfied she was the town's queen of good looks and my eyes were just for her.

In holiday season, when city Scintillans came home to the family farm, there was more competition—there was slinky fashion to leer through. If I wore sunglasses Tilda had me remove them on the grounds that it was rude to talk to people when they couldn't see you properly. I said, 'Harsh sunlight gives us cataracts.'

'So what! Cataracts are not cancer.'

I should have touched wood more on Tilda's behalf. I don't believe superstitions work but we're all nagged by an inkling there may be something out there. If there was it channelled its worst powers into the fluids of Tilda's right arm. It happened just as her two-year examination by Roff was getting close. The twelve-month milestone had been one thing—twelve months clear of tumours tipped the odds a little in her favour. A little was enough to warrant champagne, proper French stuff that cost the same as a fortnight's groceries. The two-year test tipped the odds in a bigger way—she might end up having a decent lifespan. She walked around the house with her fingers crossed, chanting, 'Two years. Please, please, let me be clear.'

The night after I filed my final plague-related story—500 words on how demand was hiking seed prices, cruelling efforts to replant crops—Tilda asked me to come into the bathroom. She wanted the full glare of my shaving bulb angled on her. 'Do you notice any difference?' she asked.

Tricky question, I thought. Be careful. She hasn't changed her hairstyle. She hasn't changed a thing. Best wait for her to prompt me. A towel was tucked around her. Her arms were at her side. She urged me to keep looking.

'You've got me, I'm afraid. I don't see anything obvious.'

'Good,' she exhaled. 'Must be in my head.'

'What's in your head?'

'Look at my right arm.'

'I am looking.'

'See any difference?'

'Nope.'

'Good.'

'What am I meant to be noticing?'

'Nothing.' She shrugged that it was just her overactive imagination.

But next day I was called in again and told to look harder this time. Concentrate on her arms. Was her right arm larger than her left, in terms of width, in terms of puffiness?

'No.'

No wasn't adequate for her. No didn't reflect reality, she reprimanded. 'How can you not see any difference? Look at my fingers. They're larger. My wrist is larger. Look at how the veins run down my arms. My left vein sticks out like normal, but my right doesn't.' She pressed her thumb to her skin and told me to watch: 'Indentations.'

There did appear to be a fuller outline to her right arm. Her fingers were fuller, redder, as if blood was trapped. I did not want to speak and cause panic over a smidgeon of swelling. In fact, the more I looked the more I was convinced there wasn't any.

On the toilet seat Tilda had laid out a length of string, a ruler, piece of paper and pen. By a pinching process she used the string to take the size of her biceps. She looped it around like a tourniquet, pinched the ends together and in the same action made a fingernail dent where the string crossed. Holding the string taut along the ruler allowed her to read the measurement: 24 centimetres, upper arm; 20 centimetres, forearm; 15 centimetres, wrist. Each finger, each thumb, down to the 4.5 centimetres of her pinkie. She said she did this yesterday, not once but four times, and her right arm was now larger by 2 centimetres at the biceps. Bigger all the way down the limb. '*You* take the sizes,' she ordered. The string was twitching in her grip as she held it out.

I tourniqueted and pinched according to her example.

'That's too loose,' she complained.

'Is that better?'

'Now it's too tight. Concentrate. Concentrate.'

'I am concentrating.' I was impatient at her impatience. I sighed a sick and tired sigh of resentment at being spoken to like that. I said, 'Your right bicep is not 24 centimetres. It's 22.'

'Take it again.' She raised her voice. 'I said, take it again.'

'Not if you speak like I'm a servant.'

She bowed her head and apologised. 'Could you please take it again? Please.'

I did. It was 22.

For a second this appeased Tilda. The 22 measurement might mean the arm *had* been swollen but was now thinning back to normal. Or another explanation could be my faulty string tension when I stretched it to the ruler. My tension produced 22. Her tension, the correct tension, produced 24. 'We'll have a break, a rest from it, then take a new round of measurements. In the meantime, where are the brochures?'

The brochures Roff gave me to safekeep. We'd put them away somewhere, as if away somewhere would keep the cancer at bay because hiding discouraged cancer. Tilda recalled there was something in those brochures about arms and swelling. Something revolting to do with 'worst-case scenarios'. First they were kept in a drawer with her medical scans. Then transferred to a suitcase in the wardrobe. Then an even further-off spot under the staircase with the broken venetians.

Would I get them out, please? Would I read what they say on the subject of arms? There were photographs, if Tilda remembered rightly. Ugly photos designed no doubt to scare the wits out of patients, bad taste examples of doctor humour. She didn't want to see photos of that kind. She asked me to read out what the brochures said and see if anything related to her.

Lymphoedema. When lymph nodes are removed, as they had been in Tilda's right armpit, impurities could not be flushed from the affected arm. The swelling was elephantiasis—lymphoedema. There was a corresponding photo for the word. I tilted the page away so Tilda couldn't see it but she was too upset now not to be shown. She snatched the brochure from me and groaned at the sight of a woman's arm fat with fluid, an elephant-human, fingernails like toenails on buckled finger-toes. A leg-arm that belonged on an obese person's hip, not attached to an ordinary-sized shoulder.

I pulled the photo from her. She didn't resist. 'That won't be you,' I said.

'How do you know? Are you a doctor?'

'I'm just saying let's be confident it won't be you. Look, here, what it advises. It says there are procedures you can follow. You must put your arm over your head and massage. And you've got to keep hygienic with your hand-health. You can't get cuts or pricks or the like.'

'Pricks.' She squinted and repeated the word a few times. 'When I had the operation, wasn't there a fuss over a needle in my hand? It was in my right side and should have been my left? Remember?'

I remembered. 'But they said it was a minor fuss.'

'I'll sue them. They've made me into an elephant-woman. I'll sue them for every fucking cent they have.'

For two hours she directed vengeance at the medical profession, cursed doctors and nurses as negligent and heartless; they should be bankrupted for her arm. Then she ran out of logic to support the blame. Her life had been saved, she conceded. That was the important thing. The medical profession had done its best by her in that regard. If her arm was worse off for a hospital prick, so be it. Besides, the swelling was probably her own fault.

'It's not about fault.' I patted her red hand for extra weight of rationality. Her skin was hot as fever but I didn't dare say. I patted and smiled, careful not to seem too casual. Too casual might be mistaken for not showing sufficient concern.

'Paints. That's what I'm talking about. *Paints.*' She wiped my hand away. 'The filth of paints. The lead and cadmium. The turpentine, the dust, the dirtiness of the whole pointless art activity. I will never paint again. Ever.'

'But you haven't been painting.' I said it not too sarcastically.

'I *have* been. Well, not painting so much as thinking about it. I might as well give up and have clean hands and not risk swelling from it.'

I suggested she try a dishwashing glove.

She guffawed. 'Too sterile. Imagine Van Gogh with pink rubber gloves! You either give your all, hands-on, not caring about cleanliness or swelling, or you give the game away and leave it to others.' She wished she knew someone to bequeath the Vincent flake to. She wanted to pass it on to a *real* artist. She was not worthy of its ownership.

I re-patted her hand. 'In my opinion, you need more ideas, that's all.'

'I haven't got any.'

'Maybe I can help you.' My saying that was not premeditated. I had no help prepared. My bold mouth simply opened and out dropped an epiphany. 'Why not paint a portrait? Enough of landscapes. What's the name of that prize for portraits I've read about, the big prize for painting famous people?'

Tilda wrinkled her brow. 'The Archibald?'

'That's the one. Paint a portrait and enter it.'

'I don't know any famous people.'

Again my mouth opened. 'You would have heard of Cameron Wilkins?'

'No.'

'Oh, he's very high up in the writing field. He'd be a perfect subject.'

'The Archibald.'

Open went my mouth but this time it went one word too far. I mentioned Wilkins's cancer. I meant it as inspirational: he with his trials of it; her with her own. 'Like a bond you'd have,' I said. 'A talking point. A common interest.'

Tilda's lips tasted the lemon-sourness of my sentence and she grimaced. 'That's all I'd need. What a depressing talking point! Jesus. I want to forget about cancer, not give it paint-life.'

Understood, I nodded. Understood. I chided myself to keep my mouth good and closed. Besides, it was tempting trouble, her embarking on a Wilkins project. Imagine her meeting Donna. One look at her splendid mother-to-be glow and it could have stirred up Richard and Alice memories: 'Cameron Wilkins gets cancer and there's no harm in *him* breeding,' she was bound to say.

'Where's the justice in that? There is none.'

As well as brochures the staircase possie contained the Roff questionnaire. In the panic of diagnosis Tilda never completed it. Probably too late to be of use to him now but she filled in the spaces anyway, just in case:

Do you smoke? No. *Have you ever?* Yes.

How often do you drink? Do you exercise? Do you have a family history of illness?

Page three got intimate to the point of asking about VD. *Have you ever contracted it? If so, what variety?* She ticked *No* with an offended flourish.

Have you ever terminated a pregnancy? If so, how long ago? She swotted at the question with the back of her hand, disgusted. 'Why do they want to know that? What relevance does it have to anything?'

'I guess it's a standard question.'

'But why?'

I gave one of my shrugged *don't knows*. I said it probably wasn't important.

It *was* important. In theory at least. Perhaps more than theory. There was certain evidence, there were studies, statistics—what Roff called *possible links*. He told Tilda this during her two-year check up. I was out in the waiting room chewing my nails for good news and wondering how it was that anyone facing dying would want to waste what life they had left reading *Women's Weekly* and *New Idea*. Yet copies were stacked there on the magazine table for flipping through. Liza Minnelli's Latest Battle with the Bulge. Ryan O'Neal: Booze and Brawling—Ex-lover Tells.

It took an hour but Tilda walked out a free woman. She was sore around the ribs from Roff's prodding examination but she was clear, she was free. She clasped her hands under her chin to restrain them from wildly applauding. She waited to be out of the clinic door before letting off a hoot of jubilation. She skipped onto a fence, a low brick border for weeds and flax bush. She star-jumped to the footpath with victorious fists, squealing, 'I've done it. I've made it. Two years!'

I barracked: 'Brilliant' and 'You've done it. Fantastic. Good girl.' I ran up to hug her but she pushed me sideways, lurched from my hold and skipped back onto the bricks for a dance. She was too free for human holding, I presumed. Free of death-fear for now, and that needs dancing not constriction. I leapt up to dance with her. She star-jumped straight down and strode off and skipped some more, her plait swinging with flicky pendulum energy.

When we got to the van she told me to wait before I turned on the ignition. She was breathing heavily, not from skipping and dancing, from anger. 'Do you know why all this happened?' She pulled her plait to her mouth for biting. 'Have you any idea?'

I thought she was attempting a philosophical statement. I expected her to continue with 'It has happened to help me grow as a person'—like people do on TV chat shows. But she meant the questionnaire question about abortion.

'Do you know there are possible links? Do you know that you not wanting our baby could have so fucked up my hormones it brought cancer down on me?'

When someone says such a thing to your face you can only answer no firmly and be silent. I was no doctor; I had no grounds for arguing science. My only defence was a puny 'It was your decision too.' I did have the wits to follow up with, 'Why rake up that shit? You want to spoil your two-year milestone? You want to spend it having a fight on what are deemed *possible links*?'

'You really do owe me. You will always owe me. I own you because of this.'

'What do you mean, *own*? Nobody owns anybody.'

'I own you.'

'Bullshit.'

'I will never be free because of this cancer. And therefore you can never be free. That's your punishment.'

'Who decided I have to be punished?'

'I did.'

'We can't own people.'

She nibbled a crunch of flesh inside her bottom lip. Her face skewed into a fighterly sneer as she bit deeper. I dreaded a rifle or weedkiller moment was imminent. It seemed a logical leap to there from this human-ownership rubbish. Not that it was rubbish in Tilda's mind. It was justice to her.

I don't see justice in ownership of people—I didn't then; I don't now. If she mentioned rifles and weedkiller I promised myself to let her have it. I would serve up a new strategy: I'd say, '*You* go buy a fucking rifle, go on. *You* buy weedkiller. You drink it or shoot yourself or whatever you want to do. Don't drag me into it. You're on your own.'

This would be Swahili to sensible people. I don't fully understand some of it myself. I don't understand how she could talk punishment of me one minute and start laughing the next. That's what she did. She laughed like it was April Fools'. Laughed as if her ownership statement was just her quirky humour. She apologised for going too far. 'I don't expect to own you,' she said. 'You're so easy to wind up sometimes.'

Maybe I am, but it did feel scary. I wanted to bolt there and then. Maybe not forever. Maybe only an hour, to prove I was still a free man.

She could well have been fishing, trying to work out how far she could push me before I left her. No one abandons a person who is facing dying—it's a low act; most people are too decent or guilt-ridden. But Tilda wasn't dying any longer, not in the near future. It made sense she would want to test my commitment by using a bully-bluff technique like the ownership argument: if I stayed after that, I must love her. A strange way to ascertain love? With our Swahili everything was possible.

Massaging is best done first with the fingertips. My fingertips had to stroke both sides of Tilda's fingers. I then pushed my palm over her knuckles, her wrist, forearm, elbow. Heavier stroking the further up the arm I got, forcing the fluid towards her shoulder, and up and over her shoulder to disperse it behind her ribcage. I stood in front of her and she sat elevating her arm for my cradling. Someone observing from a distance might have thought I was planing timber, given my action.

I used my left palm for starters until it tired. Then switched to my right hand and planed in long flourishes—a hundred strokes. A minute's break. A hundred more. The swelling was not always easy to shift. It was a stubborn liquid, thick and treacly. I could feel it squash and ripple under my touch. In between strokes it flooded back in and flattened out under Tilda's skin as if attempting to avoid me. Liquid can't think but it can harden into pea-sized lumps, form a row of lump peas that grow up overnight and refuse to leave the next day. Sometimes it took two weeks of stroking— once in the morning, once at night—until I hit the sweet spot of weakness and the peas burst like inner blisters.

In between my stroking Tilda performed her own massages, her right arm aloft over her head, left palm sweeping along it. Roff said the more massaging, the better. She took that as an instruction to do it always. He prescribed she wear a special medical sleeve, elasticised and matched to tone with her skin pinks. It came with a gauntlet to keep pressure tight around her fingers. 'A gauntlet,' she grinned. She liked the soldier sound of gauntlet, the warrior implications: what could be more suitable for her elephant war!

Before and after stroking I always touched wood that all her fingers had so far remained fingers, had not turned to toes on her. She added bandages to the ritual for extra pressure after massaging: small bandages for her fingers, bigger hand ones, large crepe rolls for her arm. She practised binding herself without needing my help. A mummy look was preferable to an elephant, she said. She never wore the look outside. The sleeve, yes. But not the mummy. Only I bore witness to it in the privacy of our home.

Bandaging through the night became essential when Tilda measured that her arm was 4 centimetres wider one morning. 'You don't mind sleeping next to this, do you?' she asked.

I said I didn't mind at all. She said we could swap sides in bed if the mummy was an obstacle. She meant an obstacle to my comfort in sleeping, but an obstacle to congressing was also implied.

I said, 'So what if it is an obstacle? Your arm is more important.' It astounded me that she could think I'd want to congress with the mummy present. Couldn't she look in the mirror and judge objectively herself? The wad of that arm was an ugly impediment. I never let on, of course. I was blank-faced discreet. Not even the advice of vodka, too much of it of an evening, got me cruel enough to make elephant jibes. I kept them under my breath.

What a relief when the wad—it must have weighed 10 kilos fully trussed—whacked me one night and made my nose bleed as Tilda stretched out in her dreams. 'It was an accident, sweetheart. Sorry.' She petted my forehead and gave her hankie for my blood.

I overacted the extent of the pain to make her apologise more and admit that the arm was a hideous and dangerous weapon. I then said, 'No, it's not hideous,' but that was just to have her contradict me and curse the wad.

'You shouldn't be in the same bed as me,' she said.

'It's fine.'

'It's not. I've just hurt you. People will think I did it deliberately.'

'It's nothing.'

Tilda suggested that from now on I sleep in the futon room, for my own safety. To think of it as a practical measure until her swelling issue was resolved.

Okay, I relented, not so fast as to seem pleased. I blew my nose to string out another trickle of bleeding snot.

It was quite something to get into a bed alone after such a long time. A true sanctuary, as a bed should be. Not just the extra space but the solitude. No expectation to kiss or have to caress or worse. Between the elephant and the massaging, the hair-counting and weedkiller, I had lost desire for Tilda's body. That's natural, isn't it? I did not want intimate contact. Even a servicing did not tempt me.

My massage duty has continued from that time till now—two sessions a day. There are no oils involved: oils dull the friction. There must be heat from the contact of skin on skin; it helps the elephant juices flow more freely; the veins and muscles yield like reeds in a current. I must have a knack for it, massaging, so Tilda always reckoned. I've done the arm a power of good. Since my first goes at it the swelling has mostly been contained. Just 1 centimetre refuses to budge at the wrist; and where the gauntlet stops mitten-like above the fingernails there is a tendency for inflammation, especially in hot weather. It has stabilised, she says. Not elephant anymore, just hefty human.

To be honest, if I didn't massage I doubt there'd be much difference. I do it anyway. Tilda calls it 'precautionary'. I think of it as habit. It's the most physical contact we have. It has often crossed my mind as being a form of substitute congressing for her: she closes her eyes as if in ecstasy.

For me it's the opposite. I tend to bow my head and swallow a lot to keep down nausea. Massaging the dry way we do creates a noise like static as our chafing skins warm up. I've worn earplugs in the past—bits of cottonwool pushed in deep so Tilda wouldn't see them—but they make the static switch to a deeper register, a distorted humming. I hear it in my insides; my stomach squirms like a bout of motion sickness. I stroke quicker these days to get the session finished.

It never helped the nausea to have an image repeatedly circulate in my head. An irrational one that I was sure had no firm basis in science, but was awfully convincing: my nausea was the direct result of Tilda's cancer or lymphoedema exiting her body and, via the massage connection, trying to penetrate mine. The static was the push and pull of my immune system mounting a defence. It was too late for defences, I was certain some days. I felt so unwell I believed a dark quantity must surely have got in.

Before massaging I have touched wood in so many sets of threes I've believed calluses might form on my hands doing it, ones so tough it would be impossible for infection to drill through.

My new futon sanctuary got my mind ticking along clearly and helped my swagger return. Being alone in bed can do that for you. You are less reminded that you share your life with someone. It sharpens your resourcefulness, your self-reliance. I would lie in my sanctuary, scheming. I was making plans that did not include Tilda. I had decided to activate my backstop. I had decided it was time to ring my father. It was time to tell him, 'Norm, I'm coming home.'

I wouldn't say I was estranged from my parents. I had written three or four letters, all neatly typed to look professional, like I was knuckling down to grasp basic technology. I left out details that might give the wrong impression: my pitiful pay cheque, for instance; that I lived among mouse plagues. Scintilla was a thriving agricultural Eden by my telling. I was *benefiting from observing another culture and other farming methods.*

I hardly mentioned Tilda. When I did mention her I used the term *my lady friend* rather than name her. Backstop logic. They wouldn't worry they were losing a son to some woman in a foreign land. They wouldn't get it into their heads to fly out and inspect her like marital livestock. I wrote of Tilda's cancer in a way that big-noted me: I was being a rock to this lady friend until her recovery was certain. The implication was that I wasn't permanently shackled.

In their replies I could hear Norm dictating his news to my

mother: mortality rates for spring lambing had been normal; weekly rainfall for the year had been average; an average number of hay bales was expected in the summer cut; he intended locking up fifty acres to grow winter silage; his Noble Bijou gelding, Stride For Stride, placed third at Otaki, then won at Te Rapa in the wet. The old girl spelt it out in her embroidery longhand but his serious tone came through predictable and comforting to me. They were letters that kept a polite distance. I wasn't interrogated, which I took as clever: they didn't want to push me away with questions and judging.

I rang the morning Tilda popped out to register for Social Security money. Social Security! What other two words make a grown-up feel so fallen? Tilda saw it as her right, given her health. She made it sound like illness had its virtues and rewards. To me welfare money signified failure and indolence. Name me anyone who comes from rural stock who thinks otherwise. Handouts are for bludgers. Tilda was going to take one anyway.

I sat down on the hallway phone stool and composed myself. I had not called them for almost a year and this call would take some swallowing of pride. Yet I convinced myself no swallowing was necessary. It was my Norm I'd be talking to. He'd be so excited I was coming home he'd say, 'I'm over the moon.' He'd say, 'I'll put champagne on ice.' I couldn't wait to hear the emotion in his voice, his manly effort of holding back tears. Me and him and our thousand acres.

'Son,' Norm said. It was him doing the swallowing. 'Son. Colin. How can I put this? Your mother and I have decided to sell up. We've come to the conclusion it's time to retire, take it quiet.

Wind down. The worry has been killing us.'

'Worry? What's the worry? I want to come home.' I presumed by *worry* they meant worrying about me. 'Aren't you excited?'

'Son, the last few years have worried us sick and dealt us some blows.' He swallowed loudly, a choking wet squelch. He said, 'Sorry.'

'Sorry for what?'

He swallowed again. Sorry for the '87 stock-market crash. Sorry for listening to his damned accountant. That's who he blamed for dangling too tempting a carrot in his face. Borrow big and buy shares instead of land and sheep. Build up strong off-farm assets and enjoy tax breaks and dividends. The market soars and a man gets richer than farmers ever are. Pipedreams! Markets soar all right. And markets also collapse. This one did with an almighty thump and brought Norm down with it. Since then he'd spent three years fighting bankruptcy. If he liquidated everything— property, sheep, cows, tractors, fertiliser spreaders, horses—he could clear his debt to zero and have enough cash for a modest townhouse, a nice porch to rock a chair on.

'We didn't want to worry you with it. I thought it could be resolved.' He swallowed again and said another sorry. Said it pleadingly, as if the word was really his hand and he wanted me to hold it and forgive him his folly. 'My ticker's been playing up with all the pressure of juggling the finances. But you yourself are fine? You yourself are okay?'

'Yes.'

'That's the main thing. You're in a good job going by what you've written to us. You sound settled, you with your lady friend and all. Is she over her troubles? Seems like you've taken on quite a responsibility. I'm proud of you for that, son.'

He was waiting for a response from me. I didn't give him one.

He said, 'You were never much interested in running the place anyway. Farming wasn't your go. You had greener pastures. It's no skin off your nose, then.'

My mother could not come to the phone. Norm said, 'She likes to bend the elbow in the mornings these days. To be frank, I figure if it makes her happy, why stop her?'

I said, 'Fair enough.' I could not bear to hear him anymore. I said, 'Fair enough. No worries,' without parting my teeth. I said it with hate and love and anger. I was never one for talking back to him. He deserved talking back to now, I was sure of that. I had in me a savage talking-back, but the pattern was too ingrained. 'It is skin off my nose. But not a lot of skin,' was all I said. 'You're right, I'm doing well. I've landed on my feet. In fact, I have to go. I'm up to my ears in work.'

He hoped I would write to him regularly, and that we'd talk again soon.

'Sure. No worries.'

He thanked me for taking the bad news so well.

'Sure. No worries.'

Write regularly? Talk again soon? Write nothing, say nothing was the punishment he deserved. I vowed it with all the fury of unsaid words.

If you bawl and sob when you are alone, no audience of others, then you mean it. It's not a performance. The tears have welled up in your humid head and need a way out. It's like looking underwater. A breeze of light brings flies through the window. They want to nest in your hair and drink from your nose, and you let them. Enough alcohol injects a general deadening but it's only short-term. You are senile with headaches and slow eyesight afterwards.

They say when parents die we are left as orphans. No matter how old we are, that's our loneliest. When they go broke—I can attest to this—you are loneliest too. The home that founded you is over. You are lost, fixed to nothing. You are frightened and shambling. You cry. I lay in that state in the futon sanctuary.

It could fix anything, this sanctuary, with a solitary sleep and a stretch and a yawn. Not this time. By morning it was as if my body was trying to burst. My legs had turned a puce colour. From the kneecap down, like a burn on my shins, lumps hard as pebbles appeared. Four skin-marbles so sore the slightest air seemed to punch them.

My feet had gone blue-purple. I hadn't been woken by the usual cranky crows and pigeons in the spouting—it was pain that stabbed me awake. I sat up intending to swing my legs to the floor and stand but my legs had too much extra weight. They were not my legs, they were lead legs with lumps and a bloated surface. My feet were like kitchen gloves when you blow into them. The ankles no longer showed knobby bones but were flesh-balloons in the blue-purple colour, turning kindling-red in patches. My shins too.

I pinched and rubbed my thigh skin. It felt normal and painless. Whatever was happening to me stopped just short of my kneecaps. The skin there had formed a powdery layer—I could lean forward and with a puff make my skin go *puff*. Beneath this powder my flesh was splitting and peeling like sunburn. There were hundreds of splits going longways and crossways between the lumps, some exposing the moist quick.

I slid off the futon and eased myself to the floor. As soon as my legs were no longer horizontal, fire-blood filled them and I lost my breath from the agony. I dragged myself up into the lying position, flat as I could to make the blood subside. 'Tilda,' I yelled. 'Tilda!' I yelled 'fuck off' to flies parking on my sticky pain. 'Tilda!'

Naturally I diagnosed the massaging as the cause. Never mind good sense, my massaging of Tilda was contagious after all. I wanted to accuse her there and then as she rushed to my calling but I had no breath for forming sentences.

She bent over my lower half and gasped *Jesus*.

'Don't, don't, don't.' I waved to her not to breathe so hard. The air she spoke with was too heavy on my skin.

She diagnosed spiders somewhere in the bedding. It had to be a white-tail. If not, bull ants or centipedes. She had bare feet and jigged her dislike of creepy crawlies as if they were mounting her toes. She demanded I allow her to reach over and around me to check in the sheets and blankets, lift the pillow. She picked up one of my sneakers, shook it upside down in case of insect infestation and grasped it as a killing weapon.

It was no more spiders than Tilda's fluids leaking in me. It was rheumatoid arthritis, and those lumps and flaming skin were a complication called *erythema nodosum*, explained Dr Philpott, kneeling by the futon and *mmming* his fascination at my ailment. 'Quite a rare condition, and boy have you got a doozy of an outbreak.'

'I'm only twenty-seven. Arthritis is for old people.'

'No, no, no,' he corrected me, pricking my artery for a blood sample. 'We inherit these things. It's in our genes. All we need are triggers. Has something happened to trigger this in you?'

'Maybe,' I replied, and mumbled 'family worries'. I left it vague as that. 'Usual trouble, type of thing.'

I was ashamed I was fathered by a bankrupt. I had no backstop left—my father had made me a bankrupt too. *Estranged*. From then on I used that word to eliminate the subject of parents from my life. I used it with a casual shrug, dropping my chin to signal weariness. *Estranged* and shrugs go well together. People think: Ah yes, the usual family tensions. No further explanation required.

Now I am ashamed to have been ashamed.

The treatment was simple: lie flat on my back, legs uncovered because the sheets weighed a tonne. Tilda brought cups of tea, soup and finger toast because my appetite withered the bigger my legs grew. *I* was the elephant now. Philpott prescribed a white lotion to cool the pain but its application was sadism: tongue depressors are the gentlest of implements; they could have been broadswords when used to smear my legs.

The worst discomfort was toilet time. I could drag myself there, keeping the legs flat and free of pain. I didn't need Tilda for this section of the ordeal. The journey was merely thirty seconds long. It was the toilet bowl I needed Tilda for. For lifting me onto the seat and holding my legs up while I directed my penis downward and pissed. The fire throbbed less if my legs were held level with my waist. She held them at bath time too. Her seeing me splash my privates clean didn't faze me in the slightest. It was all part of what happens when you're a couple and one is offering the other helpfulness.

Where I drew the line was bowel movements. Bowel movements are our *own* business, given the smell and fart noise, the brown sight of what we store in us. She could turn her head away and close her eyes but not her nostrils and hearing. I made her leave the bathroom so I could get on with it alone.

I was able to hold my bowels in for two days. Not the third. By the third I was packed hard and needed releasing. Tilda supported me with her good arm until I was throned in position, then I made her scamper out the door while I exploded, leaning sideways, legs splayed upward like doing sit-ups. I had to empty out fast before my legs gave way and crashed down. If that happened I needed Tilda to come and pick them up in the presence of smell. I practised my toilet sit-ups in bed. I could last thirty seconds if I gripped the cistern with one hand for balance. I wiped myself by lurching left and twisting side-on and using the toilet roll holder for purchase.

It took four weeks for the ballooning to reach its peak. By then my shin skin had turned to dry scabs. The redness had darkened to suntan bronze and itched and could not be scratched or else it brought on worse pain. My ankles were bruise-blue and would not flex. My feet lost their nails and were weeks off being ready to fit a shoe. Leprosy, I named my lower half. Tilda liked that: leprosy to match her mummification. The president-servant balance had swung more even. We had equality of deformities.

'Two crocks together,' she said, dabbing Philpott's pain-paint on me. Her tongue protruded from her mouth corner with the effort of nursing. 'We're in the same boat.' If she hit a raw section she gasped 'Sorry, sweetie' and kissed my forehead like a brave infant's.

When the job was done she prompted me, 'It's your turn now,' and wedged two pillows behind my back. She unclipped her overalls and crouched on the floor at a height suitable for my left palm to stroke her arm the hundred times without causing my legs to twist and suffer.

You would have thought my imagination would settle down

but my squirming stomach still got to me: I still had that notion of Tilda's disease trying to transfer into my system. My condition did at least provide an excuse to stop stroking before a hundred. I had physical weakness to thank for fading at fifty. 'I'm buggered,' I said, and slumped. Tilda had no option but to forgive me. She held my good hands in her fat hand and lay her good legs beside my leprosy legs and contentedly fell asleep.

I practised taking a blanket over my legs. I would have to withstand one eventually—winter nights would freeze me otherwise. But the reason for wanting to cover them was to stop Tilda looking. She took too much heart from our ugly equality for my liking.

'Your legs are not ugly.'

'They are.'

'They aren't.'

'They are ugly leper legs.'

'They are not ugly leper legs any more than my arm is ugly. Are you saying my arm is ugly?'

'We've been through all that. No, I don't think your arm is ugly.' The old lie.

'There you go, then. Nor do I find your legs ugly.' Surely she was lying too.

Yet, maybe not. She liked to wiggle her good hand into my underpants and test me for servicing. 'What have we got down here?' she said, and rubbed and handled. As much as I clenched against getting excited, as much as I gripped her wrist and told her to behave, she persisted and wanted me to kiss her. She suggested I feel into her clothing for her good breast and see if it appealed to my touch. It did. Off came her gauntlet and her sleeve. Up and over her head went her shirt, her bra and prosthetic body part. She straddled me and said in shivery whispers, 'Tell me if I'm hurting you, sweetheart. Is this okay? Your legs aren't stinging?' She didn't want servicing, she was after true congressing, the real McCoy of loving intimacy.

Here's the Swahili of all Swahilis: so did I. My distaste for the idea was gone. In its place was not desire so much as me wanting the *home* of someone. I wanted the homeness of Tilda. We must surely have been marked out for each other, fated. Cursed in body, the better for being blessed in soul. I said so to her during the gentlest of straddlings. I said, 'We must be cursed but we are cursed together.'

'Yeth. We are blethed in that way,' she whispered.

Something enfeared me that I had never experienced when I was well. 'What are you thinking?' I asked her. 'Right this exact second. Tell me your thoughts?'

'Wha?'

'This very second. Be honest.'

'I thinken nothing. I feel you move roun inthide me.'

'Nothing else?'

No, she promised. Nothing else. I couldn't let up, however. It was jealousy, you see. Jealousy, and all the desperate hallucinations it causes. I kept thinking: What if she's straddling me but in the privacy of her mind wishes she was straddling her equivalent of a Holly or Donna? I closed my eyes and searched the town for a selection of threatening possibilities. Gavin, the gardener at the duck pond park? Christ no—he has teeth missing and talks simpleton-slow. Joshua, Scintilla's liquor store attendant? Has

179

body odour and looks over fifty around his eyes.

What about Michael Farrelly, LLB? He has Scintilla's goldest shingle. Its only shingle, in fact: Attorney at Law, like Americans on TV. He wears suits, cufflinks, ties, so he wouldn't be interested in Tilda. It reassured me and insulted me that he was out of her league.

What about Vigourman? He left a get-well cake for me at the back door, and a batch of Mrs Vigourman's Anzac biscuits. *You're in the wars, you two*, it said on his card. *We look forward to having you back on board soon. My wife is always saying, 'There can never be enough Colin in the* Gazette.'

I disliked his name intensely. I couldn't even congress with vigour given my state. I was a passive pommel horse for Tilda to trot on. I also envied him his money. On my bedside table were official government forms for my filling out and signing. I now qualified for a sickness handout. What slightest appeal could I have left for anybody? Yet Tilda must have valued something. There I was beneath her, not a Joshua, attorney or Vigourman. I advised myself that this could well be as good as things ever got for me. This might be the height a man such as me can reach. It's like sinking to the bottom of your own life, thinking such thoughts. You are weightless, released. You don't want to surface; you no longer want to breathe. Which makes you panic suddenly. I came up gasping for air, grateful for Tilda in her moaning reverie upon me.

That's when I asked her to marry me. I spluttered it into her dangling hair.

She gripped my ears to steer my eyes to look into hers. 'Really?'

'Would you want to?'

'What a beautiful quethion.'

'So, yes?'

'Yeth. Pleathe. Yeth.'

Marry me is the very opposite of bad language. A bout of bad language and I crave chain-smoking. I get so thick in the neck veins—anger is blood-borne and clogs them—I need smoking and cold vodka to treat it. Then I need sleep to silence my banging brain. *Marry me* was calming to utter. More like soap and water than two old-fashioned words. I expected my blood was being cleansed of red and was now a clear colour.

Tilda was the same, though she took it one step further. What I called soap and water she called pure and holy. She said no wonder churches are the common wedding preference: even if you don't believe in God, what other place is worthy? You can do it in your living room but that insults the feeling. She set her mind on the little white place at Mallock Mallock. It hadn't been used in years but was so dignified, so simple in the Presbyterian manner. Oh, it would need sprucing up but leave it to her; she'd fix it. She skip-ran down the stairs for a pen to list arrangements. Weatherboards would need re-nailing. She had once sketched the church, made watercolours of its windy ambiance—a bare paddock and padlocked gate, ragged gum trees like sentries. She noticed two stained-glass windows were broken but not too badly. She spied through the cracks and saw cobwebs—they'd need sweeping. There were bat droppings and bat stench, the abandoned nests of sparrows or starlings. She would clean it all, scrubbing one-handed. 'My pet project,' she decreed. I was off the hook with my legs being their way.

As for a celebrant, Tilda would make a few inquiries. A minister was all we needed. There would be no catering or grandiose expense—this was *our* marriage, hers and mine, no family present. Other people get married to show themselves off, a stage production with bridesmaids and flowing veils, Rolls-Royces driving in convoy. We had nothing to show off except rotten health. Nobody was going to watch us become each other's spouse, weeping how touching it was and feeling sorry for us. We'd exchange vows in the tiny chapel in the presence of the god you have when you don't believe in any—Nature. The wheat-field winds, the sea-blue sky; tree limbs creaking around us in their own crippled dramas.

'I get the sense that chapel has been waiting years,' she said. 'Doing nothing but wait for the sole purpose of having us in it.'

She bought a catalogue from the newsagent—*Wedding Bells*. She wanted to wear white like the chapel's whiteness. Fawns, blues, greens would not do for a wedding, our wedding. They're for ordinary dos and balls. It was $500, though, for a dress with the merest satin. Instead she ordered a roll of material and pretty lace lengths and a silken bustle, part of an intricate effort to measure herself and cut and pin and stitch the fabric. She taped thimbles to her finger ends and bound up her bad hand, keeping the binding loose enough to let her bend and grasp while ensuring security against needle injury. She sat on the lounge floor and threaded her wedding artwork. I wasn't allowed to enter and glimpse it. My eyes would have to wait for the ceremony, which is the custom. The dress took a month to complete. She called it her masterpiece. It's still here somewhere, folded in two garbage bags against silverfish. I think it's under her side of the bed but I don't want to see.

I wore a suit, a hired one from a phone number in the catalogue. Tilda measured me for it during my experimenting with standing. Three months after the leprosy set in the pain was dulling enough for relearning to walk. Up the hallway I'd go, then back to bed and a pillow under my heels for draining away pangs. I practised walking twice a day in preparation for the aisle, for waiting at the altar and saying vows and escorting Tilda on my arm out of the church and into married life.

The arrangement was that Reverend Giles Hugg from Scintilla's All Faiths Congregation would do the honours for a $40 gratuity and keep it hush-hush so there'd be no sightseers. The *Gazette* would want to be there with a photo for its social page if word got out. Tilda didn't want people nattering about how lovely she looked for someone with a mastectomy. I certainly didn't want the attention. I was managing to walk again, yes, but only with a walking stick in each hand. Tilda bought me black wooden ones from the Salvos—less medical than the steel kind from Philpott but walking sticks nonetheless, like an old codger. I had put on belly weight too, from being bedridden and having my appetite return. I had, in other words, aged. I found seven grey hairs in the mirror: three on my left temple; four on my right. There were signs of sagging below my eye sockets.

My responsibility was getting a ring for her. I didn't need one—rings are optional on males and we had to be sensible and scrimp on spending. The symbol of a wedding ring was essential on women, Tilda believed. 'It's like saying, *Colin is my husband.* It's saying, *World out there, I'm the love of his life.*'

She gave me her finger size—her good hand's finger, a finger she would display like a normal wife: 13 millimetres diameter, which turned out to be size C in jewellers' language. Not that we had a jeweller in Scintilla. We had O'Connor's Manchester, which sold everything for the home and human, including orthopaedic footwear. And down the very back, in a knee-high locker, cheap watches, necklaces, bracelets and ear studs. In a locker inside the locker, accessed by brassy key, was a felt container which opened out into rows of rings of gold and silver. Wedding rings, engagement, eternity.

Of the three that fitted Tilda's measurements there was a plain gold band, price $75, which came in a little domed presentation box and included a tag saying nine carats. Me and my sticks hobbled down Main Street twice before I finally decided on the nine carats over a thicker band with a speck of diamond in it but not as much reflective shine.

It was probably the O'Connor girl who informed the town—Shona or Sheena or whatever her name is. The one with powder so densely applied it makes her face look dirty. 'When's the happy day?' she asked.

'We're keeping it very quiet.'

'Oh, do tell.'

Never confide in country people.

The ceremony would start at 11am. Tilda was having her hair done at Tracy's Salon before breakfast, which would give me time alone in the bathroom to make myself presentable. I was able to bathe on my own now—my legs tolerated water and floated painlessly under the surface provided the temperature was cool. I could step out and onto the bath towel without help, and bend and rinse dead skin from the enamel without losing my balance or feeling leg blood scalding me.

I was to dress by nine and wait at the back gate for Reverend Hugg, who had kindly offered transport. He and I would go to his house for morning tea while Tilda dressed in her masterpiece, put on her face and picked a dewy posy of flowers from our backyard for her aisle walk: lavender sprigs were in the purple of health after spring rains; oleander bloomed pink; bottle-brush was scarlet and bristling. She'd make her own way to the chapel by van so I wouldn't see her bridal look until vow time.

Reverend Hugg was worried about the van part of proceedings. What if the rickety wreck broke down? What if we stood there at the altar, he and I, and there was no Tilda? He'd put fresh batteries in his cassette player and said it would be a shame if only flies and magpies got to hear the wedding march. Also, he was booked to umpire junior cricket in the afternoon—any dallying would cause him inconvenience.

He needn't have worried. The van did its bit. We heard it pull in through the church gate with a salute of backfires. The reverend stood to attention and nodded his relief to me. He touched a knuckle to his nose to wipe away bat odour. He lit two candles and smoothed the cloth he'd brought to cover the bat-stained altar table. He didn't care whether we were believers or not, if we were going to get married in a house of God there had to be a Bible and crucifix present or we could get someone else. His cross and Bible were between the candles. He nudged them together as if aligning sensitive instruments. He was the fidgety type, short in stature, big on baritone speaking. His head was a pincushion of hair transplants still healing, pubic-like strands slicked across his skull as if he thought no one would notice. He pressed play for the organ music and immediately had to turn it down because of echoing in the empty pews.

There she was, the long white stem of her. Her arms were webbed in lace, with oversized lace cuffs in a glove effect to conceal her sleeve and gauntlet. She stood in the narrow door arch holding her posy above her waist like a nervous offering. She smiled but it was a flinching, embarrassed kind. I could see the problem. There were people behind her, half a dozen elderly women. I couldn't name them but I knew them by sight. 'Biddies', they were called behind their backs in Scintilla. 'Ladies' to their faces, but 'biddies and busy-bodies' behind. They tugged and pinched their cardigans over their bosoms, patted their candy-floss perms because Holly was there too, camera over her shoulder, blinking heavenward for the best lighting, positioning the camera tripod used for steadier social-page portraits.

The biddies clumped themselves together to be photographed,

granny-stepping through the door after Tilda. She took a deep breath and proceeded towards me. The nuisance of impostors would have to be ignored. Reverend Hugg directed me to extend my arm and invite her to be at my side. He stood on his toes and pointed for everyone else to settle in the rear pews and be quiet. He put his finger to his mouth and gave the order: *Quiet.*

I put both walking sticks into my left hand and bid Tilda *come embrace my right elbow.* I felt compelled to touch wood that she would look just as fragilely beautiful up close as she did slow-stepping from the door; that she would not become tearful from all the smiling and worry about tears melting makeup. I touched wood that I would not appear unlovely suddenly to her with my hunched reliance on walking sticks. That there would be no scene of second thoughts for the biddies and Holly to dine out on for months. Wooden walking sticks at least mean you've always got the touchings close at hand.

There was no need for touchings. Tilda held me tightly, her head bowed to display jasmine flowers braided there. She was shy and wanted my approval.

'Beautiful.'

The reverend lifted his arms like surrender. 'Heavenly father, we beseech you to be with us on this most auspicious day.'

I never knew humility was not demeaning. I never knew it made you kneel and made you tall.

I was sworn in to Tilda, and she was sworn in to me.

I switched walking sticks to my other hand for a moment to get the ring box from my pocket, spread its stiff jaw and prise out the nine carats.

Reverend Hugg surrendered his arms again. 'A ring is a symbol of commitment, of pledging love and faithfulness. Marriage is not to be taken lightly. It is our souls we are joining. Let this ring be a constant and lifelong reminder to you, Colin and Tilda, of your blessed union.'

It slid into place on her with a few budges over bones. There. Done. I leant forward and kissed my wife. She leant forward for me to kiss her longer. She whispered, 'My husband.'

Reverend Hugg announced, 'Ladies and...ah...ladies, I give you Mr and Mrs Colin and Tilda Butcher.' He began applauding us. The biddies applauded, called out, 'Amen. Congratulations. Bless you both. Bless you.' They pulled handkerchiefs from their cardigan sleeves for effeminate dabbing.

What happened next I thought was just those old girls. There was a crazy screeching like they'd spotted a ghost, or had a turn, one of them, and dropped dead to the floor. The screech was higher up, though, where roof beams criss-crossed. Dust fell to us, and dirty clots of old spider webs. I looked up and dirt stuck in my eyes. The reverend spat fibres from his mouth. 'Bats,' he coughed.

Bats don't have green feathers and flash about in green flight.

Green was all I saw—a screeching blur of it, then another louder screech as greenness descended and separated into two birds: two parakeets diving our way, merging and tilting, separating again. They arced around the reverend's head and screeched directly into mine, collided with mine, a feathery thud on my forehead, tipping me off my sticks. I crumpled over. Tilda told me later they didn't even try to alter course. It was like they'd lined me up and hit me on purpose. They swerved to miss the biddies and Holly but flew straight into me, then whooshed out the chapel door.

I have to hand it to the biddies: they tried to make me feel better. I was shaky on my sticks after climbing to my feet. My eyebrow had a bleeding scratch on it, like a parakeet sign of foreboding. 'Oh no, no, no,' they said. 'Parakeets are good luck. That's a good luck sign you've got on your head. Isn't it, Valmai?'

'Yes it is.'

'Isn't it, Ada?'

'Absolutely, Vera.'

They probably even believed it. I certainly did. I had the weather to help me believe—the softest drizzle had started up. The whole smooth sky was coming down to greet us and give that soap-and-water sensation for our outsides.

I smiled for Holly—for her camera, not her eyes. Her fringe was dyed orange, which suited her. But I had eyes only for Tilda.

Ceremonies are like surgery—they kid you along with their action and elation. The ordinary business of living is then returned to you. Our wedding ceremony lasted two honeymoon days and nights. We didn't take off anywhere special: the expense would spoil relaxing. A night in Bendigo at The Shamrock, say, was $100 before food and beverages. We appreciated the special history of the building—Dame Nellie Melba stayed there, but that was years before. For $100 we wanted her singing in person and not to feel we were financing bistro renovations.

We set up the stereo in Tilda's bedroom—I moved back there like a proper spouse. With the blinds kept down our bodies looked normal in the honeymoon dimness. We played Bruch's Violin Concerto No. 1, Tilda's favourite, over and over. We kissed, we congressed. We whispered 'sweetheart' and 'darling'. We planned the years out, defiant of illness. If welfare was all we were good for, so be it. We resigned ourselves to burdening the government—we deserved being indulged after what we'd been through.

Vows. You can't take back vows. You can't revise them later. You can't say, 'Sweetheart, you know that bit about *till death do us part*? It's a beautiful sentiment, but how do we keep the words *going*?'

Six months after taking them I resented Tilda. I got well, you see. My legs shrank back to normal. It took most of the six months but my ankle shapes returned. My shins and toes returned. So many layers of skin had been shed but fresh skin took its place, sparsely hairy. There was a tickling like loose socks when I strode, a phantom sense of baggy flesh falling. Dr Philpott said this was common and temporary. He said an outbreak like mine, so savage in one still young, might protect me against extreme recurrences in future, or so goes the research wisdom. He pronounced me fit to lead life as usual, even to begin running again. Fit to go off welfare and be in the workforce.

Hector Vigourman was delighted. He had expanded the *Gazette*—it was now The Gazette Group, with two sister publications: the *Watercook Tribune* and the *Wimmera Wheatman*. The *Wheatman* was a trade rag bought from city investors who didn't know farmers. 'Ear to the ground,' Vigourman theorised. 'Farmers want local people writing about their industry, not city nobodies. They want reporters from their own backyard, not cubs up from Melbourne to cut their journo teeth.'

Holly had quit Scintilla for a TV pipedream. 'The position is yours,' Vigourman said to me. 'Grains writer. The *Wimmera Wheatman*'s wheat man.'

I knew nothing about cropping but Vigourman reckoned ignorance would benefit me. He wanted *human* stories, not just the science of low-tillage grain-growing or dissertations on whether single-desk marketing delivers the best price at harvesting. I would have my own workstation at *Gazette* HQ *and* the Commodore at my disposal when I needed it, as if it was *my* Commodore. One day that new cellular phone technology would come to Scintilla, he said. One day they'll build a big dish for it here, meaning out with the CB and up with the Joneses. And my pay? I would be paid as actual staff. Not per story but per week, like a valued citizen—$200, which sounded a fortune. I know it's chicken feed if you're a qualified something—a plumber or vet with certificates saying so—but it was *my* chicken feed. No more twenty-four hours a day in this house, which was less a house than a hospital.

Tilda bounced with such glee at the news that her body part shook out of its bra cup and she had to catch it. No more cheap-brand bread and margarine, she cheered. No more vegetables on special because they're spotty with rot. We could buy new sheets—the old ones smelt convalescent. So did the pillows. She could afford a supply of chemist cosmetics: anti-ageing creams instead of useless Pond's from the supermarket. She bought me a sporty watch to help meet deadlines. It cost nearly a whole week's pay, which was why I didn't say thanks more than once when she presented it. She considered this ingratitude and began to cry. Cry! Cry as if it was *her* money, *she* had earned it, *she* was the one working eight-hour days and not me.

A ritual similar to our past one set in. It took a few months but Tilda began experiencing those two minds again. I would arrive home from *Wheatman* duties and she either greeted me with a cheek-kiss or an argument. If it was a cheek-kiss she handed me a Crown lager with the top already off for my immediate sipping. 'Look what I've done today,' she said, taking my hand, leading me to her studio. 'I'm on to something here. Vincent would be proud of me. Wouldn't you, Vincent?' The envelope with the flake inside was stapled to the wall as a talisman. A square of masonite or canvas five feet or so by five leant beside it, splashed and stippled with her rendering of the plains or a molten-looking sun glistening because the paint had yet to harden. Sometimes she put a picture outside to dry and gnats stuck to it like insect-birds. I admired the realism but she picked the creatures off. She said if insects weren't intended by her then the painting was just an accident. 'Did Van Gogh do accidents? Van Gogh did not do accidents.'

She liked me to sit with her and think up names for her creations: *Lava Sunset*; *Wheat Flung*; *Emanations*; *Weather World*. I had a knack for it and enjoyed drinking my beer and approaching the task as if solving a problem. I could think on them for hours and have the peace of trivial conversation: 'What do you reckon, Tilda? *Cloud Quill*? What about *Sky Halidom*?' I admit I got out the dictionary sometimes.

If the greeting was an argument-greeting it was a one-sided argument—it didn't include me at all. It took place behind her closed studio door and was with Vincent. I would knock. We would exchange hellos, then I left her to her quarrelling: '*Your* paintings were fucking magnificent, Vincent. Pure fucking marvels. Mine are pure fucking shit. Totally fucked pieces of shit.'

I'd put my ear to the door and she'd be kicking over a chair to emphasise her exasperation. Paint cans would fly. They sound like glass smashing when all up-ended. Pallet knives make no noise when hitting canvas, but clatter if booted across floorboards. I touched balustrade wood that she would keep on at Vincent long enough for me to tiptoe upstairs, change from my good clothes into running rags and slip out the back door for two hours of pounding the forest path.

Three paths, actually. The first took me uphill past the sundial at Ringo Point. I always got a laugh there: the graffiti was mostly

Tyler 4 Zoe and *Cory fux fags*, but someone had defaced the sundial with texta—north and south had been changed around. Beside it someone had scratched *I'M LOST. Santa.*

I ran across Ringo Point to an outcrop of flat rock handy for a minute of push-ups. The sky is pulled down so low to the horizon there it sweeps over your head, over your eyes like a hat brim. A third track bends east of the ridge and cuts through thick scrub and ironbarks. Even if rain blows through, the ground still crunches with dryness. The only colour not grey or black is when lemony wattles bloom in October. This is the hurdle track. This is where you can't blink in summer or you'll jog onto a snake. They curl like long turds in a sun-drugged state. Up go their heads once they sense you. It's either hurdle or get a bite on your ankle. There are little ones called flicks but little or not it's best to hurdle them, just in case.

Two hours on my running route and I wanted to applaud myself for having a heart that can keep going that long. When I arrived through the back gate I celebrated by stripping to my underwear and turning the hose on. I champagned water over me like a podium victory, which Tilda hated. It was the sight of me grinning and gulping and spitting. It was the pleasure I was taking in snorting spray and moaning as the coolness covered me.

'Do you have to do that?' she complained.

'Do what?'

'Show yourself off.'

'I'm not showing myself off.'

'What do you call it then? You're saying, "Look at my athletic physique."'

'I look athletic?' I patted my stomach to check. Yes, there were muscular corrugations. Yes, I was athletic, firm across the chest, no loose meat on my thighs. On sunny nights, nights of long dusk, my trim reflection lit up on the kitchen window glass. I turned and twisted to admire myself in the rays. I walked around the house with no shirt on, hoping for a stray breeze.

'Put a shirt on.' Tilda covered her eyes as if I was unsightly. 'You trying to rub my nose in it?'

'I'm not rubbing your nose in anything.'

'You look very striking. There, I've complimented you. Now, please, a shirt.'

Be guilty about being healthy—this was the undertone; if you can't be sick with me then at least keep your health and your fitness concealed. I liked feeling well on the inside and out. Of all the things to be guilty about, to be ashamed of!

Yet I obliged and put on a shirt. I changed my running time from after work to during. I parked the Commodore at whatever farm the *Wheatman* took me to and I ran once I'd interviewed my subject. 'Jack,' I'd say—or Wayne or Neville. 'I'm going to stretch my legs. Running helps me compose an article better.'

'Is that so?' they'd say, scratching the hatband rash on their foreheads. 'Wouldn't know m'self. Never wrote more than a cheque.'

I kept it up for one winter. Winter meant only light sweating mostly confined to my underarms. Wimmera winters last barely two months, though. By August the full sun is back. Car air-conditioning will dry your shirt if on high fan but the smell of heavy sweating stays with you and pongs the interior. I couldn't walk in to the office and reek. No one likes those sort of people, the office stinker. So I resumed my forest route, resumed my hosing, my snorting. If I wanted to take my shirt off I would take my shirt off. What life have you got if you can't take your shirt off in your home, your own private premises? I rehearsed those very words in preparation for Tilda: 'In my own house I should be free to do as I want.' There was nothing more obvious than this truth to me.

It was not an obvious truth to Tilda. 'If that's the way you feel then do as you want, leave your shirt off.' She said it quietly and meekly, as if I was bullying her. It's a clever way to trump you, meekness. It makes you back off a fraction, as if you've overstepped the mark.

'All I'm saying is, in my own home I should be able to go shirt-less, that's all I'm saying.'

'It's *my* home, remember. My money bought it.'

I backed off another fraction, then did some trumping myself: 'Well, technically, if you want to get technical, yes, it's your home. If *I* want to get technical I could say it's my job that brings in most of our income.'

'I have no desire to get technical. We are married and we share things. I was just hoping you would wear a shirt to consider me.'

I put a shirt on. But I made sure I played a sarcastic game of 'Please, Madam Tilda' when about to take a hot bath. 'Please, Madam Tilda, may I remove my shirt? May I remove my pants too, so I can wash properly?'

From this point on we didn't congress again, ever. We serviced each other, never kissing with tongues. It was quick servicing and I used old girlfriends like Caroline summoned to memory to arouse me and get it done. In bed I was allowed to take my shirt off—bed meant the night dark blotted me out. Our genitals touched but not much more of us. She hardly laid her hands on my back. She must have found the feel of it intimidating—its new drum skin and sinew span. Perhaps she used old boyfriends to pique her mood. I didn't care. I was finished with jealousy.

Tilda's jealousy was just getting into full swing. I liked it at first. I came to fear it—felt condemned by it, imprisoned.

I had begun treating Tilda like a fan: I was the important one and her job was simply to adore me. This went to my head. I started running with my shirt off for any eyes that were interested. (You can tell when curtains are being spied through—the parting flicks shut when you wave.) I kept thinking what a waste it was: Scintilla was my audience, windows with only biddies looking. When I panted in through the back gate Tilda stomped up the gravel path to have her say. 'Are you trying to provoke me? Are you trying to advertise yourself like some half-naked ape?'

I never answered, just panted 'leave me alone' and 'Hitler of the backyard.' One day I trumped her with this: 'Why don't you take your top off and come running with me?' I said it with a snigger.

'All right then, I will.' She unlatched her overalls, unbuttoned her shirt down to her navel.

For a moment I was sure she was going to do it. I glanced for any sign of parted curtains. I said, 'Jesus, Tilda, do your buttons up. Jesus.'

That gave her a victory. She had out-bluffed me. She raised her chin and smiled her satisfaction.

I trumped, 'Take your top off then. Go on, give the town an eyeful.' I headed for the hose for a champagning.

Tilda yelled that I was cruel. How else could she describe a husband who told her to go naked in public?

I didn't see her unbutton everything. I was snorting water from my face and moaning like a lowing cow. When I peeped through the spray her top was off, her overalls were already at her ankles. She wore black knickers and asked if she should take them off as well.

I leapt out of the water and covered her with a bear hug. I picked her up and marched into the kitchen. She laughed all the way, kicked her legs like paddling. When I let her down she put her fists on her hips to signal another victory, another out-bluffing. She said it felt so wonderful to at last go, 'Here I am, world. This is me, one tit and all.'

'I have a responsible job in this town. You want people saying I have a missus who runs around starkers?'

'Oh, Mr Responsible. Grains writer for the *Wimmera Wheatman* hardly makes you Prime Minister.' She gave a slow, mocking shake of her head.

Then, whether by accident or instinct, I produced the ultimate trumping. 'Fuck it, I'm leaving. No more of this shit. I'm having no more.' I put my hands out in front of me and waved: 'No more. I'm leaving.' I strode up the hall, gripped the balustrade knob and swung onto the stairs, bounding up three at a time.

In the bedroom I stomped when I walked, cursed: 'I'm off. I've had a gutful.' I opened and closed drawers with as much bang and crash as I could. I emptied my sock and underwear drawer onto the bed, same for my wardrobe shirts and trousers from the ironing pile. Razor and toothbrush from the bathroom cabinet. I was leaving. Or at least that's what I wanted to show. I had instinct enough to know this trumping needed an aggressive display of packing; not just saying 'I've had a gutful' but actually shoving possessions in a backpack.

Tilda arrived at the bedroom still topless but with one arm across herself for modesty. I snapped at her, 'Where's my blue polo neck?'

'In the futon room on the clothes horse. What are you doing packing?' There was no mocking from her now. There was shallow breathing, quick little gasps: 'What do you mean, *leaving*? Please, sweetheart. No. Don't leave. No. Don't go.'

I kept packing but slowed down my jamming the backpack full. If I finished too soon and had to fasten the straps shut there wouldn't be time for Tilda to plead more.

'Baby, please, where would you go? Sweetheart, don't.'

'I'll get a hotel room until I find my own place.'

'Darling, no. I'm sorry, darling. I'm sorry. Don't leave, please. Please.' She held my arm to prevent me hoisting the backpack to my shoulder. She embraced my neck, pressed her face into it. Her voice smelt sweetly and sourly of tea and a tooth on the turn needing drilling.

If I had my life over again I would not have my life over again. Not from this point on in the story, anyway. I would have thought more decent thoughts. Thoughts have consequences though they never leave your brain. They do damage if the bad ones get too prominent. Thinking darkly rots your decency. Among us small people—people in small towns with pipedreams over—the staleness of disappointment makes you mean. Add in dark thinking and you're history.

Two months after my trumping win Tilda was admitted to hospital. There was blackish blood on her toilet paper. A tumour in her woman's parts was her amateur diagnosis. Her cancer must be on the march.

It turned out to be a benign ovarian cyst easily dealt with, scalpelled out and forgotten.

'Get plenty of rest,' Roff advised.

'Rest is the best medicine,' Philpott agreed.

Rest, I scoffed in my thoughts to their faces. Rest is her main occupation these days. Art is too hard for her so she has a long lie down. If you spend your life resting what are you resting towards?

She had stopped her complaints about my parading without a shirt—I'd trumped those out of her. In their place, however, came *rest* and the silent treatment. That's what I called her new polite distance. Silence, I was convinced of it, was her latest trumping strategy. It never occurred to me she might be acting in good faith, trying to help me love her by letting me breathe a little. I was too busy letting my thoughts run away: I felt let down by the black blood not being cancer. I expected it would be. I expected Tilda would die soon. I would nurse her. I would grieve. I would get sympathy. I would live in this big home a widower. I was still a young man: one day I'd remarry. Till then I would play the field—one-night stands in Melbourne; a week in Surfers or Byron. I would buy a David Jones suit and act a man of means. I would wait a year or so, a respectable period, then clean out Tilda's clothes, her studio. This building would go on the market and I would exit Scintilla, make a beginning from an end.

Then Tilda broke her silence with this declaration: she wanted to embrace life with fresh resolve. She blessed the cyst as a reprieve, a reminder that life is temporary and we must make our mark before perishing—any mark, something to say we were born into this world and have lived a life that's worthwhile. She wanted me to be proud of her again, not think of her as a patient or a nuisance. She wanted me to relish her presence and not feel trapped by petty put-a-shirt-on demands. Jealousy drives the person you love away, she realised that now: 'It's a very unattractive quality. It's like you don't trust the very person who has vowed themselves to you.'

At night I faked sleeping, my back turned against her.

'Please, sweetheart, don't fall asleep yet. Talk to me. Talk to me.'

I kept my eyes closed tight.

It was her idea to ring the Wilkins household. It was her decision to attempt the Archibald Prize, nothing to do with me. I supplied the phone number, yes, but at her request. I didn't think anything would come of it.

She was almost too late: Cameron's cancer was back and in the process of killing him. He could barely sit upright; his bones were eaten out and could not take his weight. Tilda apologised for even fetching him to the phone, let alone suggesting he might pose for her. 'Art is so trivial alongside illness,' she said, tucking the phone under her chin, pressing her palm against her forehead. Her face had lost its pink cheeks and pink lips; they were sick-bed pale from embarrassment and cancer memories. 'Just forget I rang,' she apologised.

Cameron insisted she not apologise more. He was accepting of his fate. So was his wife. Dying needs its distractions too: a portrait might be the perfect tonic. There were plenty of photographs of him around, family ones, a few formal shots for book covers—his daughter, Ruth, eighteen months old, would have those images to say, 'This was my father.' But a painted portrait was another matter, he said. It's an artist's impression in oils of what's inside us, of who we are. It's an artefact.

And so it was arranged. Donna took care of the details. Thursday week; a three-hour session for preparatory sketches should do it. He'd be comfortable enough if propped on pillows, and he would doze if the morphine got to him.

Tilda maintains she never liked Donna. Right from the start she had a bad feeling about her. You wouldn't have thought so listening to that phone call. 'Donna,' she said. 'I can't thank you enough for letting me have your husband's precious time.' She hung up and smiled, 'What a woman, this Donna. Such dignity and graciousness. Such strength given the situation.'

I remembered the day at the Barleyhusk silos. I imagined I wouldn't look twice at Donna now. Women in the country go fat from having children. I imagined her no further. Not yet.

Never liked Donna. Bullshit, Tilda! You came home from the portrait session like you were smitten; like you felt a little bit lesbian towards her. The prettiness of the woman; her hospitable, intelligent nature; so loyal to her husband, and caring. Never liked Donna. You didn't spend much time telling me about painting Cameron Wilkins. It was Donna, Donna, Donna. You had made a new friend, and if the cyst had taught you anything it was that you hadn't valued friendship enough. You had locked yourself up inside this old building and it had driven you lazy and loopy. When Cameron died, three weeks after posing, it was you who insisted we attend the funeral. I said, 'We didn't know him enough to go to his funeral.'

It was you who said, 'We need to be more social.'

Never liked Donna. You're rewriting history. You liked her so much you forgot to think about me. That *I* might like her too; I might get smitten. I might end up wanting her more than I want you.

There were two lunches—one at our place, one at Donna's.

Ours was Tilda's idea, to do with Cameron's portraits and the Archibald. Three months after the funeral a series of six oils had been completed. Tilda wanted Donna's opinion about which was the best of them. The best would be the prize entry. Donna could choose a gift for herself from the others. It was a nervy Sunday lunch: would the widow be in tears? Would she look at Cameron's image and collapse on us? Her daughter, too, would she get spooked seeing her father in frame? Having no child ourselves we predicted a grief tantrum.

Death doesn't register with kids. While mummy did her choosing I took the wee girl to the park and she was thrilled to ride the plastic horse, hold on for dear life on the swings. She wept at having to dismount and hurry home with me. I didn't want to be at the park being counterweight on plastic horses. I wanted to get back and pretend not to be watching Donna. At Cameron's funeral (which involved no church, just a burial) I had kept my distance, felt an impostor. I didn't get a good view of her. Her head was bowed; relatives shrouded her in hugging. She still had that Spanish look from the day at the silos, in the hair sense, the black shawl sense. Her hair blew forward as she tossed a handful of dirt in the grave. The rest of her was hunched around a handkerchief. She wore sunglasses. Her blue dress was too long down her legs to see anything more than ankles.

But in our small living room eating dips on sticks of celery she was all bare arms and pants cut off at the knees. I focussed there—on her knees. Or rather, stared into spaces either side of her knees, taking little glimpses and keeping her on the edge of my vision. Tilda's tape-measure eyes couldn't complain about knee spaces: I wasn't looking at a face or cleft of bosom, though I wanted to. Donna's knees were like most knees—a dry-skin knob putting a blemish in her tan skin. But most faces were not like hers. I don't just mean the U-chin and dimple. I mean her brown eyes. Our culture values blue eyes as if blue eyes are purest—miniature replicas of sky. But brown eyes can have earth-dark gleams to them. Donna's eyes were this way. It was a pity not to peer into them.

I am not an open smiler. I smile self-consciously, lips askew or pursed. Donna's smile put all her big white teeth on show; not as an act, performing smiling like *cheese* for cameras, but as a pleased-to-see-you friendliness. Unless, of course, I had been fooled and she had perfected smiling for vanity's sake. That's what Tilda would say. Anyway, it was a pity not to look.

I listened instead. Donna was explaining how she was doing fine. Fine in the tears sense, in the dropping-your-bundle sense and needing a good cry. A month ago the crying stopped and in its place came money worry, and does she stay in Watercook or move somewhere urban for Ruth's schooling? If it wasn't for Ruth she would go somewhere like Darwin. A complete change, a new life, exotic and tropical. Ruth required stability, not exotic and tropical.

'I've even felt like cutting off all my hair,' she said. 'Shave it off to symbolise grief, but also for saying *there's a new me starting*.'

Cut off her hair? I jerked up my head at such a notion. I took an admiring look at it, the dark mesh of curling; then stared off before Tilda saw.

The lunch ended with an agreement to a do a lunch again, next time at Donna's place. She had been thinking of a modest party in a few months. A daytime soiree with local people she knew—neighbours and parents from Ruth's playmate group. Nothing wild or late-nightish. Would we come?

'Delighted,' said Tilda. 'Who knows, we might be celebrating an Archibald!' She kissed Donna on the cheek. Ruth too. I shook hands and said nice to see you again.

They were walking up the backyard, across oleander leaf shade, when Ruth's hairclip, a fake-glass tiara adornment, snagged on a low branch and dropped from her head, broken. Donna knelt to retrieve it, pausing in a crouch to comment how it was just a cheap old thing. I did not stare off from the band of white flesh that appeared because of her crouching—almost all of her lower back. It was so smooth and transparent you could see a faint few veins where her T-shirt rode up. And the top of her pants, the shadow and crease of her bottom.

No sooner had we waved Donna's car goodbye than Tilda said, 'You seemed very quiet. What do you think of Donna? I got the impression you don't like her, staring into space like you were bored. I hope she didn't think you were rude.'

I shrugged that I had no opinion of her either way.

'She's very attractive.'

'Is she?' I shrugged again. 'I suppose she is. I wasn't paying much attention.' If Tilda was fishing I was matching her with yawning nonchalance.

'Don't you think it's a bit early for her to be stopping crying?'

'What?'

'If it was me who died I'd want you to cry over me longer than three months. You would, wouldn't you?'

'Yes.'

'Promise?'

'Of course.'

She hugged my arm as we walked towards the back door. 'I like Donna well enough, I just think she's, you know, a bit cold. A bit hard and cold.'

'Same here.'

Tilda squeezed my arm as if relieved we were of a similar mind. She said if I died she would never stop crying over it.

The Donna lunch was barbecue-style, the cooktop sizzling like tap water running. A dozen people were arced around it, squinting at rissole smoke and decrying the lack of government research into declining wild bee populations. All the money pouring into genetically modified produce—it was a scandal. Mankind was going to make nature unnatural. These were alternative-lifestyle types who farmed alpacas or goats and lived in mudbrick houses built with their own amateur hands.

Tilda and I were out of place in our nice jeans, our clean Adidas runners. The men wore workman shorts and leather sandals, their dusty toes bulging through. They held beers like microphones kept handy for swigging, for laughing louder into each new bottle. The women wore frocks so expansive it was hard to tell if they were expecting or had let themselves go. I could not picture Donna with this crowd as friends. She was more like us in her black denims, her blue blouse with frill collar. Red leather boots with wineglass-stem heels that pocked the dirt like footy sprigs as she tended the grill. Tilda had more makeup than her, too much in fact—it looked like she was trying too hard. If she was hoping to put Donna to shame she was doing the opposite. For all her red boots Donna was just naturally better—more beautiful, I mean. She had no need of blush and eye shadow. She had no fat arm getting fatter by the minute because the sleeve was left off as an experiment for socialising.

I didn't contemplate this at the lunch itself. I didn't think she was competing with Donna—the older woman attempting to outshine the younger, radiant belle. But the Swahili between us rings true. Especially given her Archibald entry was a failure. It didn't even make the first cut. She was embarrassed but bluffed it over with anger. 'It's not what you know, it's who you know with these things. You've got to be sleeping with someone or brown-nosing the judges to win prizes.'

Such statements make a failure look bitter. Saying them at a barbecue makes people clear their throats and blink in search of a different line of conversation. I provided it by pursuing the topic of genetics. I'd been guzzling wine and it fired me up for a performance of big-noting. 'This genetically modified foods issue you've mentioned. We shouldn't be too quick to slam it. Not if it's going to stop starvation in the world. No famine—wouldn't that benefit humanity?'

I received frowns and muffled guffaws. One fellow swigged his microphone and spoke so close into it he produced an echo. 'Not if all nature is mutated.'

I rose onto the balls of my feet and returned his frown. 'Science deserves more credit than that.'

'Are you a scientist?'

'No, I'm a reporter.'

'Reporter?' His scoff blew another echo from his bottle.

'I've written a thing or two on this subject for the *Wheatman*. I'm their specialist grains person. Trials conducted at Ouyen and Boort predict a trebling of tonnage per hectare if growing oilseeds or wheat using genetic modification. The plants become drought-tolerant which, in the growing process, conserves thirty parts per millimetre of natural moisture in the soil. You can feed the world from the grain belts of Australia.'

There were indeed trials, there really were. I honestly had written two stories about them. But my 'trebling' statement was an elaboration. I couldn't remember the precise percentages. As for thirty parts per millimetre—I made that up to sound learned. Which worked. There were no scoffs anymore, just a general mutter of 'I'm still concerned' and 'We must still be vigilant.' On the subject of genetics there was deference to me.

'You've got to love an expert,' Donna said, giving the browning meat a prod. 'I didn't realise you were such an expert, Colin.'

'Oh yes,' Tilda butted in. I wanted Donna to keep going with the compliment, not have Tilda affectionately slipping her fingers down my back pocket. 'Who'd have thought that when I met him he wanted to be an actor.'

'No, I didn't.' I pulled her fingers out by the wrist.

'Yes, you did.'

'I didn't.'

'You did.'

'It was just me mucking about in my youth. I'm more practically orientated. Science is my forte. Agricultural journalism.'

There is a custom in seating arrangements that I don't understand. If a group of couples is spread along a dining table they're placed boy-girl, boy-girl so as not to sit beside their spouse. I suppose it encourages more diverse interaction, but it also encourages flirting.

You have to be quick arriving at the table if you intend to flirt. Arrive last and you'll be plonked beside the person others avoided. Arrive first and you can be selective. You can act as if you're waiting to be directed to a position by the host when in fact you are really shuffling yourself between people until paired with your preference. That's what I did with Donna. Tilda got shuffled sideways between two microphone swiggers and a wide-frocked alpaca breeder. I had Donna to the right of me, and I can't remember who on the left—I looked left only once to pass the potatoes. Right was my priority. I didn't look right often; I kept my gaze forward. Tilda was seated only four placings away, so keeping my gaze forward was safer. I had Donna visible in my eye corner to read the signs: a heavy breath of boredom if she wasn't liking me; an allowance for our elbows to touch once in a while if she was. If I lifted my head to turn her way she would avoid our eyes meeting at such close range if she liked me.

I remember the four main topics we covered in conversation.

One. She admired my stance on genetic modification. Didn't agree with me so much as appreciated my knowledge. She valued my social conscience in wanting solutions to famine. 'It's tough to take an unfashionable stance. But there's sense in what you're saying.' Cameron was robust in his opinions, she said. She'd been starved of that since his passing. She leant closer to me and spoke at a whisper, her hand over her mouth as if for coughing. 'My neighbours are very pleasant but, you know, they're simple people.'

Two. She had enrolled in a psychology course at the university in Bendigo to keep her mind sharp and critical.

Three. She intended to get fit, lose the hips motherhood gives you. I couldn't resist saying, 'Hips? They're perfect.' Ruth crawled from under the table onto Donna's knee at that moment. If she hadn't I might have continued the flattery. I'd judged by now that she liked me well enough.

Four. She intended changing her married name back to her maiden one. Not now but soon. 'I don't want to be one of those women looked at as eternally *widowed*. I'm too young.' She often wondered how long a period of grief should be. 'They say it takes twelve months. That means I'm halfway through it,' she figured.

Her saying this got me thinking: in six months she'll be out for fresh mating. I felt jealous in advance about whoever the bloke would be. A silly chill of jealousy. I shivered for it to be gone from my shoulders.

In the car home Tilda asked me, 'So, what did you two chinwag about?'

'Boring stuff. Genetically modified crops, that sort of thing. Boring.'

'I had a windbag telling me alpaca wool was a wonderful fabric. Banged on and on and on. But the rissoles were nice.'

'The rissoles were. Did you have to mention the acting stuff?'

'Why not?'

'Don't refer to it in future, please.'

'Why not? It's funny.'

'It's not.'

'It is.'

'It makes me sound flaky. Don't do it again, please.'

'Are you kidding me?'

'I'm asking you not to do it again, please. Okay?'

'Okay.'

'Thank you.'

The Scintilla Picnic Race Meeting, Melbourne Cup day. I had a free family ticket, a gift from the racing club to the *Wheatman*. I said to Tilda, 'This family ticket. I see no point in using it, just the two of us. It's a waste. Let's give it away.'

She considered that a shame given the gorgeous green tinge to the spring weather. A shame given the chance to mix and mingle. 'You have your work to get you out of the house. You get to have normal conversations. I slip back into hermit mode much too easily. I'm housebound again, Colin.' The Escort van had clapped out permanently, towed for scrap. I had the *Wheatman* Commodore. Tilda had nothing till we could afford a replacement vehicle. She said, 'I sit in my studio and go *bugger it*.' She flopped her arms down in a defeated motion. 'Take me to the races, sweetheart. We'll have fun. Let's invite someone to be our guest. We'll be like hobnobbers. We'll take bubbly and roast chicken like we're hobnobbing at the races.'

Truth is, I had every intention of going. My 'I see no point' was just for Tilda's sake. I wasn't about to come straight out with 'Let's call Donna Wilkins. I want to see her again.'

Harmless flirting, that's all I intended. I was not setting out for love or congressing. Just flirting, a bit more than I'd had at Donna's lunch. Her grieving period would be up by now, her twelve months had just been reached. We could spread a picnic rug near the racecourse rail and I would find a way around Tilda's presence to enjoy the charge of simmered yearning. No harm in that—everybody does it, I bet.

'Sweetheart,' I said—using *sweetheart* was always good politics, particularly in this instance: I wasn't sure about the state of Tilda's jealousy-guard regarding Donna. 'Sweetheart, it just occurred to me, we should probably return the hospitality of your friend Donna. It's been months since her soiree. She might be an option.' I paused—a clever pause. 'Or maybe not. We can cross her off the list.'

'What list? Our list consists of blank.'

'Perhaps ring her and ask her then. Up to you, sweetheart. Makes no difference to me.'

Simple as that. Donna was invited. She told Tilda that Ruth would adore it—the hoof-thunder of horses, it would delight and scare the wits out of the child.

I was curious to know after the call if I was mentioned. A 'How's Colin?' or something. Tilda didn't say so and I wasn't about to ask. I doubt I was, which disappointed me. But it was pleasant disappointment. I smiled to myself and winked to myself and muttered, 'Oh well, *c'est la vie.*'

The family ticket allowed us two car spaces. Donna was able to reverse her green station wagon in such a way that the tail door could be lowered as a smorgasbord table facing the home straight. The Commodore was parked beside it, which kept the next group of people along at bay. Perfect for not being too sociable with them. We even had willow shade, which added intimacy to the outing, like blinds drawn down while others sweated.

This was not like Donna's lunch, however. I did have her on the right of me again, but I did not have her to myself. I had Tilda directly on my left and Ruth straight in front. Tilda was in a talkative mood. Christ, she can talk sometimes. All her house-bound inactivity must have stored talk up in her. Not ordinary talk. *Health* talk. That's the thing about people with health problems. You give them the chance to explain their afflictions and it's as exciting to them as party time. We'd only just sat down and chinked glasses to say 'Happy race day!' when Donna asked, 'I hope it's not rude of me, but I'm curious about your sleeve. What's it for, exactly?'

Tilda put the arm behind her back and said, 'This bloody thing,' as if she despised it. She'd fretted about wearing the sleeve that day. Such a glamorous day. What was worse, having it stared at or having swelling to explain? Midday heat and sleevelessness would be heaven to the elephants in her.

Donna apologised and said, 'I just wondered if it's

uncomfortable.' She reached over and touched Tilda's thigh to try and erase her faux pas.

I thought Tilda might take all this as snideness: a putdown by a flawless woman to the unfortunately maimed. To her credit, or rather the goodwill in champers, she brought the arm forward for display. 'It's my uniform. And this little glove is my gauntlet.' She said it like a boast.

If she had left it at that I would have admired her as gutsy. But on and on she went about swelling and massages. She referred to me as Mr Fingers, her indispensable personal massage mate. I picked up a stick from the dirt and touched wood she wouldn't get me to demonstrate massaging. *Don't do it*, I touched—I could tell it was in her mind. I didn't want Donna seeing me intimate with my wife.

Tilda did it. 'Colin, show Donna your stroking method.'

'Can't. Races are starting.' I stood up and took $10 from my wallet. 'I'm off to place a bet.' I hurried away wishing Tilda would just melt into the ground. Melt and not be seen or heard from just for an hour. Half an hour would do, instead of being an interference to flirting.

I placed no bet—I'm no gambler. Gambling always seemed too sleazy an activity. I walked around the betting ring disdainful of bookies, the way they thumped their white money bags and spruiked 5 to 2 on Baron's Boy as if offering me a favour. Yet, between bookies and me that day, bookies were the more wholesome. I should have demonstrated the massaging as Tilda wanted. I told myself as much—'Do the right thing by Tilda.' But by the time I returned to the rug, topped up my glass, nibbled at a chicken thigh, I was thinking of ways to have Tilda leave Donna and me alone.

Ruth was an option. Or I could get Tilda so drunk she needed a lie down. Drunkenness would take hours, however: she held her drink like a shearer. Ruth was the better way. If only I could get Ruth to take Tilda's hand and ask her to play. There are a dozen opportunities on racecourses for children's amusement. There are jockey-midgets in their harlequin costumes. The swaying ambulance that follows the race to the finishing post. When the barrier shoots open the metal bang is bone-jarring; it's a wonder the horses don't drop dead of fright. I said this to Ruth. I said, 'I would drop dead from the terror of it. But horses have wings inside them.' I let out a great exhaling of wonder at horse wings. 'No matter how terrified they are they run and run and refuse to drop dead.'

It worked. She was O-mouthed with fascination that horses don't die from noise but sprint instead and sometimes fart very loudly from the sudden lunge.

'I reckon farting makes them run faster,' I said. I had her in stitches from saying a rude word like farting and making a fart sound with my mouth. Donna was giggling too, and burping up champers fizz. 'Ruth, I'd take you and show you, but I'm going for another bet.' She begged me to take her and show her the farting but I said no.

Tilda said, 'Don't be so mean.'

'I'm not mean, it's just—a person in my position, wearing my *Wheatman* hat, so to speak, I have to be seen *participating. You* take Ruth. You'd like that, wouldn't you, Ruth?' I tapped Tilda on the forearm to suggest she hold out her hand for the child. I said,

'Don't *you* be mean.'

Ruth had the most innocent, pleading smile. It brought on the melting I needed. Tilda wiggled her fingers to have the girl come near. The moment they touched Tilda held her close and kissed her hair. She said, 'But who's going to look after Donna?'

'As if I require looking after.' Donna reclined on her elbows, her drink almost tipping too far.

As Tilda led Ruth away it occurred to me she might pretend she was the actual mother of the girl. I hoped it would be a pleasant fantasy. I hoped it would mean she stayed away a while. I guessed their walk would take ten minutes to reach the barrier at the 1600-metre chute. Watching the horses circle around and get loaded into their gates would be five minutes. Then ten minutes' walk back after the barrier crashed open: twenty-five minutes in total.

I did not even bother with the pretence of betting. Once Tilda was out of sight I sat down and said, 'Second thoughts, I might hold off on a punt until later.'

Donna wagged her glass to ask me to fill it. 'This is bliss,' she said. 'I haven't let my hair down for I don't know how long.'

'Feel free to do it today.'

'I have to drive. I'd better watch my intake.'

'Oh, you'll be fine.'

'I'm out of practice with drinking.'

'No wild parties?'

'Hardly.'

'No romantic dinners?'

'Hardly.'

'No fellow on the scene? I'd have thought there'd be men

queuing up at your door.'

'I wish,' she blurted. The tiny sentence surprised her as much as me: the hearty frankness; the hinted crudity. She quickly revised it. 'I wish it was that simple, I mean. Oh, never mind.'

'Go on. Don't stop.'

She stood, one hand visored over her eyes for a view of how lovely the horses looked in the mounting yard. From our distance they appeared to be all one colour—shiny bay with a silver feather of perspiration in their flank.

'You were saying?'

'Forget it.'

'Why?'

'It's awkward to explain.'

'Why?'

'Just think on it for a second.'

'Think on what?' I was still excited by that initial frankness-crudity moment. 'I'm afraid you'll have to be explicit with me.' Using *explicit* in this context sounded frank and crude as well.

Donna got re-seated, snuggled between two ridges of willow feet. She spoke to her glass, not to me directly. 'I am a mother. I am a mother and a widowed mother at that. A man, well, it is expected that a man will keep company—let's call it that: *company*. A man will keep company. He will seek it out, even. I've heard of men whose wives die and they're off seeing people, off in the sack with people, a few weeks later. It's not considered improper in their case. It's considered *nature*. But a woman, a mother, *we* have to be proper. Or feel we have to be proper. I do, anyway.'

I did not believe any of this was for my sake. It was innocent

222

drink-talk. Or perhaps there's no such thing as innocent. A lump of breathlessness rose in my throat. I gulped on wine to treat it. That's what lust is—breathlessness. Then the old sweet poison. Then, worst of all, love deranges you in the whole confusion of the process. It does in my case. I was still a way off being at the deranged state. About twenty-four hours. That's how fast the deranging gets a hold. There was the following clumsiness to get through first. 'So let me get this straight. You want—*company*?'

'God yes. Of course. Who doesn't?'

The champers refluxed into my sinuses. I fought back a sneeze. 'I'm astonished nobody has made a move on you.' I sneezed.

'Bless you, for the sneeze and for saying that. I mean, there's nothing wrong with me, is there?'

'No. Jesus. No. You are very—desirable.'

'Thank you. Very kind of you.'

'It's true.'

'I wonder, is it me having Ruth?'

'Ruth seems a nice kid.'

'Is it that men feel a bit put-off because, you know, my husband died and that makes me sort of jinxed or something? Is it that they're overly respectful of my widowhood? Such an ugly word, widow.'

I managed to get out, 'Who can say?' through the breathlessness.

'I have one friend, Ian, a neighbour. He wasn't at my barbecue—he was sick. He gets colds and flu and any bug going round. Which is one of the problems. He's single, he's available, but he's a wreck. And he's not handsome. He's actually quite unattractive. I look at his mouth and I think: Do I want to kiss that mouth? No, I don't want to kiss his mouth. If you don't want to kiss their mouth, then it's very—clinical.'

Whoever this Ian was, I loathed him for being in consideration for kissing from her.

Donna sat up straight. She said eagerly, girlishly, 'At university, in my psychology class, there's this boy. He'd be eighteen, nineteen. To me that's a *boy*. Him I could kiss. He's so incredibly beautiful. He's dazzling. Him I could really kiss and keep very nice company with. But what am I supposed to do? Ask him out? I just can't pluck up the courage.'

'Don't do it.' I spoke so forcefully it made Donna flinch. 'We're all beautiful in our youth. It's nothing unusual.'

'No, he is very beautiful.'

'He'll soon go to seed. And besides, where does a relationship with a nineteen-year-old take you?'

'That's true. I've wondered the very same thing. It takes you nowhere. But it does give you physical gratification.'

I scratched at the dirt around me. What I wanted to do was scratch this boy's image from her mind. Scratch him out and put me there and ask, *Would you care to kiss me? Is my mouth worthy?*

What I did do was say, 'I'm attracted to you, Donna. I know I shouldn't confess it, but there, it's said. I'm very attracted to you.'

No reply. Not a rejecting motion of the hand; not a willing welcome of her eye. She was too busy taking in my indiscretion. Finally she uttered, 'Oh. Oh.'

The whole scene was spread out over twenty minutes. One minute at least just for Donna's two *Ohs*. She too found dirt to scratch in. I considered letting my finger scratch closer her way but was glad I didn't, not in the open like that, with Tilda surely only a minute off. Less than a minute. There she was skipping between car rows; Ruth at the end of her arm, jumping and stumbling in horse mimicry, smacking herself like a whip.

I stood up and patted my trousers clean of grass dust. Guilt and worry were so cold on my face my blood must have fled heartward to hide. Tilda would tell I'd done something just by my colour. I thumbed my wallet for cash to look busy. I timed walking off like a purposeful betting man just as Tilda called delightedly, 'Your daughter has worn me out, Donna.'

I used horse rails and tree trunks to touch wood that Donna would not tell on me. The count went into the hundreds. She didn't tell. She went quiet instead.

As we packed up the picnic I wanted to whisper, 'Donna, thank you for keeping mum.' But there was no chance. Tilda was too near. She said later, 'Wonder why Donna went so moody?'

Next morning I fed coins into the Hastings Road public phone. I had to speak to her immediately. I could not wait until lunch and the empty office. I certainly could not take the risk from home— my excitement was not that stupid.

I did not feel dirty making the call. The handset was dirty from public fingers, stinky from cigarette breath, ice cream was smeared on the glass, but I did not feel dirty in myself. I was embarked on the higher purpose of Donna, or so the deranging had it. Whatever wrong I was about to do felt wondrous.

The ringing kept on so long that Donna's whereabouts concerned me. If she was at university, was she talking to that boy? Was she wetting her lips and imagining kissing his? If the phone rang out I had a powerful impulse to drive to her, find her class and interrupt the lecture. This was no time for manners or niceties. The phone clicked.

'Hello, Donna speaking.'

'Hello. It's Colin. I felt I better call.'

'I'm glad you did. I wanted to try you at your work but held off and off.'

I had no speech composed. 'I thought I...I just wanted to say if I said anything yesterday that offended you...' I left the sentence incomplete, for her finishing.

'I wasn't offended. More surprised. Very surprised. But listen, we can just forget it. Put it down to the champers.'

'Is that what you want?'

'Is that what *you* want?'

The course of life, such a long, large thing as life, can have a simple yes or no change it. One tiny syllable and it's changed, or gone.

'No,' I said. The certainty of the sound was itself emboldening. I repeated it. 'No,' I said, 'I do not retract what I admitted to feeling.'

Donna let out a whistly exhaling. 'I see. Wow. Are you sure?'

'Yes.'

'I mean *really* sure. Take a moment to think before answering.'

'I have.'

'Truly?'

'Yes. I've thought of nothing else.'

'Nor have I.'

'Really?'

'Someone says what you said and you don't sleep. You just think.'

'Good.'

'Listen. Let me say this: I have no wish to be a roll in the hay. I have no wish to be a...mistress or something. Some grubby *affair*.'

'Of course not.'

'You sure?'

'Yes. I understand.'

'Obviously the big question for me is, what's the state of your marriage?'

'I am dying from it.' The words came out like a plea. What relief to say them! A light breeze of truthfulness blew through my chest. I said, 'I don't know if any of us has the right to say we deserve a shot at joy. But I want to say a shot at joy is what I crave. I don't have it now. I have the opposite. But I want that shot.'

'But Tilda is a...very pleasant woman. I like her. She isn't a good friend, but a friend nonetheless.'

'What are you saying?'

'I'm saying I feel very uncomfortable. Naturally I feel very uncomfortable.'

'If I wasn't with her then you'd be interested in me?'

'Yes. I would. I have thought to myself: What an attractive man. But I have not let myself think it in a serious way because you are with Tilda.'

'Would you prefer I hung up and we dropped this, cast it from our minds?'

She hesitated. I heard her sucking her lips, troubled. 'No. No I don't want it cast from my mind.'

'Good.'

She hesitated again. 'What are we going to do, though?'

'I want to see you.'

'We need to talk this through.'

'This afternoon I could swing it.'

'This afternoon? Where?'

'I could come to you?'

'Okay. Just to talk, though.'

'Yes.'

'Let's be clear about that.'

'We are.'

'Come on, are you sure?'

'I promise.'

'Talk and nothing more.'

I arranged a job in Watercook. It's more a sheep town than grains but I figured I could concoct an article with a herbicide-resistance angle—I'd heard resistance in rye grass had become a problem in Watercook. It was common in Scintilla. My story would say it was now spreading eastward.

I arrived at Donna's a little after 3pm. Good timing for Ruth to be posited at the living room television. We had the kitchen table to ourselves. We sat opposite each other like negotiators. She began proceedings with an offering of coffee and a formal introduction to her house, as if it were people. 'Over there is my own handiwork—I designed the stovetop area and glued the benches together myself.' She stood up, nervous. 'This is the porch. Gets the west sun from midday. Great in winter; hot as hell in summer. The cupboards were Cameron's doing. He liked to bang in a nail when he was up to it. See how the hall kinks to the right in the middle? That's deliberate—the previous owners had some eccentric notion about it being eye-catching.'

Talking on the phone was easy. There we were in the flesh and avoiding everything but house and land chatter.

'It's a very nice place you have,' I said. I really thought it spartan. I had been spoilt by our big Scintilla building—two storeys and a forest for a town fringe. Here the brownlands were dealt out in buckle-fenced rectangles: two or three acres with a mudbrick dwelling in the middle. 'It's pleasant here,' I said. 'Bit of country life, bit of suburban feel all in one.'

The important thing was that we were taking every opportunity to look at each other. Doing it while the other wasn't noticing, though of course we *were* noticing. You don't need eyes for noticing. You watch each other with your skin. I scanned for her every blemish, any petty reason to criticise her. A final excuse to curb my deranging. I could not find a single problem. Nor could she in me, going by our hour together. We did not touch. We did not kiss. There was no embracing. We were standoffish in a courting way, quaint old-fashioned courting. There was no chaperone but might as well have been.

Two issues were most on Donna's mind: if we wanted to take our attraction further there was Ruth to consider. 'As I've said, I won't do a cheap casual fling. If I was twenty and childless...But I am not twenty and childless. I don't want a daughter who grows up thinking her mother *entertained* men.'

'Fair enough.'

'If, say, we went further with this, are you okay with taking on a child? Ruth comes with me, to state the obvious. Are you sure about that?'

Ruth had not crossed my conscience. Donna's 'taking on a child' had a forbidding ring. But the deranging doesn't consider anything except its own immediate needs. 'I'm sure. Absolutely,' I said, turning up my palms as if never so certain in my life.

The second issue was Tilda. Donna did not like the prospect of another woman being hurt. A woman who has never harmed her, never done her wrong. 'Has she ever harmed you?' She asked me this as if hoping for *yes*.

'No.' I was tempted to make up something, some lie about Tilda being unfaithful to me. There was no time to construct a credible tale complete with lover's name and sordid details. Nor did I fancy the image of me as victim: a heartbroken man did not appeal to me as manly. What's more, I did not want to fill her pretty ears with ugly lies. I mumbled off a list of marital complaints, trying not to sound too whiney. I was locked into a life of lovelessness, I said. I was far too young when I settled down. I told of the abortion and said it was all my doing. I hoped my honesty would impress her as brave, a full airing of dirty laundry. In a modern world only the welfare classes and the dumbest boys father children when they're not much more than children themselves.

She nodded agreement at my reasoning. She said she'd never had an abortion but would if necessary.

I did mention Tilda's rifle and weedkiller moments. Donna shook her head and said, 'That must be difficult.'

I avoided mentioning Tilda's cancer directly. It could only make my courting Donna sound disgraceful. But she wasn't about to let it pass. 'It does add another dimension,' she said.

'It's in remission.'

'Even so.'

'Yeh. You're right.'

'Who knows what would have happened if Cameron had lived. Would we have lasted? I presume so. I was content with him. He bore his disease lightly. He was not a complainer and I loved him. I never felt the desire to stray. Therefore I was never tested. But you have been tested. And I'm in the position of being the accomplice, if that's the word.'

'Does it put you off?'

'It makes me take a breath. Then I think: It would be prefer-able, of course, if there was never mess or pain when two people are drawn together. But it's not always realistic.'

'So you are definitely drawn to me?'

'I am.'

I wanted to reach across the table and feel her hand, get contact with her skin. She must have sensed this and considered skin contact wrong just yet. She leant back and checked her watch and said, 'It's close to five. I have to organise dinner for Ruth. What time will Tilda start wondering where you are?'

'Good point. I better go.'

What a deliciously awkward few seconds came next. I stood and wanted to step forward and kiss and smell and caress her. Restraint is such a delicacy. I was teetering on the edge of her body and could not move.

We agreed I would ring her tomorrow. I was to let her know immediately if I changed my mind. I said I had no intention of changing my mind but she reserved the right to be cautious: she feared letting go of her heart and having me change my mind and stay with Tilda.

'I won't change my mind.' I did step forward at this point. The teetering was too much—I had to act on it.

Donna held up a halting hand. 'Don't,' she motioned with her head that Ruth might come in.

I apologised for being impetuous. I opened the sliding door and smiled goodbye. I drove home.

If you could call it home. It was no home to me now. It was a place I was forced to part from Donna to go to. It was a place I did not want to arrive at. Then, having arrived, loathed. It was nothing but a place to be hostile in. Me, the betrayer, blamed Tilda for it all. To become the betrayer makes you *turn* on the betrayed. Why? Because they are the obstacle to your desire. They are the reason for your guilt. Hostility is the only option. The mere sight of Tilda brought it out of me. From the moment I got home to my un-home I ground my teeth and mocked Tilda in my thoughts. Can't you see I do not love or need you or care for you anymore? Can't you tell where I've been? Don't you see Donna in my eyes? Are you blind? Are you stupid? Surely you can hear her in my silence.

She tried to kiss me hello: 'How was your day? Would you like a beer?'

I was not going kiss her, no way, not even a peck. 'No, I do not want a beer,' I said with raised voice. 'No, I am not hungry. No, I have not had a bad day. No, I am not in a bad mood.'

Couldn't you decipher my secret, Tilda? I'd had the most glorious day. A day of craving the body of another woman. A day of being in lust and plummeting in love. Couldn't you make that out in me? 'No, I am not going to massage you tonight. Can I not have one night off? One night of freedom from stroking that fucking log of an arm?'

I told her I had no intention of naming her new picture tonight. Call it a pile of shit for all I care. I complained about the smell of turps through the house. 'Fuck, I hate the stink. Air it out. Fuck! I'm sleeping in the futon room tonight. The turps is soaked into your flesh. It's like sleeping with petrol. Am I supposed to be attracted to petrol? I don't care if I am being hurtful. I am speaking my mind. See my lips move? That's me speaking my fucking mind. Goodnight. I'm off to bed. You just stay there crying, there's a good girl. Here, borrow my handkerchief—you can't say I don't comfort you.'

I felt entirely justified in my cruelty. I felt powerful and right. I quipped, 'You might want to consider skolling some weedkiller like you used to promise. Whatever happened to that promise? Why don't you buy some tomorrow? Or get a rifle? Do yourself a favour and top yourself. Goodnight, sweetheart. Sleep well. Don't disturb me.'

I got halfway up the stairs before Tilda's sobbing got to me. I turned around, hung my head, trudged towards her intending to be kindly and say I was tired, overtired from being busy at work. She was seated on the edge of dinner table, weeping into her hands. I turned back to the stairs, mounted them quickly before the weeping did its job and had me weakened and apologising and acting tenderly. I congratulated myself for not having given in. I muttered, 'Do yourself a favour and top yourself, Tilda. You'd be doing me a favour as well. That would solve my problem.'

In bed I wished it upon Tilda, death. I wished it like saying my prayers: now I lay me down to sleep, I pray she dies before the end of the week. I wanted to kill her. How could I do it and not be found out? Was there a way of stopping her breathing without evidence?

Sleep brainwashes us clean like a natural remorse system. If it wasn't for sleep we might act on all our impulses, never have doubts to keep us rational. If it wasn't for sleep I might have smothered Tilda with a pillow that night. Sleep did the decent thing and dreamt it out of me, sweated it out of me with horror-dreaming of being utterly alone, desolate. I was in a paddock and mourning, not for any particular person, not at first. Just mourning my own desolation. Then I realised I was also mourning for Tilda. She was dead in my dream and I was begging the dream to bring her back to life. The colour of the dream was like photo negatives.

I brought her breakfast in bed next morning—Vegemite on toast and a mug of milky Nescafé. She gave a faint nod of thanks but did not squeeze my hand when I cupped hers, or respond with a nuzzle into her pillow when I kissed her temple. Her temple was dank with hot hair. I could see where a crow's-foot of tears had rolled over it through the night and dried crusty.

I began saying, 'I said some awful things last evening. I'm...I get wound up in my work...I feel dreadful and I want you to forget I opened my cakehole and said those awful things...'

She made no attempt to assure me I was forgiven. Not so much as an eyelid twitch of recognition that she had heard me.

'Eat your toast before it gets cold,' I said, touching her chin. I was resolved to driving to the Hastings Road phone that instant. I was going to lay down the law to Donna Wilkins. 'I am not going to pursue a relationship with you,' I was going to say. 'Finished. Over. I am not going to break my wife's heart. I can't do it. I don't have it in me. I can't do it.'

I whispered 'I love you' to Tilda, kissed the lobe of her ear. A desperate *I love you* to reel back the life I was only yesterday prepared to let slip. There was still no eyelid movement or parting of the lips from her. 'Oh well, then,' I sighed. I was impatient for a reward for my gentle effort. I was prepared to relent to mutual servicing if she showed gratitude for my tenderness and kiss. I expected a return *I love you too* even if it sounded automatic.

I deserved the silent treatment. But as I drove to Hastings Road I could not help but feel an injustice. Why couldn't she have blinked or relented with one little lip-corner smile? Why couldn't she have given me something to go on with instead of blank rebuffing? Just one little lip-corner smile. By the time I pulled onto the gravel beside the phone box I was brooding on being taken for granted by Tilda. Was I supposed to beg and crawl to her? I'm worth more than silent treatments.

I was in no good humour to queue to make a call. Three girls—aged fifteen, if a day—had wheeled their baby prams into an arc of waiting and smoking. A fourth girl was in the box on the phone. Housing Commission types with oily unbrushed scalps, tracksuit pants, black moccasins.

'Excuse me,' I said gruffly, as if interviewing them. 'Is there a problem with this telephone? I'm Colin Butcher from the *Wimmera Wheatman*. There have been reports of vandalised public phones. I have to check this one for a story I'm doing on how viable our phone network is to cope with bushfire season.'

That got me to the head of the queue, huffing loudly enough to rush the current user into hanging up. Once in the box I said, 'Do you mind all standing back, please. Back further, please. Thank you.' It got me privacy.

I was still determined to finish it, the Donna thrill. The brain-washing horror-dream was still fresh in me. Daytime does reduce the power of nightmares, however; the sun shines down a calming light. But I was determined to finish it. I just hoped it would not be too brief or blunt a call. I intended to explain that I was not a weak man but I was resigned to the dutifulness of my marriage, even at the expense of my happiness or the affections of my heart.

Passion too has a brainwashing ability. Once in your system it makes bad dreams fade from the memory fast. I did not finish things with Donna during the call. It felt too good to be on the end of her voice. Too good to hear her excited at hearing my voice. She asked if I had changed my mind, and when I said I hadn't she said 'Excellent' and 'I was worried you might.'

'No need to be worried. I'm very sure about what I'm doing.' Just saying this made me feel surer and stand more fixedly in my shoes. I told her there was tension between Tilda and me. I did not mention my cruel tongue, of course. I used 'frosty' to describe us. I used 'a difficult evening with unpleasant exchanges of words.' I said, 'There is a...what's the word...a realignment happening inside me. Like I've changed my focus. My focus is you—you're who I think about. Not Tilda.' Which sounded so clear-cut. I even told her Tilda and I slept in separate beds last night. 'I can't sleep with her any longer. It's like I'd be unfaithful to you.'

Donna gasped that she wished she could hold me and give me

strength for what must be so harrowing.

Yes, I would love to be held, I replied. I reckoned I could swing another Watercook trip in the afternoon if she wanted, on the pretext of more work being needed on the rye-grass-resistance story. I said I could swing anything if it meant seeing her.

'There's a playgroup in town. I could leave Ruth there for an hour.'

I liked Donna's term *keep company*. It had her smell on it—citrus and aniseed from the gels she showered with. I liked her long, coy way of saying the word—*commpanyyy*. She made it sound like a foreign language. Tilda's *congressing* was pompous, like she was better than fucking, too good for it.

I never intended keeping company in Donna's house. When I arrived I was hoping for her to hold me like she said she wanted to, but even that seemed unlikely given her shyness and hesitancy. I had to make the first move. I asked her, 'Can I have that embrace we talked about on the phone?'

She kept her head down and took two slow steps my way. I took a step her way to meet her more quickly. *Contact.* We made contact. Slow and tender contact, as if our skins might bruise. Citrus and aniseed were all through her hair. There was a peppermint breeze from her lips as they parted upward onto mine. She was shorter than Tilda, which meant a more physical kiss: I had to strain and lower my head down more.

We almost didn't go further. I pulled away on seeing her brass bed reflected in the hallway mirror. It had four pillows—two each side. Her and Cameron's pillows. *Their* bed, not Donna's and mine. I tried to ignore that line of thought. I adjusted my kissing position to a deeper and more strenuous hold. I stepped towards the bedroom, still kissing, keeping Donna in step with me. I was not rushing her. I stepped and stopped, stepped and stopped, and she kept in time—a walk-dance. At that moment I thought of Tilda: how I was breaking faith with her. But it was a thought no more than a heartbeat long. Breaking faith was easy. I had given over completely to breaking it now. I slipped my fingers under Donna's blouse and rubbed the small of her back to test her willingness. She pressed on tiptoes to kiss her *yes*.

But the mirror reflection kept bothering me. We could not do it on his bed, Cameron's bed. We could not do it in his house. You don't have to be alive to be a presence. I unkissed my mouth from hers to explain: 'It's not like I'm feeling his eyes looking on. It's just, I'd love somewhere neutral. Somewhere *ours*.'

Her eyelids were half closed with willingness. She came down off her tiptoes, pulled her blouse straight and licked her bottom lip like a way of kissing herself to keep the kissing going. This drew me back to kissing. Then to stepping. The 'neutral' idea could not compete against resting my hands on her hips, running them up over her ribs to her bra strap. Then a breath, a pause to concentrate and savour what my hands were about to do. They were about to shift around onto two breasts. Two not one. No scar, no elephant fatness in the sandy shaved pit of her arm.

I could not stop looking at them. As we crabbed onto the bed her breasts transfixed me—two not one, as if two were unusual and I had never seen them before. Their little noses of nut-nipple, softer than Tilda's body-part nipple. We were unwrapping each other from our clothes yet I had to slow up and stare at them, give my lips the pleasure of rubbing both. I said nothing of this to Donna. I just revelled in her to the point of over-delight. I had to close my eyes or else I'd need mathematics. I concentrated on removing my shoes, taking a moment to unlace and settle. Two breasts not one. And ribs not poking out but covered with a healthy layer of flesh. Rounded buttock and thigh, strong not skinny.

It is impossible not to compare one lover to another, even as you're climbing into them. I was thinking how Donna's diaphragm was not as deep in as Tilda's. I butted its rubber and refrained from thrusting quite so deeply.

I could feel Cameron's shape in the bed. The scoop where his body slept on the mattress. Even if I changed sides his scoop was still there under me. Donna put it down to my imagination but conceded somewhere neutral would be preferable. She agreed it didn't seem right stepping over children's toys and dolls in the hall and then doing what we were doing. Having been spreadeagled in one another's arms, it was hardly romantic to get up and wash us from the sheets because Ruth liked to get into bed with her mother in the mornings.

What about we use the forest at Ringo Point? I suggested it because a motel was difficult: we'd have to drive halfway to Melbourne given the risk of tongues wagging. No one hires a motel room for the day in the country, not unless they're up to no good. Besides, there was the expense of it. I knew all the forest at Ringo. I knew of clearings and cavities in the scrub where only kangaroos would see us. There was the risk of the odd reptile but that was okay, I would shoo any away and we could throw a blanket down. Consider it a temporary measure, I said, until I left Tilda. And I would leave Tilda soon, I promised.

The forest became our arrangement. Tuesdays and Fridays— Donna's non-uni days. She dropped Ruth off at playgroup and drove an hour to me. We used an old doona cover she had, spread it at a spot three minutes' walk west of the sundial where there was plenty of bush to screen us. Ironbarks stretched out enough for two people to keep company in shade. The ground was hard but smooth. There were no bull ants. We codenamed it Neutral Motor Inn.

For six weeks we made a brief bed there, never fully naked in case we heard humans. We did a drill, just so we'd be ready, pulling our clothes up as fast as possible. We were never interrupted except by parrot voices. Afterwards we shared water from Donna's thermos and watched the ticker-tape effect of sun through the swaying branches. We could not remember, either of us, being so happy, so peaceful.

I said, 'You're the love of my life.'

She answered, 'I'm very respectful of Cameron, but I feel love like you do too.'

Her saying that always gave me such resolve. I would go home from Neutral Motor Inn determined to tell Tilda goodbye. I whipped myself into a state of contempt for her, the right frame of mind to deliver the ruthless news. I rehearsed it: 'I am leaving you, Tilda. I am walking out. I am not in love with you. I am in love with Donna Wilkins.' I walked in through the back door without so much as a 'Good evening.' My jaw was clenched for conflict. I hadn't showered, hadn't washed Donna from me. Surely I reeked of the off-smell of wetness dried and clotted in my trousers. I deliberately breezed by her so she might catch the scent, but failed to provoke her into getting the whole smithereens of us underway. Call me spineless but I baulked at igniting it myself.

Those six weeks provided me a sordid balance: I had Donna waiting in the forest and still had a home to return to afterwards. I had it both ways.

I began writing these pages in the first of those six weeks. My daily regimen. I suppose I was hoping they would help me make my decision. The unhappiest people in the world must be those with too many decisions to make. Even one is too many. In my case, Tilda or Donna.

Donna pressed me only slightly. She said, 'Promise Neutral Motor Inn is temporary?'

I promised. And I did mean it when I was with her, though I avoided giving an exact timeline.

The excuse I used was Tilda's health. Towards the end of the six weeks she got so thin. She didn't eat, stayed in bed as if wasting away. Surely this time it had to be the cancer. How could I leave her in that predicament?

'You can't,' Donna said, tears in her eyes. 'This could drag your leaving on forever and ever.'

'It's not my fault.'

'I know it's not.' We pulled up our clothes and lay in sun-leaf dapples. The only obvious utterance to make was: maybe Tilda will die and leave the way clear. We bit our tongues. Neither of us was going to reveal that we were capable of such a statement.

Anyway, it wasn't cancer. It was me. Tilda didn't need Roff to confirm that for her. She'd put the whole heartwrecking puzzle together.

Donna would park her car at the sundial area. I always left the Commodore out of sight up a narrow track half a kilometre from Neutral Motor Inn. In all the years I had run up the track I had never seen another person. It wasn't our cars that gave us away. Nor did I ever call Donna from home—the phone bill didn't spring us. Yes, I overused the Hastings Road phone box in broad daylight but I couldn't help it: when you're in love you simply have to hear your loved one's voice constantly. I called from the office three or four times but I made sure everyone was out on a tea break.

It was the underpants I bought from O'Connor's Manchester. I believe I set out to sabotage myself. Brand new underwear after years of the same old saggy ones. I was ashamed of saggy ones with Donna. I replaced them with bright blues and purples—four pairs, tight-fitting with bulgy Y-front pouches.

I didn't take care to rinse off the stains before throwing them on the wash pile. Surely it was sabotage—my way of telling Tilda without actually telling her. I was letting dried wetnesses do the work for me.

I was standing at our backyard oleander, running the filter end of a cigarette around my mouth to simulate Donna's nipples. It was here I had first seen the crease of her bottom. I smiled at how far we had progressed from that to Neutral Motor Inn. I lit the cigarette and had just drained the dregs of a vodka and ice when Tilda walked up behind me. Her arms were crossed tightly. Her hair was frizzing loose from her plait as if it had been picked at. There was such a narrow-eyed strain in her face you'd have thought she was lifting a heavy invisible weight. She said, 'Have you got a problem with your water works or something?'

'Ay?'

'What else would leave these kinds of stains?' Her fist threw me the purple underpants I'd worn yesterday, which was a Donna day.

I held cigarette smoke deep in my lungs for courage. Let it stream out of me like a long, calm purge. I did not answer.

The weight in her face got heavier. 'It's Donna Wilkins, isn't it?'

Here it was—the smithereens. I filled my lungs for more courage. 'Yes,' I said. A pitiful whimpered yes. I was so scared. Scared of life itself for being so different with that yes—so wild and shattered and free.

Tilda locked her two fists into one and threw her head back and made an awful vomiting sound. 'I am such a fool,' she said to the sky. She took one lunging stride towards me, eyes and nose teeming. 'Get out. Get out of this house. Get out of my home.'

I attempted a consolation *sorry* but she covered her ears to keep sweet-talk out of her mind. 'Get out!'

Plenty of windows would have heard her. I headed to the back door to get out of sight of neighbours.

I ran up the stairs, stood in the bedroom, thinking: What do I need? What do I need? I need clothes, of course. My cheque book—it was a joint cheque account with Tilda—I had the right to keep my half of our money. My typewriter, I needed that.

Toiletries—razor, toothbrush. Take a flannel, some soap, a towel. All would fit easily into the Commodore boot. If I needed to I could sleep on the back seat overnight.

Then panic hit me. I could go to Tilda and undo the *yes*. I could lie that I was joking. Or I could beg with many apologies and congress with her until she wilted and changed her *get out* to *please stay*. Oh, I was scared of life all right. So scared I slowed my packing hoping she'd come and save me with kisses of tender absolution. I piled belongings on our bed and folded and shoved and slowed.

Eventually fearlessness straightened me. Donna's face, her two breasts were restored to my brain; her voice, her *I feel love like you do too* to my ears. I was in such a penduluming madness—packing, slowing down, terrified, ecstatic, *Come save me, Tilda* one minute, *I'm on my way to you, Donna* the next—I did not smell smoke until the air was faintly foggy with it. Even then I sniffed my fingers to check it wasn't cigarette stink.

It wasn't. It was fire. The fog was denser the further around the hallway I investigated. It was coming from the bathroom. Smoke was blacker there and petrolly in its stench. It burst up out of the bathtub, curled off the top of rearing flames with chunks of half-burnt newspaper. Tilda was feeding the tub with splashes from a turps bottle. The invisible weight was still in her face but she had a sneery smile now, as if achieving something.

A paper chunk broke up and blew my way. I stomped it to ash on a patch of threadbare carpet. Another chunk smoked and crumbled onto the lino at Tilda's feet. She yelled for me to 'fuck off' when I tried to stomp it. She held the turpentine out like a liquid threat, gave it a shake to warn me off. I saw my Donna underpants, every pair, burning in the tub.

Tilda let me stand and look at them. She smiled wider and said, 'Every drop of the bitch's cunt juice is going to burn. Fucking burn. Every rancid trace of her. It's like burning her, that's what it's like. Wouldn't that be justice and beautiful to burn her to fucking bits? Tell me you want that. Tell me she deserves it.'

At which point the smoke got into her breathing and she gagged and threw the bottle into the tub and coughed her way past me to gulp fresh air. Flames flicked faster; half the shower curtain was melted. I turned on the shower head by dabbing the taps open with my thumbs—the steel was stinging hot. My arms had to bear a few seconds among flames before the taps were open enough and water ran. I yanked the window up as high as it would go and used a towel to fan away smoke.

Surely neighbours would have called the fire brigade by now. How was I going to explain a burnt bath? I fanned and thought up excuses: an art experiment with burnt clothing as a medium. I kept the water running to rinse the tub down into a minor-looking incident. I didn't know where Tilda had gone. I concentrated on fanning and throwing my sodden, flame-chewed undies out the window. I scooped ashy newspaper into the toilet and flushed.

The neighbours were not a worry. I had put the fire out in time. If they were spying from their curtains they must have thought we'd taken to having barbecues indoors. Tilda was the problem. She was downstairs dialling the phone with a stabbing finger. She kept getting the number wrong she was stabbing so hard and furiously. She must have reached innocent people more than once because when I arrived she swore 'Fuck, not again!' into the receiver. She poked her fingernail into the back of the phone book where we jotted numbers. She recited Donna's number with seething slowness.

I ran up to her, snatched the receiver. 'What are you doing? Give it to me! Give it here!' She snatched it back and hissed and elbowed my jaw to keep possession. Donna had answered. I could hear her saying 'Hello. Donna speaking' down the line.

Tilda let fly: 'Slut. You fucking slut whore. You betraying slutty bitch. How could you? How could you touch my husband, you fucking lowest form of life?'

I made another snatching attempt. Tilda grunted and gave me a shove, shouting, 'Watch my arm! Don't you dare hurt my arm.'

I wasn't hurting her arm. I had my hand on hard phone plastic, not her, but I retreated anyway to stop her accusing me. I tucked my chin to my chest to beg a truce but she jabbed the receiver into my cheek. I hunched to deflect another hit but *bang* came one on the bone behind my left ear. *Ding* on bone higher on my head.

White wires of electric water fizzed across my vision. My skull went numb, then seared. *Ding* again between my shoulder blades. The cord had pulled out from the wall. Tilda followed, swinging the phone like she was batting.

I took each blow, resigned to deserving them. What else could I do? I couldn't retaliate—my size against hers? I would break her in half. So I took the hiding. Walked up the stairs more proud than defeated. The white wires and the searing were punishments I accepted. I withstood them. They were worth it to be able to be with Donna. They helped drive me towards Donna. I would be with her tonight. I was getting my belongings and leaving.

I came back down the stairs, backpack on shoulder and reached for the Commodore keys on the hook beside the back door. They weren't there. They should have been my priority, the first belongings I packed. Instead they were in Tilda's fingers and she wasn't about to let them go.

'You are not going anywhere.'

'Oh yes I am.'

'Oh no you're not.'

'Give me the keys.'

'No.'

I reminded her that the keys were the property of the *Wimmera Wheatman*.

'So?'

I put my hand on the doorknob to keep my leaving flowing. I turned the knob. The door was locked. I had no way to open it— my house key was on the Commodore ring. 'Hand it over, Tilda.'

'You are not leaving me.'

'I am.'

'You are not leaving me and going to that fucking slut.'

'Give me the keys.'

'This is where you live. You are my husband. You are to take me upstairs and congress with me like my husband.'

'You've got to be kidding.'

'Take me upstairs, Colin. Show me that you are my husband.

Because that is exactly who you are. You are not leaving me. You are not going to that filthy piece of shit. Take me upstairs. I said *upstairs. Now.'*

'What would that prove?'

'It will remind you that I am the only woman in your life. By *law.'*

If she had locked me in a tiny cell she could not have suffocated me more. Not being allowed to go here or there. Not being able to seize a key because of the grabbing and tearing and hitting I might have to do. I shouldered my backpack and said, 'Okay. Okay. Let's go upstairs.'

'Good,' she grinned. She nodded for me to go ahead of her so she could keep an eye on me.

At the bedroom she ordered me to cover my eyes while she decided where to hide the keys. She checked that the window latches were closed. As if I was going to jump out! It was straight down two storeys with no pipes to climb on. The bathroom window was a different matter. It had a drainpipe against the bricks and was still wide open from the fire. Tilda seemed to think the bedroom was her cage for keeping me in and nothing else existed outside it, least of all the bathroom. She pulled down the blinds. She slipped the keys somewhere—under the mattress or a flap of carpet. Keys were not my focus now. The bathroom was.

'You can open your eyes,' Tilda said. 'Take off your clothes. Do it please. Now.'

I unbuttoned my shirt. Tilda unclipped her overalls and peeled off her sleeve. 'Take your pants off, please. Now, please. Then lie on the bed and invite me to bed with you. I want you to hold out your hand and invite me properly and formally as your wife.'

I unfastened the tongue of my belt but did not unfasten the belt altogether.

'I said, hold out your hand and invite me to bed as your wife.'

I distracted Tilda from demanding I get undressed by taking her good hand's fingers to my lips and kissing them. She knelt on the bed and I distracted her more with kisses on her cheek and chin. I said, 'Please come to bed with me properly and formally as my wife.'

'Thank you. I shall.'

I lifted her shirt to remove it over her head and get her naked. Nakedness would slow her running after me when I upped and dashed to the bathroom window, shimmied down the drainpipe to be gone.

'Not so rushed,' Tilda frowned, using her elbows to block the shirt's removal. 'Properly. Do it properly, like you adore me.'

It took more kisses than I could stand. It took an effort of open-mouth ones. It took some biting of her neck and making breathy carried-away noises to get her bra and body part from her. I managed to keep my belt buckle clasped. My own shirt was still on, and most importantly so were my runners. I pretended I was trying to heel-to-toe them from my feet but that my passion was so great it was affecting my co-ordination. Tilda smiled, eyes closed, surrendering to my performance.

As she eased her knickers down over her knees and said, 'You may touch me and enter me,' I ran. I scooped up the backpack and ran. Tilda screamed for me to stop. She hopped after me, pulling her knickers on, but I had already thrown the backpack out the window and was negotiating the pipe before she could cover herself. My only problem was thorns of pipe paint, years of them formed from undisturbed peeling. They stuck in my palms on the way sliding down and made me jump the last six feet and hurt my ankle.

I didn't care. I had the open air and no locked door or Tilda. I sprinted for a second, west up Main Street, then jogged so as not to attract attention. *Just going for his usual exercise* was the dignified impression I wanted people to get.

My plan was to run to Donna's, the entire ninety-five kilometres to Watercook. I would cover ten kilometres every hour, sticking to the highway for a smooth surface. I hoped the stars stayed unclouded to light the way.

It was a bad plan. Nine hours of running? Not with my ankle starting to throb. I decided to call Donna to come and get me. I turned left off Main, ran across Kitten Lane—the little street we used to access our back drive. I was headed for the Scintilla forest. I intended to take a breather there, elevate my ankle before walking east to Hastings Road, using the forest leaves to hide. The cover of leaves seemed sensible because I expected Tilda would be after me, searching the streets in a desperate temper.

I was right. She was searching. Not on foot either. She was tearing about in the Commodore. I had made it through the Methodist carpark, past Philpott's place and onto the forest fringe where the tarseal ends when I spotted her—or, rather, spotted the Commodore with its shiny bullbar and CB aerial, *Wimmera Wheatman* lettering on the side. It was on the next street along. Tilda spotted me too and yelled for me to wait, stop. The car squealed, skidding to a halt. It reversed with another squeal and fishtailed into a right turn, the rear wheel clipping the curb. I sprinted up a dirt parting in the scrub in the direction of Ringo Point. Did so out of habit—Ringo Point was the opposite direction to Hastings Road. I kept running there anyway: its ironbark clusters would make me invisible. I got in among them and crouched to catch my breath and my heartbeat. I slumped the backpack to the ground but didn't take off my runners. My ankle would have to ache and swell—this was no time to care about ankles. Dusk was setting just the other side of the treetops. A dark breeze was leaning heavier on the branches. The sky was cloudy, which meant the forest would blind me soon. I needed to stay in sight of street-lights to keep my night bearings.

A car was going up the Ringo Point road. The Commodore, I was sure. But I wasn't about to peep to check. I remained in the ironbarks' protection and listened to the wheels grinding gravel. A sift of dust moved through the vegetation. I had so many choices of trunks to touch wood on I touched a dozen within two steps of me: 'Tilda, if that's you, go home. Don't stop. Don't get out and search for me. Keep driving, touch wood. Touch wood you're keeping driving.' But wood was only ever wood. The car slowed and Tilda's voice called out, 'Colin? You here, Colin?'

At first she sounded clipped and angered. Then she called my name more sweetly. 'Colin, sweetheart? Darling? Please, sweet-heart, please come home with me.' Then sharpish again: 'At least do me the courtesy of answering. At least give me the respect of speaking.' Her voice cracked as if she were talking through crying. 'Come to me now, Colin. Come here, now,' she yelled, so high-pitched she started losing her voice. She gave one last 'Come here, you bastard' and went silent for a few seconds. Then the car ripped away up the road in the sundial's direction. I heard the faint rasp of it turning around on the loose surface, sliding from too much speed off the mark. Back down the road the car came. I touched wood it would not stop for more of Tilda's yelling. It didn't. It ripped past like a signal of good riddance to me.

She might have been playing games, parked up the road to catch me as I emerged, so I stayed among trees till the last impression of light offered me vision. Then I limped to Hastings Road. I'd untied my runner to let my ankle blow out and had to spring myself along on my toes.

I had no coins for the phone so I made the call collect via the operator. Donna's number was engaged. I waited five minutes, sat on the sandy grass out of the streetlight's glow, and tried again. Still engaged. Another five minutes. Engaged. I kept trying but the operator said, 'Sorry, sir, the line is busy.' The phone was off the hook, that was the logical reason. Who could blame her after Tilda's hateful serve? I imagined Donna pacing about, wringing her hands, wanting to put the receiver back in case I rang. I expect she was desperate to hear that I was bearing up to the acrimony. I expect she wanted to say she loved me and express support. Thinking that heartened me.

I hobbled from the phone box to a council toddler park near the Housing Commission project. Not much to speak of, as parks go—a garbage bin, swing, plastic slide, plastic tree house—but I decided the tree house was good for spending the night. I climbed into it. I had never slept in my clothes before. I tried to think of it as an adventure, not a homewrecking. I had the injured ankle of an adventurer but the rest of me had the scared-of-life sensation; too much of it for easy slumber. I counted the lorries and their earthquakes. I held my nerve, though, and did not limp home to Tilda.

I fell asleep eventually. Woke many times through the night

but the earthquakes were enough of a distraction to have me count them until I dozed off again. I woke for the last time at 7am. Scintilla was well daylit by then. Seven is peak-hour for traffic in the country—cars and one-tonners going past at a rate of one every fifteen seconds.

I splashed my eyes with water from the park tap and set off for the *Wheatman* office. My gait was a hop-shuffle given the ankle but I hurried as best I could to avoid gossip: 'What on earth is Colin Butcher up to, lame and head down like he's trying to hide?' The office opened officially at 8.30 but compositors were usually in before then. My intention was to slip by them, grab the Commodore's spare keys from the front desk drawer, then sneak into my own backyard and retrieve the vehicle like a just thief.

Very proud of his heritage is Vigourman. He was waiting for me, new lamb-chop sideburns framing his face. The centenary of his family settling in Scintilla was a month away. What better way to commemorate the occasion than copying his sepia great-grandfather's features?

The salt-and-pepper fuzz aged him. So did the sleepy redness in the gutters of his eyes. 'I've hardly had a wink,' he said, stirring black tea at the staff basin. 'Half the night I've spent in consultation with police. Your ears must be burning.'

'How so?'

'Come with me.' He indicated my desk would do for a serious discussion. Then changed his mind—it was too close to the compositors to be private. He brushed past me, dripping his tea, ignoring it splashing his shoes. He opened the storage room door and told me to sit on a pile of *Wheatman* back issues. He perched on the taller *Gazette* pile. He was his usual full-of-himself self, shoulders back, chest and stomach spinnakered, but his voice wasn't normal. It was muted. He hardly parted his lips to let the words out. 'You are aware of what Tilda did last night?'

I presumed he meant the bath-burning scene. A neighbour must have witnessed it after all and blabbed.

'It was an experiment,' I began explaining—but Vigourman was not referring to underwear.

Tilda had driven the Commodore to Watercook and threatened

to kill Donna, burn her house down and let her and Ruth burn in it. She had splashed turpentine at the back door, set it alight and only the fact the house was brick and the door was a glass slider stopped the premises catching fire. She then rammed Donna's car in the drive. There was a heap of damage to the Commodore's front end.

Vigourman had insurance concerns given Tilda was not the authorised company driver. 'All because you were tomcatting. Oh, this is very distasteful. Very distasteful indeed. This is deeply embarrassing to the *Wheatman*, to me, to Tilda, Mrs Wilkins, you. It reflects so poorly on you I am more than disappointed, son. More than disappointed. Your whole future in my employment is under review, I'm afraid.' He sipped his tea but was too infuriated to swallow. He spat the mouthful back into the mug. 'How could you do it to your poor wife? After what she's been through, to do this to her goes directly to your character, or lack of it.'

I leant forward, my hand held up to request more details from him. 'Is Donna all right? Ruth all right?' Last on the list was Tilda.

'Yes, yes,' he replied irritably. 'That's something to be thankful for. I have, I think, convinced the Watercook police that this is a very private matter and no charges should be brought against Tilda to embarrass us further. Mrs Wilkins can try and force the issue but she will not necessarily find a sympathetic ear in the senior sergeant. None of us have much sympathy for her—her husband still warm in the ground and she's off tempting you into tomcatting. This community embraced you as a Scintillan, Colin. *I* embraced you and gave you a start. And you do this to us.'

'I'm sorry, Mr Vigourman.' I called him Hector normally but

sitting up on his paper pile he had the distance of a magistrate. 'I'm sorry for what has happened. But I have strong feelings for Donna. Very strong.'

'Nonsense. You've given over to your urges instead of your decency.' He shook his head as if I must be a halfwit not to recognise such obvious wisdom. He voice lowered to a confidential register. 'We all have urges. If we live with the same woman for a number of years we get urges. But that doesn't mean we go tomcatting. There are ways and means to satisfy yourself without fouling your own nest. You take a business trip to Melbourne. Do I have to spell it out? You take your urges to Melbourne. There are places you go to. There are ladies who are professionals. You take care of your urges that way and keep your home life intact.'

'You've done that...*professionals*?'

'Did I say I had? I said no such thing. I'm simply telling you: there are ways and means.' He took a sip of tea. 'Tell you what I'm going to do. I'm willing to treat this escapade of yours as a one-off. You were temporarily bewitched by a loose female, someone who had lost her husband and was not in her right mind from grief. I am aware that sacking you also punishes your good wife. She needs a provider for a husband, not a jobless so-and-so.

'Therefore, here's what you do. I suggest you go to Tilda, get down on your hands and knees and beg to be taken back. You do the right thing by her and I'll do the right thing by you. Poor woman's up in hospital this minute, bawling her eyes out despite sedation. Dr Philpott fears the trauma of all this could kickstart her cancer. What a terrible, terrible thing to have on your conscience.

'As for Mrs Wilkins—let's never speak of her again. Do I make myself clear? These are new conditions to your employment. So, what's it going to be? You can go to Watercook and be with that... that widow if you want. But if you do, I wipe my hands of you. And don't think you'd find work in Watercook either. Not Watercook or anywhere the length and breadth of the Wimmera Plains. I will see to it that your name is mud. Understand?'

I am glad I never gave Vigourman the pleasure of replying, 'I under-stand.' Saying 'I understand' was the same as saying 'You're right, Mr Vigourman. It was all urges and nothing more. Not love. Not a shot at joy. Just the equivalent of professionals in Melbourne.' He could threaten me all he liked but my feelings for Donna were greater than worries about being called mud could ever be. Greater than any job with a Commodore. Greater than a bad conscience. What's conscience when you'd rather die than beg to a woman you no longer loved?

Donna was another story. Her I could beg to if needed.

I left Vigourman to his smug tea-sipping; turned my back on him, breathed my chest and stomach out so they made a spin-naker of their own. I limped from the storeroom without a word. Donna was my priority. I went to my desk and couldn't care less if Vigourman eavesdropped. I was going to speak to her like a man speaks to his loved one. I dialled. Her phone was working again. She picked up immediately.

'Donna, sweetheart. Are you all right? You fine?'

'Physically, yes. But rattled. Extremely rattled.'

'Sweetheart, don't be rattled.'

'Why not? I've never had someone say they want me dead. I thought she was going to do it, kill me. I held Ruth and I thought: How do we defend against this kind of hatred? Abuse over the phone is one thing, but to come to my home and stand at my door

screaming she will kill us. Try to set us on fire. Ruth was so terrified. I have to keep her in my arms or she shakes.'

'I wish I could just fold you in my arms.'

'I tried to lay charges. I was told: *bed-hopping* disputes aren't
why police are paid. You made your bed, you can lie in it, they said.
I feel dirty. I feel I have made a dreadful mistake. And I have a
child shaking in terror.'

'Let me come to you right now. I will need to organise
transport...'

'No.'

'The train to Ballarat leaves here at noon...'

'No.'

'From there I'll get a connecting bus.'

'No, I said.' A sharp no with a wet growl in it.

'But I want to.'

'Let's have a break. Let's do that. Let's have a break from each
other.'

'A break?'

'I need to take stock of things.'

'A few days' break?'

'I don't know.'

'A week? How long?'

'I need to get Ruth back to normal. I want just her and me and
a wholesome feeling back.'

'How long a break?' I was aware of being weak in voice
suddenly. I was starting to beg. I bent forward over my desk, hand
cupped around the mouthpiece so only Donna could hear. 'How
long a break?'

'Indefinite.'

'That sounds more than a break.'

'Yes.'

'Are you saying forever?'

'I'm sorry, Colin.'

'Are you meaning the end?'

'I'm sorry.'

'Why don't we say a couple of weeks? Let's say a month while you get over this.'

'What then? Looking over my shoulder for Tilda? Looking over Ruth's shoulder? I can take on small baggage. But this is not small.'

'Let me hang up now and call you tomorrow.'

'Please, no calling.'

'Or a few days. Have a rethink and I'll call you in few days.'

'No.'

'Please.'

'I'm taking Ruth out of here tomorrow. We're staying with friends interstate to get away from this and feel safe.'

'Whereabouts? How can I reach you?'

'No. No calls.'

'Donna, please.'

'I have to go.'

'Donna.'

I said I loved her. I said, 'Remember our Neutral Motor Inn; remember our happiness there.' I was pleading so loud I didn't hear her hang up. There was just silence and the seashell noise of air through the phone wires.

I called back straight away. No answer. I tried again. Same thing. I envisaged her standing at her phone, fists clenched against the temptation to answer it, against reconnecting our voices, our lives: *No more of this man I may love but who is too much trouble.*

I waited a few minutes, dialled but got nowhere. She must have unplugged the line. This did not put me off. She would have to plug it in eventually. I spread the latest *Wheatman* edition on the desk and thumbed through it to look occupied, reading headlines aloud as if testing their petty poetry:

> *Soaring freight costs go against growers' grain.*
> *Boomspray ban near Wimmera waterways.*
> *Agronomists warn over-till is overkill.*

Vigourman was washing his cup at the staff sink. He dried it and put it on the tray beside the taps. He whistled a few notes with trills in them as if that would soften his officious mood. He kept whistling all the way up to me, scratching his sideburns. He complained how growing whiskers made a man itch. He leant close, put a hand on my shoulder.

He said, 'Shouldn't you go up to the hospital, to see Tilda? Don't you think that's your first priority?'

I bent down and rubbed my ankle. 'My foot hurts.'

'I'll drive you.'

'I've got a call to make.'

I dialled, delaying pushing down on the last digit until Vigourman had retreated. All I reached was the seashell static but pretended I had made contact.

'Hello?' I said. 'Hello.'

I motioned to Vigourman that I'd go with him soon. I bowed my head, closed my eyes and rested that way a minute, stopped my life from anything more happening just yet.

Vigourman dropped me at the hospital.

He said, 'You've come to your senses, I hope.'

Yes, I nodded, an automatic gesture.

'Good man. That's the way. Good luck to you in there.'

He turned out of the driveway so slowly it was obvious he was checking for equivocation: my duty was to go directly and beseechingly to Tilda, not duck around the side of the building or hesitate at the glass entrance. I did hesitate but pushed through the front door anyway. It required a barging with my elbow to release the suction of the hinges. The cool inside air puffed my hair pleasantly but put a taste of antiseptic into my breathing. I stepped outside to spit out the taste.

Vigourman stopped his car and wound the window down. I waved to him that I was simply having a good cough and clearing of the senses and would be heading inside in a second. He returned a wave and resumed driving.

The hospital was all shiny lino and scuffed cream walls. The corridor ran left a short way, and a longer distance right. I went right, expecting someone in authority to appear and give directions. The six rooms either side of the corridor had beds in them, neatly made with blue covers. There were no patients.

I dreaded facing Tilda without people present. There would be less of a scene with people near. Tilda would be inclined to curb her fury. The dread put such a weight onto my head and shoulders

I had to lean against a wall and double over, hands on knees. What marriage did Tilda and I have now? What future was there for me if I lived cap in hand? What kind of man would accept such a life? The only honourable course of action would be to kill yourself. That would be the only future, suicide.

And with that I stood to attention. I issued myself the following instructions: go to Hobbs' Timber, Tacks and Twine this instant. Get a length of rope—make sure it's twice your height. An inch in width should be strong enough to take your heaviness and not slice the skin or snap from tension. Do not engage in conversation with old Jock Hobbs. He might pat his leather belt and scare you away with, 'What's this for, the rope?'

Or go to Ringo Point and flush out a snake and stomp on it, taunt it to bite you. A tiger snake, not a red-bellied black. Red-bellied blacks are far less poisonous. Do not fear the pain. Pain is only temporary and then nirvana. Don't dither, do it. What are you worried about? The *other side*? You don't truly believe in God. Yet still you worry. What if death is not just the blackest darkness? What if you wake afterwards into this world's complicated sequel—long-dead relatives pointing their accusing fingers; or Richard or Alice with ghostly infant faces wishing upon you the sewer life you condemned them to?

Do it, now, kill yourself and then good riddance, you're gone.

No. I want to be alive. Even if it is only a second-best life. A life that *will do*. Who's to say we aren't all living that way—from Prime Ministers to Vigourmans, we're all settling for second-best love; we just don't let it show, we accept our fate in secrecy.

A voice from up the corridor spooked me. 'May I help you?'

A thin woman, in a white smock a bit baggy for her. I tried to pick if I'd seen her around town. I had, in a just-another-face way. She'd had no presence like she had now in that white uniform. She looked into my eyes as if to challenge. There were deep spokes of skin around her mouth, a smoker's wheel, made more obvious by her pursing.

I stood up. 'I'm looking for my wife. My name is...'

'I know who you are.'

She glanced at the watch on her lapel. 'Tilda should have finished the little meal I gave her by now. Follow me.'

We went to the end of the corridor and turned right into an alcove where a metal ramp led outdoors. The nurse directed me along it. 'She's on the deck. I've set her up in a nice spot in the sun. Dr Philpott wants her to rest here for a few days, and I am going to treat her like a queen.'

'Thank you.'

'Don't thank me. I'm doing it for her.'

I couldn't see Tilda at first. Sun lit the metal railings around the deck too strongly. Leaves from a lattice climber were too transparently green and shimmering. Then my eyes adjusted. She was on a canvas banana chair, dappled in shade, placing the glass of water she was sipping onto a tea trolley beside her.

The blouse she had on—it was the yellow one, the sunflower one from my first sighting of her in London. I'd forgotten we'd kept it. Eight years in a bottom drawer and now its moment had come, given a sentimental airing to re-arouse my love for her, or so I presumed. Her hair was plaited her favourite, stump-tailed way, pulled back tight, very tight. It had the effect of distorting her face, stretching her skin smooth. The nurse must have helped her get the tension. Her makeup was tan-like and shiny.

She raised her chin and smiled, a proud, triumphant show of teeth made to seem whiter by silvery red lipstick.

She said, 'Some females are doormats. Others can wield a sword. I think I've proven I'm the latter.'

Her grinning disgusted me.

'Come closer,' she said. 'I want you to see something. I love Scintilla. I love the people. The people are so kind and compassionate. See these? Delivered first thing this morning.'

She was referring to two cards in her lap. The get-well and greetings sort with Monet-type landscapes on the covers, lots of purple wisteria and blue.

She read, 'Dear Tilda. My wife and I extend our sincere sympathy and support to you during this tumultuous episode. Signed, Hector Vigourman.' She shook her head. 'What a decent and dignified man. If only more men were like him.'

'Is that so?' I said.

'Yes.'

'He didn't appear so decent just before, advising I use prostitutes.'

'What are you talking about? Why do you want to say dreadful things?'

'It's what he said. Go to Melbourne and use prostitutes.'

'Don't make up lies to me. I don't believe anything you say anymore. This town is all I've got left and you want to taint it. At least leave me that, while you go off with your Watercook whore. Why aren't you with her?'

I blinked and lowered my head but made sure I lifted it up immediately so I didn't look defeated.

Too late. Tilda had noticed: 'Doesn't she want you anymore?'

She grinned and read from the other card, 'You showed him, dear. Signed, the ladies of Scintilla.' She held the card for me to see. 'These people understand the pain I'm feeling. A simple card like this and I think: There are good people left in the world. I think: If Colin wants to go off with another woman, then he can go off with another woman. He doesn't deserve me. I will go off with another man. I will find a better man than he could ever be. I've proven how much I can love someone. I am prepared to kill to prove it. That's how much I can love. Jealousy is proof of love.'

She began to cry. She covered her face with her right, gauntleted hand. Her fingertips were especially red and swollen. She must have done some violence to them at Donna's.

'Bastard,' she said. 'What a bastard you are. That's what you've made me do, want to kill someone and humiliate myself by admitting to your face it was proof of my love. I bet you listen to me say it and deep in you it gives you pleasure that a woman would fight for you. Bastard.'

'I don't take pleasure.'

Tilda looked up at me.

'I do not take pleasure. I promise.'

But here's one final Swahili. There was pleasure. To be worth killing for is the supreme vanity. It places value on your life. And in having that pleasure I felt affection for Tilda. I didn't kid myself that it was more than affection. It wasn't the same as love. But seeing her reduced to a pathetic state was to see the power I had

272

over her. To be the cause of her misery shamed me, yes, but left me affectionate and gentle. I wanted to heal her. Me loving her was all that could heal her. I wished I could offer her that. I even closed my eyes and willed myself to. I used the first time I saw her, that London moment. I let the memory of it circulate in my mind. I willed to be transported back there in spirit and have the original raw love sweep into my heart. Yet, when I opened my eyes, I only felt affection.

Tilda could tell I was trying from my clenched eyes and prayer-like rocking. It made her suffer even more that I had to try at all. She craned forward and snaked her arms under mine for embracing.

She said, 'I can live with you not loving me. I can live that way. I can say to myself love changes and we have to change with it. I can say it's time for us to be best friends now. We can stay together and be best friends and that's how we live from now on.'

She kissed my cheek and my forehead, hard. She kissed me on the mouth. I let her, but I didn't open my mouth. She said, 'As long as there is no other woman, I can live that way. As long as there's no other woman involved.'

She pushed me in the chest and swore *Jesus* and *fuck*. I was startled and braced for another push.

'What am I saying?' she said. 'Look at what you've done to me. Reduced me to this. I hate you. And I hate her. I hate her so much.'

Tilda stood up. She stared me in the eye. I turned my head. She said, 'I have to know, when did it begin? Where did it begin? Who made the first move? That Wilkins bitch did, didn't she? She moved in on you, didn't she? Pursued you and seduced you with her big fuck-me mouth and her fuck-me body.'

'Yes,' I lied. 'Yes,' I repeated, meekly, as if I too had been wronged.

'I knew it. The bitch went after you. I knew it. The man who took those vows with me in that beautiful chapel, he wouldn't betray me willingly. You were weak and that Watercook slut took advantage.'

I drew breath to say *Don't call Donna a slut*. But where would that have got me? Tilda was showing me affection back, and pity, cradling my jaw.

She said, 'Where did it begin?'

'I can't remember.'

'Bullshit. I don't believe you.'

'The races.'

'The races? Right under my nose at the races?'

'I'm sorry.'

'What about those two lunches?'

'What about them?'

'There was nothing between you there?'

'No,' I said, trying to keep the betrayal contained and limit Tilda's recriminations.

'Nothing?'

'Nothing.'

'Meetings. Where did you have your meetings?'

'What meetings?'

'Assignations. Where did you meet and fuck?'

'Tilda, please.'

'Where?'

'Please.'

'Where?'

'At her place.'

'With her daughter present?'

'She was off somewhere.'

Tilda sucked in air. She sneered. 'Where else did you do it?'

'Nowhere else.'

'I don't believe you.'

'I promise.'

'Just at the slut's house?'

'Yes.' I was not going to tell about the forest. The forest was on Tilda's home ground. The recriminations would not be contained if she knew about the forest. 'Just at Donna's place. I promise.'

Tilda poked her finger in front of my chin. 'Never ever, *ever* utter that slut's name again. Don't even *think* that slut's name again. You can use *slutty bitch* or *Watercook whore*, but don't dignify her with a proper name.'

'Jesus, Tilda.'

'*Slutty bitch* or *Watercook whore*. Not even *her* or *she*. But especially her name. Never ever use her name. Or you can go. For good.'

'I will go for good, then.'

'You won't renounce her? You won't do it?'

'Don't tell me what to do. Don't order me to say this and not say that.'

'I *will* tell you what to do. That filthy slut broke my life. I want you to call her a filthy slut.'

'No.'

'Do it.'

I turned away.

Tilda yelled, 'Go, then. Get away from me. Fuck off.'

The nurse came up the ramp, arms at her side like she was marching. 'Tilda, dear. Shsh, settle.'

Tilda said to her, 'He won't say it. He won't renounce her.'

'Then he's a fool,' said the nurse. 'Settle, dear. Shsh. Let him go if he wants to go.'

I walked off a few steps. 'Goodbye, then.'

Tilda began following me but the nurse stood between us and tried to hug her, saying, 'Let him go, dear. You're worth twenty of him.'

I said, 'This is just between us two, thank you.'

The nurse didn't respond. She hugged Tilda. 'Worth twenty. That's the girl.'

I walked towards Tilda. 'I need a key to get into the house. I want to get some things. More clothes. Things.'

The nurse said, 'Shall we let him have the key, dear? I say, let him have the key and let him get his things and go. Let's play his game.'

Tilda nodded.

The nurse unzipped the pocket of her smock and brought out my back door key, the one usually hooked on the Commodore ring. She winked to Tilda: 'Shall I let him have it? Let's let him have it.' She winked again. She handed me the key.

Tilda started sobbing. I said goodbye to her, softly. I stood waiting for a reply but there was none. I expected a goodbye in return, then a beseeching of me not to go. But there was nothing. Which gave me a cut-adrift feeling, as if this was it, the true moment of our end, and I was as far adrift—the loneliest, the most lost—as I could ever be.

I wanted to step back out of the loneliness, back to the familiar. I wanted Tilda to call me back home to it. I said, 'So where will I leave the key, Tilda? Under the back doorstep?'

The nurse answered. 'That will do fine.'

'I was speaking to Tilda.'

The nurse let out a grunt and shook her head. 'It seems your husband wants to speak to you, dear. Do you want to speak to him more?'

'I'd like to know where he will go.'

'She'd like to know where you'll go.'

'I heard her. And I don't know the answer.'

Tilda said, 'Since I'll be in here, he can stay at the house a few days.'

'If I could do that, it would be helpful.'

'You're very generous to him, dear,' the nurse said. 'If it was me I'd say goodbye for good. Not *stay a few days*. Let him leave and go off and see what he's given up. Let's see what he's worth without you, and Mr Vigourman's charity. He'll be back, dear. He'll be back.'

Tilda's lips angled up into a trusting smile at her. Then a smile at me, of the previous triumphant kind. She said, 'Yes. He'll be back.'

The nurse guided Tilda into the banana chair. 'Too true. You're worth twenty of him. He'll be back.'

I said, 'Is that so?' sarcastically. I said, 'Goodbye, Tilda,' with a cock of my head. Bravado lifting me up on my toes.

They were still saying it to each other like a chant—'He'll be back. He'll be back'—as I stomped over the ramp, away.

The bravado lasted all the way out of the hospital, and along the roadside. I strode like a man who knew exactly his destination in life and his reason for being. No pain in my foot anymore, the bravado numbed it. When I reached Main Street I was swinging my shoulders like the town celebrity. I imagined myself the centre of attention, focus of people's whispers. The swinging said, *Here I am, Scintilla. A man who has sinned. A man with danger about him. A man who might sin again if given the chance. You better watch out, ladies, or I'll sin with you.*

Putting the key in the back door sapped that attitude from me. I was neither adrift from Tilda anymore, nor did I belong to her. I was between the two. I was nowhere, but I was in our house. I was empty, like being hungry. I wasn't hungry but even if I had been, did I have the right to eat the food in the cupboards now? Have milk from the fridge or water from the kettle? Perhaps just a little water was permissible. I filled a glass and drank it and in doing so felt like I was stealing.

What was mine? Clothes in the wardrobe, yes. But what more? Only this documenting I've done. I climbed into the roof and brought the briefcase down. I took it into my nook and read the pages. I had written up to the part just before the Neutral Motor Inn meetings. I had kissed Donna for the first time and had seen Cameron's pillows. I parted my lips and kissed her again as I read. Bent forward and kissed as if she was really there. Did it without thinking, until I saw my shadow on the wall and laughed at it and myself. The kind of laughing that takes you to the edge of crying. I didn't cry. I was alone, therefore my crying would have been genuine, but I didn't do it. I was full of too much resolve.

Not resolve that was clear yet. More an energy to *do* something, make irreversible change. If Donna could hear that resolve in my voice she would want me with her, wouldn't she? I went downstairs to the phone to try her. No answer. But it was comforting to know my ringing was making sound in her living room.

I went back to my nook. It was peaceful there, safe, with no worry about Tilda coming up the stairs in two minds. I fed paper into my typewriter and continued these pages. The process was too slow. The tapping put an ache in my ears. I switched to longhand and wrote up to the bath-burning scene. Then I phoned Donna again for some comforting unanswered ringing.

I bought potato cakes from the takeaway for dinner. I had the right to make coffee, I decided. And use Tilda's milk, or else it would go stale. I took a mug to my nook and wrote up to where I slept in the children's playground, and in writing that the need for sleep dragged my head down onto my folded arms. I slept half the night in that position, on the pillow of my desk.

When I woke my body ached. I straightened it by stretching out on the floor. I fell asleep that way, and dreamt so deeply and horribly there was no telling it from reality: I was sleeping with Tilda in the Scintilla hospital. 'Come on. Get up,' she said, shaking me. 'Come on. Follow me,' she said, pulling me by the hand to hurry up and walk with her to the forest. Walk, faster, faster, hurry, run to the forest. To the clearing in the forest. *The* clearing. The bedroom in the forest. We must take off our clothes and lie down among the twigs and insects. I must congress with her. I must not think of the Watercook whore. Tilda was claiming the clearing as hers. I must desecrate the memory of what had happened there. Congress in the forest with her, Tilda, not the whore.

I woke before the act of it. I knelt in the blackened bath and rinsed and scrubbed in cold water. Drying off I heard knocking at the back door. I hurried down the hall to the bedroom window, peeped around the edge of the blind, panicking that it was Tilda knocking.

It was Vigourman. He was looking up at the windows for signs of life. I let the blind fall shut until the knocking finished. I went to my nook.

Honesty box, help me. I must hurry and leave. I've got to leave. The future is pulling me. I don't know where. What's keeping me? Guilt? A final check of my soul to make sure all love for Tilda has gone?

Does all love ever go, or only the people?

I don't know.

I once fell in love with a woman named Tilda. Beyond that, I don't know much about anything.

Craig Sherborne's memoir *Hoi Polloi* (2005) was shortlisted for the Queensland Premier's and Victorian Premier's Literary Awards. The follow-up, *Muck* (2007), won the Queensland Premier's Literary Award for Non-fiction. His first novel, *The Amateur Science of Love* (2011), won the Melbourne Prize for Literature's Best Writing Award, and was shortlisted for the NSW Premier's and Victorian Premier's Literary Awards. *Tree Palace*, his latest novel, will be published in 2014. Craig has also written two volumes of poetry, *Bullion* (1995) and *Necessary Evil* (2005), and a verse drama, *Look at Everything Twice for Me* (1999). His writing has appeared in most of Australia's literary journals and anthologies. He lives in Melbourne.